MISSION: DISCOVERED?

The Iraqi vehicles had arrived. Like metal monsters from a child's bad dream they crouched, far larger than the DPVs of Leopard-1, diesels snorting as they came to a clanking halt, turrets moving cyclopean eyes for prey. Rather than answering with his voice, McTaggart keyed his push-to-talk button on his belt twice. The rapid clicks on the radio telling the listener that the last transmission was acknowledged.

It was impossible for McTaggart's Leopard team to move without discovery. They had to wait until the Iraqis either left or . . .

A hatch over the lead vehicle opened and McTaggart saw the upper half of a soldier rise from within. The soldier, an officer, peered around the area. The officer turned slowly, looking in a two-hundred-twenty-degree arc, peering carefully into the rocks and topography around him. The officer pulled himself up and out through the hatch, dropping gracefully to the ground. A second soldier emerged from within, this one to take up position at the 120-mm gun. In the second vehicle, still another man materialized behind a 7.62mm machine gun, racking a round into the gun's breach. . . .

SPECIAL OPS

RAPID FIRE

MIKE MURRAY

A SIGNET BOOK

SIGNET
Published by New American Library, a division of
Penguin Group (USA) Inc., 375 Hudson Street,
New York, New York 10014, U.S.A.
Penguin Books Ltd, 80 Strand,
London WC2R 0RL, England
Penguin Books Australia Ltd, 250 Camberwell Road,
Camberwell, Victoria 3124, Australia
Penguin Books Canada Ltd, 10 Alcorn Avenue,
Toronto, Ontario, Canada M4V 3B2
Penguin Books (N.Z.) Ltd, Cnr Rosedale and Airborne Roads,
Albany, Auckland 1310, New Zealand

Penguin Books Ltd, Registered Offices:
80 Strand, London WC2R 0RL, England

First published by Signet, an imprint of New American Library,
a division of Penguin Group (USA) Inc.

First Printing, July 2003
10 9 8 7 6 5 4 3 2 1

PUBLISHER'S NOTE
This is a work of fiction. Names, characters, places, and incidents either
are the product of the author's imagination or are used fictitiously, and
any resemblance to actual persons, living or dead, business establishments,
events, or locales is entirely coincidental.

In memory of Leo Marlantes,
educator, scholar, and once my commanding officer

CHAPTER 1

The casino at Monte Carlo had always been a favorite stopping place for members of the Saudi royal family because of the Principality of Monaco's proximity to Europe's appealing southern door, with its excellent weather, international cosmopolitan atmosphere and, above all, a sense of decorum befitting one royal family to another. It was important for young princes to play their choice of games in total relaxation. Besides the casino there were other refined locations in or near the principality such as its exotic gardens, the opera house, the Tower of Augustus, the Cocteau Museum, none of which the Saudis bothered to visit in person, but which lent social gravitas to their choice of vacation spots.

Adding to Monaco's attractions was winter skiing within short drives—Peira Cava, Gréolières, Andon, La Colmiane, Valberg. In the summer there were the warm sands of Larvotto beach, decorated by beautiful young women wearing thong beach suits, often without tops, their glowing breasts floating easily on bodies designed by a god other than the one Mohammed had warned about. There were additional seductions available to the men of the Levant, even as their private jets touched down at the nearby Nice-Côte d' Azur International Airport, in the form of liquid refreshments and, by special request, high-quality cocaine that they could, without much exaggeration, claim to be homegrown. Or at least home subsidized.

Visitors from the Kingdom of Saudi Arabia were more than a little welcome in Monaco for the millions of dollars they left in their wagering wake. The courtly Arabs tended to be undemonstrative by nature, never raising an eyebrow when presented with bills that would stagger other wealthy people. Nothing was too good for the rulers of the desert—from the finest food they consumed to the money they gambled and lost with almost dedicated indifference.

So when Monsieur Tans Roget, *directeur* of Casino Monte Carlo, received a telephone call from Riyadh that Prince Abd al-Aziz Al Saud and several members of the royal family were to arrive in Monte Carlo on Saturday, less than twenty hours hence, the staff of the hotel and casino shifted into high gear. An entire floor of apartments including all three royal suites were made ready and special hostesses known to be favorites of the prince were assigned to service those floors.

Croupiers, dealers, assistant managers, restaurant staff, and security personnel were made aware of the party's expected arrival. Obviously there would be no limits placed upon their play. Service for the royal family, as always, was to be unobtrusive yet instant. Their needs were to be anticipated.

Carlos Aveniedo, the casino's untitled manager in charge of special guests, telephoned the airport to get information on the estimated time of arrival of the Saudi airplane. The casino would provide limousines, of course. He was told that there was no advanced information on an arrival of the Saudi aircraft. Still, the air traffic control supervisor pointed out, a flight plan could be received at any time, assuming that the aircraft was flying direct from Riyadh. It was also possible that the flight could originate from a different location, perhaps Europe, in which case the plan might not be filed for two or three more hours.

Aveniedo was nothing if not a thorough planner, a

primary personality trait required for his position, so he made several more telephone calls. He called the harbor master knowing very well that the Saudi royal yacht was an occasional mode of transportation of the prince's. Aveniedo was informed that indeed the *Montkaj*, owned not by Prince Al Saud but a near cousin of the foreign minister's, was scheduled to make port on the twenty-seventh day of the month. The opulent Mediterranean cruiser would arrive with a party of thirteen, Aveniedo was told, at Condamine, rather than Fontvielle where it usually docked. Aveniedo thanked the harbor master and hung up the telephone. The twenty-seventh was more than a week away, Aveniedo considered, so Prince Al Saud must be arriving either by car or plane. He called the airport back and left word with ground operations that he was to be contacted at once when any aircraft transporting Prince Al Saud radioed.

Despite misgivings about intruding on what might be a very busy work schedule, Aveniedo called the ministry of foreign affairs in Riyadh and was put through to the prince's travel secretary. That department's factotum responded that the prince was currently out of the country and that his whereabouts was not public information. Thus chastened, Aveniedo thanked the man on the other end of the line and hung up.

Aveniedo discussed with the casino manager the difficulties he had experienced in preparing a proper reception for the Al Saud party. Tans Roget merely shrugged his shoulders. He proposed that they not worry. Everything that could be done had already been seen to, except local transportation for the prince's party. Since they were not mind readers they had more than discharged their hosting responsibilities. Roget sent Aveniedo away with an appreciative pat on the shoulder, then turned his attention to other important guests.

By midnight the after supper, post-opera crowd had arrived. Some would only have a drink before retiring, some would spectate, and others would play at the tables. Among those guests of the casino was the internationally recognized John Murphy. Irish by birth, Murphy was an extraordinarily rich American from fabled Santa Barbara who had amassed a fortune lending money to farm laborers at exorbitant rates of interest. Enfeebled by a lifetime of overindulgence, Murphy was totally dependent upon his trophy wife, Mary, a startlingly attractive woman half his age, who saw to it that her husband's supply of oxygen flowed freely from a tank attached to his wheelchair. While he sat docile in the chair, Mrs. Murphy gratified her passion for gaming by betting stacks of black chips—one-thousand-dollar value—on each spin of the wheel or turn of the card. There was justice in the world, Roget thought, as the Murphys remained at their customary station at the high-stakes roulette table.

Monsieur Roget paused to speak briefly with Antole Pestoche, their South American head of security for the casino. With the advent of slot machines installed in one area of the casino there had been a fear that the lower social classes would flock to them, that there would be more cheating than usual, and that the exclusive clientele built over one hundred years would turn away. Happily for all concerned that had not happened, in no small way thanks to Antole's subtle but omniscient eye on the operation.

Roget noted that the French minister of finance had arrived with his son and daughter-in-law. Arnaud d' Vouse was the French president's closest, lifelong friend and advisor for all things personal and official.

"Tans," the French cabinet member said by way of greeting the casino manager, "how are you this evening, my friend?"

"I am well, Monsieur Secretary, *merci*. The room is always a more pleasant place when you have arrived," Roget responded, and he meant it. Monsieur d' Vouse was always an impeccable gentleman and the world was a better place with him.

"Then you must never retire. I have no other welcome to match yours. Tans, you know my son, Henri?"

"Of course," Roget said, extending his hand.

"It is always my pleasure, Monsieur Roget," the young man said, smiling shyly.

"And his bride, Michelle Burgoine d' Vouse," the minister smoothly continued.

"Ah," Roget said, gallantly touching his lips to the young lady's hand. "You are far more beautiful than your newspapers pictures, Madame d' Vouse, and I thought they have all been excellent."

"Oh, *vraiment*! Now I know why these d' Vouse men spend so much of their time here. I'll never let them come alone. Thank you, Monsieur Roget. And please call me Michelle," the suddenly radiant lady said.

"I am glad that you said that, Michelle. I am the person to whom you must come for any reason when you are in Monaco. *Si je trouve que vous vous êtes niés n'importe quoi à tout sans me laisser savoir, je serai très bouleversé*," he said, faux sternly.

Roget used a house phone to advise his accounting office that the d' Vouse party were guests of the casino's hotel and were not to be presented with a bill for their stay. Roget then spoke with room service and arranged for Swiss chocolates and two bottles of the hotel's finest champagne to be waiting on ice in the d' Vouses' rooms.

By half past the hour of midnight the house was quite full. The theater crowd set the tone of dress in formal attire, while others wore casual designer clothing, men without ties and some women in khaki or denim skirts or slacks. All, however, added glitter to the magical glow of lights reflected through the prisms of the casino's magnificent chandeliers and by gems worn around their necks, wrists, and ears.

Roget's attention was demanded by a hurried messenger who, breathless, informed the manager that the Arabs had, unannounced, at last arrived. Totally confident that everything to make the Saudis comfortable had been done, Roget walked purposely toward the main entrance to greet the new guests just as they entered. They were five men, dressed colorfully in the distinct red-and-white keffiyeh, *akal* of the royal family, and long flowing *mishlahs* adorned with gold piping on the sleeves and wide gold thread brocade around the edges. Under the robes were traditional *brussa* shirts.

Roget had begun to open his arms in wide welcome when something slowed his pace. While the man walking one step ahead of the Arab contingent, despite tinted glasses covering his eyes even at night, bore a strong resemblance to Prince Abd al-Aziz Al Saud, Roget knew that it was not him. A brother? A more distant relative? There were, after all, five thousand members of the royal family. Roget reminded himself that he had hardly met them all. There had, perhaps, been a miscommunication in advance of their travel plans. That was the likely explanation, Roget thought, recollecting the series of unsuccessful calls made today by Carlos Aveniedo to not only Riyadh, but several other places the prince and his party might have been.

"Welcome." Roget smiled broadly, bowing slightly at the waist as a form of respect shown to any royal person from any one of many realms around the world. It cost nothing and the returns, Roget knew from experience, could sometimes be great. "This is a wonderful surprise and—"

The first burst of submachine gunfire caught Roget in the throat, the shooter allowing the weapon to climb slightly so that the next two rounds struck the casino manager in the head. It was an unhurried, highly disciplined piece of shooting that said volumes about the professional training it took to execute the action. The weapon of choice, an AK-47, customized for close work with a reduced stock, fired a 7.62mm round that was purposely not muted by a suppressor so as to increase panic by increasing the noise. Indeed the percussive, shattering sound echoing inside the large room had a stunning effect on the casino's patrons. The other four royal imposters swung their automatic weapons out from under their billowing garments and, in a clearly practiced formation, cut loose in every direction.

There were all kinds of screams erupting at once—

some from pain as men and women were struck with hot bullets, others from panic and from fear. The killers, in contrast to their panicked victims, were calm and their technique was measured. They were looking for two results: a high body count and the infliction of maximum horror for tomorrow's news media headlines. Also destroyed were valuable paintings, sculptures, and etched crystal. The killers advanced into the panicked, running crowd, not allowing any to reach the winding staircase that led to the second floor or to any of the exits from the main gaming room. Bodies began piling up at those exit ways.

Other patrons dove for whatever cover they could find—behind game tables, behind chairs, and behind the building's support columns. But the shooters found them in their own good time and fired bursts into their faces when possible. When one clip was used up the shooters merely ejected it from their assault rifles and replaced it with another carried concealed beneath their desert robes.

John Murphy saw one of the gunmen swinging his weapon toward those clustered around the roulette wheel. Even as a burst of automatic gunfire had caught one player nearby, Murphy grasped the arm of his wife, now motionless in disbelief, and pulled down hard with all of his strength. Mary Murphy collapsed onto the floor with John on top of her, never letting go of her arm while two bullets penetrated his body. After their searing impact to his liver and kidney areas, John Murphy knew at once that he would die. He had time to whisper into his wife's ear, "Shhh. Lie still."

Arnaud d' Vouse was on his way back to the main salon from the men's washroom when the gunfire erupted. He knew at once from his army experience that the casino was being hit by terrorists. He could have retreated unseen, almost certainly he could have exited to safety through either of two doors leading off from his present location, but the thought never entered his mind. He knew only that his son and daughter-in-law were in imminent danger. He immediately quickened his pace, breaking into a run toward the sound of the guns.

Henri d' Vouse, standing behind his wife at a blackjack table on the far side of the room, could not believe his ears at the first sound of the gunfire. He turned toward the deafening noise, but pulled Michelle from her chair onto the floor; then he continued to pull her prone body behind the table. He covered his wife's mouth quickly as she began to scream, keeping his weight atop her. To the young couple cowering behind the gambling table while around them people screamed and tried in vain to run, the firing seemed to go on forever. Finally, it stopped. Henri, who had reflexively kept his eyes closed, slowly opened them and began to turn his head. Around him bodies were strewn about the floor and blood was everywhere, soaking into the carpets. As the young man slowly rolled to the side, off Michelle's motionless body, he was aware of another person standing nearby.

He lifted his eyes upward, followed the rich crimson robes of the gunman's *jellaba* and into the bearded visage above. The man's mouth widened into a large, satisfied smile as he moved the muzzle of his AK-47 to a place only one inch from Henri's wife's ear. With a thunderous roar Michelle's skull exploded in a spray of red, white, and gray matter, leaving only wet tresses of dark hair.

Still smiling, the gunman strolled off.

Minutes later, after the terrorists had gone, Henri found his father lying face up on the main floor. Because he had been a special target, his face had been obliterated with a point-blank burst of gunfire.

Security personnel arrived, all carrying handguns, but the pistols were no match against high-powered, rapid-firing Kalashnikovs. Eight minutes after the first shots were fired, those still alive inside the casino could hear sirens at a distance. Their wails drew quite near until emergency vehicles and armed police units arrived on scene. Helmeted and uniformed, they wielded automatic weapons of their own. But by that time it was all over. The killers had walked calmly into the night.

The Arabs were seen by witnesses to have entered a gray van and driven at high speed out of the casino complex. Pursuing police units took up the chase on the A8 motorway, a highway that connected with all of the European motorway systems. The van traveled west at a high rate of speed toward Nice with police units from that city, now alerted, taking up the pursuit. At the twenty-two-kilometer marker the van veered north, onto N202. Gunfire was exchanged between the terrorists in the van and police. Also among indiscriminate targets fired at by the terrorists were pedestrians on the streets of Nice. Three were wounded, none fatally.

By the time the van had arrived at the outskirts of the town of Levan, special units of police had laid a spike strip across the road. The strip ripped out both of the van's front tires and, within two hundred meters, caused the machine to come to a complete halt in the middle of the road. Rather than surrender, the terrorists used the vehicle for cover, opting to shoot it out with authorities despite the fact that they were hopelessly outnumbered.

Inspector Luis DeGault, the official in charge of the interdiction of the escaping terrorists and who wrote the definitive report, felt that there was more to the final minutes of the terrorist's last, seemingly futile stand against the police than met the eye. He said that despite the poor cover offered by their vehicle and the firepower arrayed against them, the terrorists were completely disciplined in placing their shots and in the way that they moved as a cohesive unit. As a consequence, the French police suffered two officers dead, both from head shots, and five injured. Nor did the terrorists surrender. Rather, they fought to the last man who, at the last moments of the firefight, severely injured two officers by pulling the pin of a hand grenade, attempting to take their lives along with his own.

A search of the bodies revealed identification that had

been forged, but extremely well done. The forgeries, which included passports, credit cards, and drivers' licenses from various European countries, were far better than could be bought in most criminal undergrounds.

It was several hours before DeGault, working backwards from the killing grounds of the highway to that of the casino in Monte Carlo, could discern that there were five men in the initial assault, but only four found dead at the hands of police units. Could there have been a mistake in various witnesses accounts? After all, with guns going off and people screaming in utter confusion, might there have been only four and not five?

Definitely not, Mary Murphy affirmed, quite calm while raging with anger at the savagery she and the others had witnessed. Five. Not four.

The leader of the group, a Palestinian by the name of Nabil Zibri, had exited the casino with his colleagues in murder, but while they made straight for their nearby rental van, Zibri had turned left onto a narrow walkway, entirely cast in the shadow of the large building he had just exited. He tossed off his keffiyeh and *akal,* dropping them into nearby shrubbery along with his AK-47 and his combat suspenders that held up the extra ammunition clips. He paused only long enough to remove soft leather, beige lounging slippers from a pocket on the suspenders, and pull them onto his feet. He pulled off his false black beard and moustache, exposing a clean-shaven face underneath, and with the removal of his *akal,* his hair appeared bleached blond.

Zibri, now clad in comfortable chino slacks and a plain but expensive designer shirt, walked calmly along the main section of Monaco, quite comfortably blending in with tourists as well as locals who had briefly paused in their festivities to inquire about the sirens, helicopters, and fast moving police vehicles dashing about the countryside.

"Ce qui s'est passé?" Zibri asked a couple standing in the doorway of a nightclub.

"We don't know," the young man said in English that was clearly his native language.

Zibri shrugged in passive agreement, then stepped inside where the music had begun playing again.

Peter Fischer and his wife, Nicole, waited at the table of their favorite restaurant for Tony and Barbara Barr to join them. Pancho's would never be listed with stars behind its name in the guide books of Los Angeles eateries, but for people who were addicted to Mexican food no one made tortillas like Pancho's. Peter and Nicole would likely have adopted the place anyway because the two had met there sixteen years ago when Peter had been attracted to Nicole's nose. It was probably the worst pick-up line she had ever heard and she told him so. Peter pointed out that many women with generous noses in adolescence could easily pass into middle age with noses the same shape and size as a lightbulb. The nose, made of mostly cartilage, never stopped growing, he reminded her. The same was true of men, of course, but he was not romantically attracted to men. Four months later, Peter gave up his apartment on Tenth Avenue in Manhattan Beach and moved into Nicole's two-bedroom house on Shell Street in El Porto.

There was an argument carried on for years among the local denizens of the area as to whether or not El Porto was officially a part of Manhattan Beach or El Segundo or a legal entity unto itself. The issue could have been settled easily enough by any one of a number of methods, such as a telephone call to city hall or an Internet query, but the bottom line was that mail got through and the distance was still fifty yards to the beach or five blocks to Pancho's, the nighttime hub of social activity. Despite their marriage two years later, an event that had spoiled not a few beachfront romances, their mutual attraction remained a pleasant mixture of physical and intellectual. While real estate values rose around them like winter high tides, the Fischers found their lives on the beach a source of great contentment.

Though he was twelve years older than Nicole's thirty-nine years, each day Peter clamped a helmet on his distinguished, prematurely gray hair, and rode his Harley-Davidson chopper to work at TRW. It was a lifestyle statement of independence for him and, in the process, beat the chronic Manhattan Beach parking problem.

Nicole's professional life was equally convenient. She was an air traffic controller at LAX. Her route to the job was a delightful zip down Vista del Mar along Dockweiler State Beach to West Imperial Highway. She usually took the short way, turning from Imperial onto Pershing Drive, then onto the employee access road about one-fifth of a mile from there. She seldom got her Mercedes 350 out of third gear on the trip that lasted ten minutes in moderate traffic. Being an ATC at Los Angeles International was a high-stress job for most people. But Nicole did not seem to feel the same pressure that forced a number of her fellow workers into quitting outright, disability retirement, or other forms of mild to severe psychological damage if they stayed around long enough. Nicole was blessed with an outstanding ability to handle a number of complicated scenarios at one time due to an excellent short-term memory and a clarity of imagination.

She had learned the theory of multiple dimensionality as a math major at UCLA and practiced the art during a five-year tour as an army helicopter pilot. The images on a radar screen were rational to her at all times and her situational lucidity was somehow translated to pilots who flew fast jets or slow props into and around LAX. She and Peter still ate dinner at Pancho's at least twice a month, a good excuse to suck up margaritas, see pals, and listen to music that was never very good but always danceable.

"You act like you've never seen that menu before," Tony Barr said as he and Barbara slid into the red leatherette booth opposite Peter and Nicole.

"We check it just to make sure nothing has changed,"

Peter said. "Sit down. Our guests won't be here for a few minutes."

"What? Oh, God. Did we get the night wrong?" Barbara said, a small hand covering her mouth like a character from an illustrated Brer Rabbit story.

Tony shook his head, eyes closed. "How many times has he done that to you, Barbara? Fifty? Seventy-five? You know why he does it? Because he's fascinated. I'm not, but he is. Christ," he said.

"Oh," Barbara said, flipping her hand in the air, dismissing the joke just as she usually did.

Tony shook his head and rolled his eyes. "Send any airplanes into the mountains, Nicky?" he asked the ATC expert.

"Hey, if they don't talk nice I put 'em right into the Rose Bowl," Nicole said.

"I'm retiring. Bring us a couple margaritas," Tony said to a waitress who appeared at the table.

"Not for me," Barbara said. "Maybe a Coke."

"Make it a pitcher and four glasses," Tony said, ignoring his wife's plea.

"When?" Peter asked. He had heard it before, but even at age fifty-five Tony Barr, a wiry, fast-thinking Secret Service agent, seemed as though he could go on forever. And might want to. Peter knew that the head folks at SS, Washington, had offered to waive mandatory retirement rules for him. They needed his expertise in counterfeiting on the West Coast.

"Put in the papers yesterday. Effective July First. We bought a house in Palm Springs," he said.

"I hate it there," Barbara said.

"So do I," Nicole said to Barbara.

"So, I guess we'll never see you again," Peter said. "Let's drink to it."

"I raked off enough of the best counterfeit to take care of all of us," Tony said.

"I wondered where you got all the dough to spend on Nicole's jewelry," Peter said.

"What jewelry?" Barbara said, swiveling her head around to her husband.

Tony bit into a taco chip and looked back into Barbara's eyes without blinking.

"Do you like chili rellenos, Barbara?" Nicole asked.

Barbara shook her head.

"Give me the taco salad and a side of refried beans," Tony said to the waitress.

"That sounds good," Peter said. "I'll have the beef enchilada. Hey, Barbara, why don't you try Poncho's East Texas chili? If you got worms, this stuff will kill 'em."

Barbara closed her eyes. Nicole thought she was going to cry.

"Nice talk, Pete," Nicole said sarcastically.

"What?"

"It worked on him, Barbs. He's just trying to save you a big medical bill," Tony said to his wife.

Tony, tired of the wait, suggested that Nicole try the combination seafood platter and, when she hesitated, informed the waitress to write it down and go tell the cook to get busy.

"Barbara, I'm sorry. I only tease you because you're so much fun. I don't tease Nicole because I don't care about her. At all. And I remember when you were the best looking thing on the beach. I was the guy with his tongue hanging out—the one you wouldn't talk to, remember?" Peter said.

"Of course I remember," Barbara said, glowing. "Wasn't that fun? It seems like it was just last week."

"It was thirty-six years ago," Tony said dourly.

"I was five years old," Barbara giggled.

"And still a virgin," Tony observed.

"What were you doing thirty-six years ago, Nicole?" Tony asked.

"She was pulling up on the lower strand of barbed wire so her mother could crawl underneath," Peter said.

Nicole put her head back and laughed. "That's right. Daddy didn't think the Border Patrol would shoot a kid. I was three about then," she said laughing and punched Peter hard on his shoulder. The two of them kissed.

"I thought you were French Canadian," Tony said.

"That's right, she is," Peter said to his friend.

They ordered a second pitcher of margaritas and a glass of Coke out of mercy for Barbara. In the breezy exchange of family intentions, Peter confessed that lately he had considered retirement. They could move to a less crowded locale, maybe Arizona. They had bought a couple of lots years ago near Sedona and they would probably build something there sooner rather than later. Plus, Nicole might be able to get a job at a smaller airport, maybe a grass strip, where she wouldn't be able to hurt so many people in the event of a crash.

Tony allowed that he was surprised that Peter hadn't moved straight to a place like that, Arizona, when he left the army. He was a young colonel then, still in his early forties. But he had quit rather than continue in the service of the Company. He was referring to the CIA. He had been the military attaché to the embassy in Ankara, then continued as a CIA special advisor attached to TRW, an important defense contractor.

At the end of the meal Tony won the privilege of paying the bill. Peter handled the tip, which he dug out of Nicole's purse. The foursome walked for almost an hour along the beach promenade before calling it a night. Peter gave Barbara a heartfelt hug and assured her that he and Nicole would see them regularly in the desert.

At one A.M. Peter and Nicole made love. It was as good as it ever was, and it was always wonderful.

Three days later Peter was in his "athletic" position on his recliner watching the Dodgers playing the Giants. It was the eighth inning and there was only one light on in the room that had become dark when the sun went down. Nicole was using the single 60-watt bulb to read a book that had been recommended by a talk show hostess. She was deeply engrossed, but continued to listen to her husband's baseball commentary as she read.

"No way he's going to do it this year. They won't pitch

to him. I'm surprised they did it last year. Hell, Bonds is one of the greatest players ever and I'd sell my mother into slavery to have him on the Dodgers, but . . ."

"But what?" Nicole said without looking up.

"But they won't pitch to him. Would you?"

Peter squinted into the brightness of the television, wiping his eyes first with one hand, then another.

"Nope," she said.

"How many home runs did he hit?" Peter asked rhetorically. "Seventy-two? So if I'm throwing to that guy he gets nothing but high and outside."

"Seventy-three," Nicole corrected, glancing up at her husband and back to her book.

"Seventy-three. And he's still a young man," Peter observed, accurately.

Nicole thought her husband looked slightly distorted in the dark shadows of the evening and she looked up again from her book. She was sitting to his right, on the sofa, her feet supported by an ottoman.

"Pete," she said.

"Yeah?"

"Have you got something on your ear?" she asked.

"No."

But Nicole continued to peer through the gloom. His head was back, well sunk into the soft leather cushioning on his favorite chair. His ear was nearly touching the leather. To see better she leaned to her right. The flickering television did not make her vision more clear.

"Peter . . ."

"Yeah?"

"Look at me," she said.

"He's got 'em! Yeah! He might have stolen forty bases last year, but he won't have that one in his stats," Peter said and wiped his eyes again, this time with the sleeve of his sweat shirt.

With the third out the network went to commercial and Peter swung his chair toward Nicole's place on the sofa, a satisfied smile on his face.

Nicole stared at him. For the first time in her life, she was shocked into insensibility. Then she began to scream.

Blood was leaking out of Peter. It had seeped out of both ears, down his neck, and soaked into the shoulders of his once-white sweat shirt. His eyes were puddled with blood that was dark in color. The sleeves of his shirt were wet where he had more than once attempted to wipe them dry. Blood was dripping from both nostrils and as he smiled at Nicole she could see that his mouth was filling with blood, outlining each tooth like a dentist's test for bacteria.

As Peter sat, hardly feeling, robbed of his senses, Nicole dialed 911.

Peter was rushed to St. John's Hospital in Santa Monica. The emergency surgeon on duty, Ron Gleason, immediately ordered three units of whole blood and called UCLA Medical Center. UCLA was a Level 4 containment facility, the only one in the city. There, all medical personnel attending him would wear complete protective clothing as well as filtered respiratory equipment that St. John's didn't have.

Gleason did not have a diagnosis for patient Fischer except that whatever the cause, it had attacked the man's entire body. Blood tests could be conducted while Fischer was being transported to Brentwood. Liquids oozing from his anus were also collected for study.

At UCLA the patient's wife, Nicole Fischer, had a remarkably clear head and was a valuable source of diagnostic information. Still, she insisted on staying near her husband. Short of physical restraint, medical personnel were helpless to make her stand aside. While Fischer was being wheeled into a Level 3 ICU, intensive care unit, Nicole remained outside at the request of communicable disease specialists (CDS), and rendered a pre-illness case history. The CDS person who took Mrs. Fischer's statement, Dr. Silvia Corrall, was astounded that the patient's wife could relate almost a minute-by-minute account of her husband's activities for the prior seventy-two hours. Dr. Corrall used a digital recorder in the debriefing as well as making notes as fast as she had written since she was a student in medical school.

At first glance, Dr. Corrall, as well as two other consulting doctors, believed that they were dealing with the Ebola-Reston virus or a hemorrhagic fever of which there were several—Rift Valley Fever, Marburg Hemorrhagic Fever, Kyassanur Forest, and others. Yet even while they were discussing treatment strategies and integrated laboratory exploration with CDC in Atlanta, early test returns appeared to contradict their first impressions. There was no fever, nor was he delusional.

As a further complication, according to Mrs. Fischer's revelations of her husband's recent travel, he had not been exposed to locations around the globe where such diseases, as their names implied, might have been contracted. That was not to say that Fischer could not have been exposed to any of the hemorrhagic diseases through other forms of contact closer to home—a blood transfusion, for example—but there was nothing in the data received from Nicole that offered a source for Peter's distress.

Even as expedited blood and body fluid tests arrived in the treatment room, Dr. Corrall and her colleagues could see that Fischer's body was under full assault from a malevolent agent. His liver function had dropped more than seventy percent, his body organs in total were losing tissue definition, and Fischer, fully awake and his brain alert, began to experience nerve inconsistency. Waves of nausea struck him suddenly and he projected bile from his otherwise empty stomach.

In addition, brown stripes, dark blotches, and discolored swellings began to appear over his entire body. His skin, still oozing blood and a yellowish excretion through his pores, became taut and warm.

After twelve hours, Fischer's brain began to lose function and he no longer responded to sensory communications. In ICU, while his body was being fed oxygen as well as highly concentrated vitamin and electrolyte fluids, tufts of Fischer's hair began to fall out and his skin was painful to the touch. Continuing blood tests revealed that something was killing Fischer's white blood cells. His bones were decaying and his blood turning to plasma. His saliva glands were atrophying.

Sixteen hours after Fischer arrived at the UCLA medical complex one of the toxicologists on the staff, Robert Waters, said that he didn't think the man was infected with a biological agent. He believed the symptoms exhibited by the patient were similar to rare cases of radiation poisoning. Despite the fact that absolutely no evidence existed that Fischer had been exposed to an isotope of any kind, those specific topological tests were administered.

Peter Fischer died at 10:00 A.M. the following morning. An autopsy revealed that his organs, indeed virtually all of his innards, had turned to a kind of protein soup. Dr. Waters's enlightened instincts were correct. The agent of death had been thallium that had been subjected to intense radiation that had caused the metal to disintegrate into microscopic particles. When injested with food the radioactive particles spread to virtually every tissue of the body.

At the insistence of the U.S. Attorney General's Office, after consultation with the Director of Central Intelligence, the Los Angeles Homicide Department working with agents of the FBI investigated the death of Peter Fischer as a potential homicide. Conferring with the UCLA medical staff to establish a mortality time-line, the investigators were able work backwards to isolate the location where Fischer had eaten food that was either not prepared at home or prepared for him in particular away from the home. The food source was thought to be Pancho's restaurant in Manhattan Beach.

All employees of Pancho's who had worked at the place within five days before, during, and after Fischer and his wife had dined there were interviewed at length and their backgrounds checked. All were more or less permanent and reasonably longtime employees with two exceptions. The first was a young waitress named Janine Receda, age nineteen. Janine had been employed only one day before Peter and Nicole Fischer had eaten their last meal at Pancho's. She was a high school drop-out and was on probation from San Luis Obispo County from a suspended sentence for grand theft auto. She had only one prior for petty theft—shoplifting. She had permission from her parole officer to leave the county so that she could stay in Redondo Beach with her mother and new stepfather.

The second newest employee, a cook's helper, had been hired twenty-eight days before the Fischer's last meal. He was Lamie Arturo, age twenty-three, Mexican, living and working in the United States illegally. He was questioned extensively, as were all other employees. He claimed to be married, living with his wife whose name he said was Christia. They had two children. His wife worked, he said, cleaning houses in West Los Angeles. Arturo gave an address on Firmona Avenue in Inglewood. Investigators could find no such address. Arturo was arrested before he could leave work that day and held by the INS on a federal warrant on a number of immigration violations. In a second round of questioning by federal agents who wanted to interview Mrs. Arturo, Lamie refused to cooperate by providing them with a "good" address. He was afraid, he said, that they would be sent back to Mexico.

While other possible leads as to where Peter Fischer might have been poisoned were checked out, FBI officials and LAPD Homicide detectives had little confidence that Fischer's killer was in custody. The assassination entailed no small degree of sophistication and none of the investigators on the case believed Lamie Arturo was capable of behavior that complex. Rather, they came to believe Arturo's explanation that he had given investigators the phony address to deflect attention away from his wife and children who, quite likely, were in this country illegally as he was. A "hold" was placed on Lamie Arturo, but few law enforcement personnel believed that they had solved the crime.

The other Pancho workers who had been on the premises that night had all been employed for at least nine months or more. Detectives David Joyce and Harlan De-Vore, while believing that the source for Fischer's poisoning was other than Pancho's, nevertheless went through the formalities with each worker. Included in that group was a dishwasher named Jorge Santana. Santana was short, ill-kempt, about thirty-five years of age, painfully shy and, to put the finest point on it, not very bright.

Santana lived in the city of Los Angeles, a two-hour bus ride each way. His address was confirmed when it was revealed he had a small place to sleep among four families who shared three bedrooms and a single kitchen and bathroom. He answered the detective's questions in Spanish. He said that he had come from Chiapas, near the border of Guatemala. His village was Pecesula. He admitted that he was in America illegally.

"Jesus," David Joyce said later to his partner, DeVore, as they drank coffee and completed their day notes at the Culver City station house. "What do you think that guy Santana makes an hour washing dishes huh? Four bucks? Five? And he rides two hours each way on a bus. Know something, Harlan, I think I'm gonna quit bitching about life in general. Some people have it really hard." He continued to flip through his notes on the day as DeVore worked on his.

"Yep. Makes about enough to pay the bus fare," De-Vore said without looking up.

"You'd think at least he could wash dishes closer to that shit hole where he lives," Joyce said, shaking his head as he nudged aside his cold coffee mug.

"Maybe he's got a 401K he's building up," DeVore said. DeVore pushed his reading glasses onto the top of his head rather than take them off as he rubbed his tired eyes. He still had an overtime report to submit. This wasn't their station house, but he knew where to look for the forms. He found one in a sloppily kept pile and began to fill it out. He knew that Joyce would wait until he had finished before using his, DeVore's, as a template for himself.

"Well, you know, he's not the brightest dishwasher to hit L.A. in the last couple hundred years, either. Can't hardly handle his Spanish."

"You notice that, too?" DeVore said, looking up. Neither he nor his partner spoke Spanish fluently, but they could get by if things didn't get too fast.

"Yeah, but he's from way south. Probably an Indian. None of them can talk Mexican, anyway." Joyce reached over and gently pulled DeVore's nearly completed overtime statement toward his side of the table.

DeVore leaned back on his uncomfortable, unsupported stool and closed his eyes. He was tired from a sixty-hour week and it was only Thursday. Their line of work could be a ball buster, but at least it was interesting. And he made more money than an immigrant dishwasher.

"What was that?" Joyce said, now writing with dispatch since he did not have to think about the places he had been and the time he had spent there. It was all right there on Harlan's sheet. "What did you say?"

"I said fuck me. Fuck you, too, idiot," DeVore said, leaning forward toward his partner.

"Why? What'd I do?" Joyce asked.

"You nailed the case yourself a minute ago, but I had my head up my ass and so did you. Simple, man. Santana could have sold pencils on his own street corner and made more money than he did washing dishes at Pancho's in Manhattan Beach. But he didn't. Why didn't he? Because he liked working for nothing? Nobody can be that dumb. He rode to Manhattan Beach because he wanted to be there. And why did he want to be there?"

DeVore waited for his partner's light to go on.

But Joyce was already on his feet on his way out the door.

They turned on their flashing lights and punched the

siren to clear traffic ahead of them as they raced down Lincoln Boulevard, turned hard right on Rosecrans. They cut the noisemaker a good mile before arriving at Pancho's, but when they made their way inside, DeVore entering through the kitchen in the rear, they were too late.

"He took off after you guys left," one of the bartenders said to the detectives. "A couple, three hours ago. About that."

There was no trace of him save a photocopy of Santana's I.D. that Pancho's manager kept on all of his employees to show any INS officers who might want to know. The detectives relieved the manager of his photocopy and told him, untruthfully, that they would make sure he got it back. Also before leaving, DeVore went to the trouble of lifting a number of latent prints in and around Santana's working area. The dishwasher had been careful enough to leave almost nothing behind, but the spoon that he might have used to stir his coffee was put into DeVore's evidence bag.

The detectives passed the photo of Santana on to their federal colleagues who, in turn, put it through their Terrorist-Threat computer system. At first they got no hits because, they suspected, the quality of the photo of a photo was too low-grade. So the picture was overnight air shipped to FBI Washington, D.C. where it was computer enhanced. It was scanned again for similarities to other faces in the computer's data base. This time they got a hit.

Fingerprints lifted by DeVore on the coffee spoon were a match as were matches of prints later taken from Santana's Los Angeles residence. The T-file revealed that the suspect's real name was Mustafa Al Jahani, age twenty-eight, a Jordanian Arab, who had been an al Qaeda instructor in Afghanistan until the arrival of American troops. Al Jahani had been wounded in the fighting around Kandahar and taken prisoner in November, 2002. With the secret connivance between Pakistan President Musharref and the royal family of Saudi Arabia, Al Jahani had joined thousands of other al Qaeda fighters aboard Uzbekistani Russian-made Antonov transport planes flying in the dead of night out of Konduz. Those al Qaeda and Taliban fighters were delivered to various Arab countries, out of the reach of American forces.

Al Jahani and several hundred others were clothed, fed, rested; then sent to the Bekka Valley in Lebanon where they were paid back wages, re-armed, and began special training for a new program of terrorism against the West.

CHAPTER 2

The envelope containing the announcement had kicked around the house, moved unopened from a countertop to a table, to still another table for weeks. He made a point of treating communications from the U.S. Army as junk mail, either throwing it away unopened or scanning it briefly just in case it mistakenly contained a check. The rank of Lieutenant Colonel should have been his by age thirty-two, not forty, considering the kind of work he did. Young in Special Operations teams was, of course, a relative term. It took a long time to train a team member in all of the things he must do to become a fully qualified SpecWar operator.

Still, while a professional athlete was thinking of hanging it up at age thirty-five because of advancing years, a SpecOps soldier was just becoming extremely valuable to his team. When Julia asked him, as she often had during the two years they had been living together in San Francisco, why Special Warfare people willingly stayed in the army or the navy for a career, he had trouble making her understand. In the process of trying to tell her why, he had come to realize that there was an intangible element, a source of ultimate satisfaction, in being on a team with other men who were the world's best at what they did.

Then there was the fantasy factor. Every kid's dreams were made real in SpecOps.

The toys you had to play with! Great big tanks. Real fast airplanes. Big guns, little guns, sniper rifles, machine guns, knives, and parachutes. Glasses that let you see in the dark! The world's biggest game store and the nice people that owned the toy store encouraged you to go in and help yourself. What was hard to understand about that?

But there was a flip side. Joe Mears knew about the scary stuff, too. Every toy store had its horror games. There were things which, once they got inside your head, you couldn't get out again. The bad stuff would slip in and wait, crouched there in the blackness, in the very distant recesses of your mind. It fed itself on your brain until, one day, it had emptied you. You died, then, with your teeth chattering. That's how you paid the price for your toys.

Once Joe and Julia were watching television while a group of army veterans were being interviewed about their experiences in a past war. Their war had been over for half a century, but some of the veterans still couldn't speak about it. Julia thought it was just beautiful. A kind of touching thing.

Joe had to go out into the backyard where he cried so hard he gagged on his own spit. And he had left his war only a few dozen months ago. There were times when he tried to make deals with the crouching monster. But the throbbing fear stayed right where it was, gnawing away in the blackness.

Joe had a healthy respect for dying, but he knew there were lots of times in a man's life when dying would look like one hell of a good deal.

Stepping out of the army and into life with Julia felt good from the outset and got better every day. The past months spent with her, almost two years, was even better than he had hoped. No wonder people got married.

He had never told her, of course, but he found her career as a sports reporter so utterly superficial, so totally without the need to have an original thought, that he loved it. Citing stats, commenting on coaches hired and fired, players graded and traded, games won and lost, was the whole job and none of it made a bit of difference.

Plus, nobody got hurt. Sports itself was a great activity that required nothing more than hard work if you were still actively involved, and nothing but a slice of emotional investment for your team if you were just a fan. You couldn't lose a leg. Break one, maybe, but not lose it. You wouldn't be tortured for information by the other team.

Joe envied Julia her work. He patted her butt and stroked her hair when, on the rare times she got depressed about her business, and reminded her that thousands of people, her readers, her peers, fans everywhere, depended upon her insights into the teams she covered for their daily fix. She could be proud.

Her career reminded Joe that there were such things as positive scams—like churches who solicited money. Church officials, for example, loved to get it and their followers experienced joy in giving it. It was a win, win situation.

He thought the Catholic Church was silly to have ever stopped selling absolutions, dispensations, and commutations. It made everyone involved happy, especially the priests, bishops, and popes who received it, and the many wealthy purchasers who shed their sins could face the future with new and improved optimism. Except for maybe a few puritans. That's why Joe liked the deification of sports. While it made money for the owners, the people who bought tickets were delighted with the pageantry of the games they had made possible—except for the occasional boring blowout.

Through Julia, then, Joe was keeping the dark monster in its cave. Even if his classes were becoming more routine than he wanted to admit, and not a few of the young military people who matriculated through the Monterey language school were about to take up arms in a cause that continued to stir his heart, he was almost content.

He kept his class work at a minimum. Also, to save everyone's time, especially his own, he erred on the side of giving too few homework assignments rather than too many. He spent most of his time staying in physical shape by running five miles a day around the Presidio and working out with a martial arts group that met three times a week at the post gym.

Julia had an idyllic life, as well. She had said that to Joe more than once. She, too, maintained a muscular body by regular workouts, which Joe appreciated. They could share that interest for several reasons. They made love like a couple of rabbits, though Joe would be the first to admit that he had never made love to a rabbit. He imagined that his and Julia's reproductive impulses had to be similar. If there were six-billion rabbits in the world, he thought, that would prove it.

"What?" he said, dunking a biscotti into day-old coffee as he watched a television news reporter quizzing a retired marine sergeant explain what was wrong with pentagon strategy in Afghanistan.

"I said did you listen to your messages on the machine?" Julia said from the kitchen.

"I can't hear a word you're saying," Joe responded over the volume of the television.

Julia appeared in the doorway of the kitchen. "The answering machine, Joe. There were three messages on it when I came home. One of them was for me. I've been invited to spend the night in the dorm of the Stanford baseball team before the game this weekend."

"Gonna go?" Joe asked, dribbling coffee onto his chin from the biscotti.

"Haven't made up my mind. Living with a guy your age has its limitations," she said.

"I know just what you mean."

"Living with a guy your age?" Julia asked.

"Certainly. Who would know better than me?" he said.

"So? What did they want?" she said, referring to his

telephone message from Bruce Coggin, now a lieutenant general.

"I don't know," he said, untruthfully.

"Why didn't you call back and find out?" Julia asked, her chin moving upward a half-inch.

Joe considered for a long moment, regarding her soft brown hair and green eyes. She sat next to him on their extra large sofa that looked better than it felt.

"Good news never comes over the telephone," he said, exhaling.

"Is that one of the things that spies know and everybody else doesn't?" she said.

"Nice tits," he said.

"I thought you and General Coggin were good buddies?" she said.

"We are. That is, I respect Bruce Coggin enormously. I like him, too. But the call today didn't come from him directly. It came through his office. In other words, the general wants to talk to you, Colonel. See the difference?"

Damn, he thought, she really does have knockout tits. He reached for the buttons on her chambray shirt.

"I'm going to take a nap. If you want to get laid, you're going to have to do it by yourself. Doesn't he know you're not in the army anymore? I don't understand the dodging and weaving," she said.

"Being out of the army is like a fat girl winning a marathon. It's a great idea, but it ain't gonna happen. If you accept the king's commission you are in for the rest of your life, plus ten," he explained. "Saving yourself for the Cardinal baseball team?"

"So you didn't talk to him?"

"Yeah. I talked with him," Joe said.

Julia leaned slowly back against the end of the sofa, her eyes never leaving his.

"So?" she said.

"So? So nothing."

"What did he want?"

"Nothing. He just wanted to shoot the shit," Joe said, clicking on the television.

Julia took the remote out of his hand and clicked the TV off. She waited.

Joe took a deep breath. "I'm going to be away for awhile. Not long," he finally said.

"You're going back into the army?" she asked.

"No," he said, hiding behind the sheerest veil of truth. "I'm just going to travel for awhile. On business."

Julia picked up the small pot holder she had brought in from the kitchen. It was made in the shape of a brown bear. Its companion, a wolf, was part of a Goldilocks set. She pushed listlessly on its padding.

"Julia," Joe began, but paused when she waved her hand in the air at nothing in particular. "I love you, Julia."

She nodded.

"About time I went to work, anyway. Real work, back at the paper."

When they arrived in the California Bay area she was more than willing to change her environment. With her parents dead and no family except cousins still on the East Coast, Julia took to California's beaches and mountains like every day was a vacation. She had picked up a reasonable advance for the sports book she was now writing and if she wrote one a year she could support herself. They had never talked about marriage, she thought, because of Joe's tenuous occupation. She felt, no, she knew, in the back of her mind, that they could reach out for him in some way and if they did he would go.

"Okay," she said, turning toward him. "That's it, then."

"No, that isn't it. I said I loved you. And you love me, too." He looked for a reaction from her; then said, "At least that's what you say when you're drunk."

"Yeah, well, that's just when I'm drunk," she said, then laughed. "Okay, maybe I do. It's getting harder to think about life without you, so that's probably what love is. Part of it, anyway."

She moved close to him as she put her hand in his hair before kissing him gently, briefly.

"Julia, we could get married," he said.

"Why? So I can't have dates while you're gone?"

A man who called himself Hesam, meaning "generous by nature," rose before dawn as usual, and tidied up his tiny room that resembled a monk's cell. There was little to make neat as he slept on the floor with a single wool blanket that had fed several generations of moths and beetles with only a rough cotton thobe rolled to serve as a crude support for his head. In the small room was an equally small wooden table and a single chair, for Hesam had no need of another. From a ceramic bowl suspended from the ceiling to keep its contents safe from rats, Hesam took two pieces of fresh fruit he had purchased the day before in the bazaar. He daily walked six miles to work each way and the fruit would provide much needed nourishment for his long day in the city.

Finished with his room, Hesam slung over his shoulder his small wooden box containing shoe polish, rags, and a prized soft bristle brush. He used a short aluminum ladder that had once been attached to a swimming pool to lower himself to the second floor of the three-story house. The highest floor, charitably so-called by its owner, was the least desirable because of the extremes of temperature. In the summer months, when it was one hundred twenty degrees in the city, the coolest location was the first floor. Hesam used a creaking wooden stair, built on the outside of the house, from the second level to the street. He briefly considered using public transportation, but in the end decided that he would save even the few dinars the ride would cost and walk as he usually did. Once three Iraqi dinars brought an American dollar. Now it took 1,900 dinars. The Iraqi "street" traded in tangibles rather than currency whenever possible. Hesam accepted pieces of fruit, a small cut of cooked meat, part of a loaf of bread, for his services.

Still, he did not complain. He was the envy of more than one medical doctor or engineer who earned less income. The signs of economic distress were everywhere to see in Baghdad. In the marketplace one could find family heirlooms selling for a day's worth of food. Personal jewelry, televisions, refrigerators, and furniture were sold gladly by families who were desperate for money.

Hesam walked with many others over a bridge that spanned the Tigris River. On the streets and highways there were few vehicles, among them only worn automobiles with dents in the doors and trunks, broken headlights, and bald tires. None were newer than ten years old. As he continued west, nearing the center of the city, Hesam paused to look at the window of a clothing store that once boasted an inventory from the best manufacturers in the world. Now they sold Chinese-made jeans for $7 while a Syrian-made sweater went for half that price.

He arrived at the Al-Rashid Hotel off Yafa Street before 6:00 A.M., ready to catch businessmen coming to or going from breakfast before they began their daily appointments. Hesam had purchased his treasured location by paying first a baggage handler who, in turn, paid the bell captain above him who, finally, paid the concierge for the privilege of shining shoes in one of the garden areas outside the hotel lobby.

The quality of his shoe shines was excellent, because he used plenty of wax and an inexhaustible supply of energy to make the soft leather of Middle-Eastern shoes brightly reflect the sun. Hesam liked the work. It gave him access to parts of the city he would not otherwise have reason to see. Also, he met all sorts of people on every level of society. That gave him opportunities he valued most highly despite the fact that virtually all of those people did not acknowledge him. Indeed, did not speak to him. But he knew who they were.

He made mental notes about important members of the
Baath party, the Great Leader's own political supporters,
and members of the armed forces. He had seen, and
shined the boots of colonels, generals, and once a secretary of state. Foreigners who had business with the leaders
of Iraq also stayed at the hotel. Hesam could not have
been blessed with a more advantageous place to work.

One day, in the late afternoon, when the intense heat
had kept many indoors and the city was waiting for the
worst to pass, Hesam looked up from his shoe box to
see a military figure standing over him. The uniformed
man dropped one foot onto the box.

"Shine these shoes and be very quick. I have no time.
What is your name?" the officer said.

"Hesam, sir," he said, setting to work on the shoe
without delay.

The man grunted at this unimportant piece of information, the name of a shoeblack. Hesam could tell by his
insignia that the officer was an army colonel. He affected
a mustache, of course, and wore it neatly trimmed as
was his black hair over which he wore the customary
black beret.

"I have not seen you here before," the colonel said.

"This place of business has been mine for three
months, sir," Hesam said, not slacking the pace of work
on the officer's shoe.

"And where are you from, Hesam?" the officer asked,
his gaze drifting away, indicating little interest in Hesam's antecedents.

"An Neff, sir. It is in the west. A very small village.
And very poor."

Hesam realized that he might have said the wrong
thing and added: "But our leader, Saddam, will soon
make it better."

"Yes. Of course." The colonel turned his eyes slowly
back toward the bent man shining his shoes. "Tell me,
Hesam, is your village near Akashat?"

"Yes, Colonel, sir. Thirty kilometers to the south,"
Hesam confirmed.

"Approximately," the colonel said. "You mean approximately thirty kilometers."

"No, sir. The distance is exact."

The colonel's eyes were now locked unmoving upon the head of the shoe shiner.

"You are sure."

"Yes, Colonel. I am sure. Your other shoe, please, Colonel," Hesam said.

The colonel opened the slender newspaper he carried under his arm. Because of the lack of newsprint caused by the illegal sanctions against Iraq, there were few pages. The colonel scanned them quickly, then glanced at his wristwatch.

"That's enough," he said, dropping several dinars carelessly near Hesam.

"Thank you, sir. May Allah bless you," Hesam said to the colonel's retreating back. Hesam quickly scooped up the generous payment and placed the paper money into an inside breast pocket that he himself had sewn into the material. He buttoned the inner pocket to make sure the money would not be lost.

Though quite late in the afternoon it was not yet dark when Hesam's work day was finished. His labor had been so profitable that he made the decision to take a bus from the hotel. He crossed the expanse of Zawra Park, turned northwest, and walked to Dimesha Street where he waited only twenty minutes for a bus. Hesam, among the last to board, clung perilously to a handrail as the bus continued in a westerly direction down Mansur Street, the opposite direction from Hesam's home on the east side of the city. Hesam exited the bus at Arbataash and began again to walk.

He arrived at a small café at a time when coffee houses and eateries were beginning to fill. Men sat in groups at sidewalk tables smoking their pipes and sipping the bitter Arab coffee that stained their teeth and, at least for Hesam, made the heart race. Over the entrance of the café was a hand-painted sign that read: *Khdim*. The sign was bleached by the ultraviolet rays of the relentless sun and abraded by tiny grains of sand blown by strong desert winds. The word meant server or slave.

Hesam stepped inside, his nostrils at once flooded with distinctive odor of deliciously spiced roast lamb. Instinctively, Hesam knew that the scent would derive not from a roast but from a soup. Even perhaps from starved lamb rib. Nevertheless, Hesam realized that he had not eaten since the fruit from early morning and he determined that he would at least eat Khubz Arabi, the delicious round bread, as soon as possible.

"Ah, Hesam," a friendly voice sounded nearby. Amza Abdullah touched Hesam's shoulder with deliberate warmth. "Good to see you, my friend. Why have you been staying away?"

The shoeblack nodded his head deeply in respect for Amza the longtime proprietor of the *Khdim.* "Amza Abdullah," he said, smiling. "I am embarrassed. You have been good to me for so many years and I have done nothing for you. I don't suppose I could shine your shoes?"

Amza put his head back and laughed heartily. "Come, come, let's go into my room and talk of our daughters and our donkeys," the café owner said to the man he had met only once, two months ago.

"Coffee?" Amza asked as the men settled into straight-backed chairs in a small but adequate room the café owner used for an office as well as storage space. There was, of course, less space needed for supplies that were impossible to obtain for the past ten years.

Hesam shook his head. He appreciated the fact that Amza had survived as long as he had, a northern Kurd of the Sunni sect. Amza had entirely lost the distinctive Kurdish language in which he was born and raised. Hesam knew that the language of the Kurds was not at all related to Turkish or to Arabic, but was closer to the Persian dialects or to Pashto, which was spoken in Afghanistan. In Baghdad these days were secret listeners who could find traitors among the citizenry by such simple things as an inadvertent language slip.

"I have no time," Hesam answered. "Do you have the chemicals?"

"Yes, of course," Amza said to Hesam, a man he had accepted on faith alone, silently leading him through yet another door to a room that was very small, like a water closet.

Hesam waited for the café proprietor to leave; then closed the door. A single lightbulb hanging from the end of a frayed cord illuminated the cramped room. He lowered himself to his hands and knees, reaching underneath a crude workbench. He searched blindly with his fingers until he found a small release mechanism; then manipulated the catch until he felt it come free. From a hidden cabinet door, he carefully withdrew a number of items he would need, including a second lightbulb and other small items which he placed atop the tiled workbench.

Upon the countertop there were now two bottles of opaque glass and a smaller bottle that contained a fluid dropper. Also on the counter he placed a pottery water pitcher near a flat porcelain saucepan. From the pitcher Hesam poured water into the saucepan until the level was only a few millimeters from the bottom. From his pocket Hesam removed a slender can of shoe polish and, after placing the water pitcher aside, used the cover of the can as a measuring device for the precise parts of fluid from each of the two bottles, which he added to the pan of water. When he had satisfied himself that his ratios were correct, he added a third ingredient, this from the bottle containing the glass dropper tube. He carefully counted the drops he added into the water solution.

Hesam now removed the all-but-worthless dinar notes that he had earned throughout the day, which, folded, had created a large roll in his baggy pants pocket. These he set aside before withdrawing still more dinars from his breast pocket, the ones that he had accepted from the army colonel. There were four bills, and he placed each of these carefully into the solution, prodding them lightly to make sure they were entirely submerged. He stooped once more underneath the workbench to retrieve a watch that was missing its band. Hesam placed the watch near the solution and made a mental note of the time. He remained motionless, looking at the notes, for several minutes. The shiner of shoes reached up to the white lightbulb and gingerly, because of its heat, unscrewed it. Moments later the room was relit when a new bulb cast the room in an indistinct, purplish-red glow. Hesam put a jeweler's loupe of great magnification over one eye. Fishing one of the bills out of the liquid and holding it up to the red light, words in neatly written Arabic lettering appeared on the currency in microreduction.

Hesam removed the bills from the solution, one by one, reading each with great care and taking his time. He memorized the parts of each he thought most important. He had lost track of time when he heard a gentle knock on the door.

"It is time."

Hesam recognized the voice of the café proprietor.

"A few more minutes," he responded. Hesam heard muffled footsteps fading away; then continued with his work of memorization. On the final bill there was a message different from the others. This one was written in English, by hand; then reduced to ultrafine printed characters.

Again time stole away from him and Hesam sensed, rather than heard, the footsteps return. He had to make the decision of destroying the bank notes, leaving them on the premises, or taking them with him when he left.

"Hesam," the whispered voice could be heard through the light wooden door. The proprietor's voice sounded stressed despite his attempt not to unduly hurry the man inside.

"Yes, I'm coming."

Impulsively, Hesam gathered up the bills, which by now were virtually dry, and put them into his pocket along with the fruit of his labor that day. He quickly replaced the chemicals and other items he had used in their place behind the wall, remembering to exchange lightbulbs once again. As he stepped into the brighter light of the storeroom, he found Amza waiting for him.

"A man is here," he said, inadvertently betraying nervousness by licking his lower lip.

"Who?"

"His name is Solaimani," the café owner said.

Hesam did not know the man but he knew the name. *Mudiriyat al-Amn al-Amma.* The Iraqi Secret Police. The eight-thousand-man organization ostensibly existed to pursue criminals engaged in smuggling and theft, but in fact it was a brutally repressive agency that ferreted out the slightest disloyalty to the regime of Saddam Hussein. Once located in the Baladiat district it was now quartered in the Al Baladiat area of the city, a place Hesam knew well from his perambulations through Baghdad. While its target priority remained the same, its relocation necessitated a change from item Number 9 to item Number 14 on the USAF strike map to be executed in the first twenty-four hours of the coming campaign.

"Is he a regular customer?" Hesam asked calmly.

Amza shook his head.

"You are sure that it's him?" Hesam asked.

"Yes, I am sure."

"Is he alone?"

"Alone, yes. He has a table in the back of the room. He insisted," the proprietor said as though it was not his fault.

"He could be looking for the perfect cup of coffee. Or mint tea," Hesam suggested, not for a moment believing it himself. "Walk out of your door as though you are going for fresh air. Go slowly down the street to the north; then cross in the middle. Don't hurry. You only want to stretch your legs."

"What will you do?" the café operator asked, a bead of sweat now appearing upon his balding head.

Hesam could hardly blame him. While he had not met Solaimani, he knew the man by other means. Solaimani came to the attention of Barzan Tikriti, Saddam Hussein's half brother and head of the secret police, when the then junior officer personally threw the living, screaming person of Republican Guard Captain Abd-al-Muttalib into a thousand-degree furnace. The young officer had uttered words of defeat in 1991, during the war against America. The personality twist of Solaimani's that most endeared him to Barzan was that he had whispered into the tank officer's ear that very soon he would be joined on the white-hot coals by his wife and two small sons.

In point of fact, Solaimani had merely jailed the woman and sent the boys, each under the age of ten, to distant locations, neither to see the other again. Although Solaimani had not executed the woman, Barzan Tikriti felt that it was the thought that counted and he rewarded the secret police officer with rapid advancement through the ranks. Solaimani reported directly to Barzan and to no one else in the black labyrinth of the Baghdad government. His boss had never been disappointed.

"I'll be near," Hesam said. As a matter of practical fact, Hesam had to know if Solaimani was suspicious of the café owner. Amza was risking much to help the United States. Even if his primary motivation was to serve the cause of Kurdish establishment, it was nevertheless important that America not be perceived again as deserting its friends. It was also the case that if Amza was under suspicion it was entirely possible that Hesam was also suspect. He hoped that Solaimani's visit to the *Khdim* was entirely benign. Even secret policemen had to eat and drink. But if there was the slightest doubt, Hesam would have to kill him.

Amza paused at the door, inhaling deeply, as Hesam emerged from the back room. He immediately espied the policeman in the back of the room, his chair placed close to the east wall. Solaimani looked even younger than his grainy file photographs had been able to reveal. His beard, Hesam could tell even from this distance, was far less thick than most and Hesam wondered if perhaps Solaimani had grown the immature thatch only to appear older than he was. He had, after all, been in the torture and murder business since his late teens. Hesam guessed he was now about thirty.

As Amza stepped from the doorway of the café onto the sidewalk, Solaimani rose from his chair and, leaving his tea and small sweet cake, followed the proprietor. Hesam shifted his own position so that he could see every customer, including those sitting at tables outside. Hesam waited. Sure enough, a man whose attention was focused on Solaimani left his chair behind the wrought iron partition circling the tables, and began to keep pace with Solaimani. This man, Hesam judged, was Solaimani's age, perhaps even younger. He had the strength and grace of an athlete for he was light on his feet and his arms swung easily in rhythm to the movement of his legs. Before Hesam left the premises, his hand touched a tabletop and closed around a spoon. The spoon was metal, but its handle was plastic and made to resemble bone. Unobtrusively, he dropped the spoon into his trouser pocket and stepped into the night air.

The man, whom Hesam now followed at a discreet distance, wore a dark shirt and an expensively made jacket, perhaps Italian wool. There was no question in Hesam's mind that the man was secret police and that he would be armed.

Hesam allowed Amza get an entire block ahead of the two policemen before darting into the street behind a badly abused panel truck. Because the sun was now down the truck had its lights turned on. Only one headlight was operating and one taillight, the lens of which had been broken and was covered by a red rag. Hesam had no trouble keeping pace with the vehicle as it lurched and belched along the narrow street that more resembled an alley. As the truck turned to its left at the next corner, heading west, Hesam stepped quickly into a doorway, completely shielded from the policeman who continued to track on Solaimani.

Amza now crossed to the other side of the street. He paused briefly there to light a cigarette. He raised and lowered himself several times on his toes, as though relieving fatigue. Solaimani did not break his measured stride. Without looking at the café owner, the secret policeman stopped at the opposite corner as though he would wait for a city bus. When Amza resumed his stroll, now circling back roughly in the direction whence he had come, Solaimani fell into pace, keeping well back before crossing to the same side of the street. For the moment Hesam was concerned less with Solaimani than with neutralizing his athletic assistant.

When he was certain that the second policeman was within about forty meters, Hesam stepped out of the shadows of the doorway and turned the corner. He was now moving toward the policeman, who, while aware of Hesam's progress on the same sidewalk, was nevertheless focused on his superior and the man he was following. As Hesam closed on the policeman he kept his eyes averted. It was a condition of self-effacement common to the lower classes and almost expected by people of power such as the police. Just before the instant of passing, Hesam saw the policeman look directly at him. Then away. It was at that moment that Hesam moved.

The curvature of the spoon was securely nestled in the palm of his hand with only the stubby handle protruding between the fingers of his clenched fist. In a fast, continuous motion, Hesam brought his hand upward and without hesitation slammed the handle of the spoon into the policeman's throat. Aimed at a spot just above the man's breastbone, the blow was delivered with tremendous accuracy and force. It was the result of years of work in martial arts and physical conditioning.

The secret policeman's hands flew immediately toward his neck, but the damage had already been done. By crushing his trachea and smashing his larynx, Hesam knew the man could not breathe or make a sound other than soft gurgling. Without looking back, Hesam continued his unhurried pace down the narrow street while the large, muscular, policeman fell to his knees, then onto his face, then died. The spoon remained in Hesam's hand.

Solaimani had closed behind Amza. Even as Hesam

crossed the street to be near their position, Solaimani had stopped the Kurd and was speaking to him. Hesam could not yet hear what was being said but it didn't matter. Hesam was committed. Amza put his hands into his pockets and came up with what appeared to be documents of identification. As he handed them over to the taller secret policeman, who was taking a very close look at the papers, Hesam closed.

At first Solaimani merely glanced at the shoe shiner who might have appeared to be innocuous; then he turned his attention back to the café keeper. But some kind of alarm went off inside the head of the secret policeman. He turned back toward the approaching Hesam. As he did so he reached a hand inside his coat pocket. There was no doubt in Hesam's mind that the man would come up with a gun and that Hesam's spoon weapon would do no good. Hesam sprang forward low, onto his hands; then swept a leg in a hard kick.

The maneuver was intended to knock the man off his feet. Hesam was only partially successful. Solaimani's balance was lost as he attempted to jump backward from the powerful leg strike, and he reached out to steady himself on the stone wall of a nearby building. It was his gun hand. In the space of a second, the time it took Solaimani to steady himself, Hesam was upon him. Hesam went immediately for the eyes, hooking the middle finger of his right hand into the eye socket and squeezing hard. He could feel the soft, viscous material give way, but he was very aware that he had failed to reach both eyes and that his opponent could still see. To the Arab's great credit, he did not scream from the agony that Hesam knew was intense. The policeman was aware that he was in a fight for his life and wasted no time on thinking about his own pain. He threw a knee at Hesam, which caught him in the groin, but the blow was not direct and Hesam was able to absorb the shock.

Solaimani's gun discharged within millimeters of Hesam's head. The explosion was so close to his ear that he was almost deafened on his left side. While he attempted to consolidate his tenuous grip on the policeman's forearm, Hesam received a head butt on the cheekbone. Stars and other kinds of pyrotechnics exploded into a variety of colors inside Hesam's head, almost dropping him to his knees. But he knew that to relax his attack even for an instant would bring certain death.

Solaimani was a well-trained fighter. Using all of his strength and agility, Hesam crossed his right arm over to Solaimani's right side, blocking the Arab with his shoulder, and managed to get both hands on Solaimani's right arm. Hesam pushed down hard, dropping all of his weight onto that appendage and twisted quickly.

He heard, and felt with satisfaction, the snapping of the Arab's ulna. The gun fell to the sidewalk where it discharged for the second time. Hesam was aware that gunfire would bring police and that little time was left. He was now on the ground with his quarry. Hesam slammed his elbow into the man's jaw once, twice, and again. A groan escaped from the policeman's bleeding mouth, but a glint of metal then appeared. Hesam expected in the next moment to feel the blade of a knife rip into his flesh. The knife did indeed flash but it was wielded by Amza, and it was plunged into Solaimani's ribs, penetrating vital organs. Amza struck hard and repeatedly until the policeman stopped moving, an audible hiss of air leaving his mouth and nose.

Without exchanging a word the café owner and the shoe shine man pulled the policeman's body down a narrow walkway between the buildings. Hesam, following Amza's head movements, helped carry the Arab's inert body into a small courtyard where there was a large trash container. Hesam assumed Amza was going to push the body into it, but Amza shook his head violently in the negative.

"No, no. Leave him here," he said.

Literally dropping the body where they were, Hesam followed Amza to a different way back to the street, several buildings away. When they emerged Hesam could see that the first policeman's body had already been moved. Amza followed his gaze. "The police have no friends here. Come."

They traveled a circuitous route which eventually returned them to the *Khdim*. There were soldiers in the streets, but they were not directed, milling about in response to shots having been fired. They had no idea where to look. While customers sat at their tables sipping coffee and mint tea, a policeman entered the premises. He first asked Amza if he had heard the shots. Amza nodded and said that he had. Where? They seemed to come from that way. But he could not be sure. Anyone else? the policeman asked, raising his voice. No one responded. The policeman saw no point in querying each customer so he went back into the street.

"When they count heads back at the *Mudiriyat al-Amn al-Amma* and find out who is missing, they'll be back," Hesam said to Amza.

"Yes."

"And someone will talk, I think. If I were you, I would leave now," Hesam said.

But the Kurd shook his head slowly. "There is nowhere to go. Do you remember the attacks?"

"I was not there," Hesam said. But he knew of what Amza was speaking. On March 16, 1988, Saddam Hussein attacked his own citizens with poison gas. And with biological weapons, as well. Tens of thousands died unspeakable deaths. Hesam was in Iran at the time, but he crossed into Iraq three days later. All of the dead were not yet buried.

"My family lived in Halabja," Amza said, his eyes steady on Hesam's. "My mother and father were there. My father was a dentist. I had two sisters and two brothers. Saddam's troops positioned artillery on the road outside of the town and began shooting. All of my family died. Even our cow died, lying on her side, crying from the pain. It was the family pet. My oldest sister's skin fell off her bones while she was still alive."

Hesam had knowledge of these things. The Iraqi army used a variety of chemical and biological weapons. They wanted to see how they worked on human beings and the Kurds were ideal. Saddam Hussein wanted them dead because the Kurds owed him no allegiance.

"A woman in our town went insane when she saw a pack of dogs eating her son. She was being held by the soldiers and before they released her the dogs had eaten him all. Can you imagine such a thing?" the Kurd asked Hesam.

Hesam slowly shook his head.

"So I will not run away," Amza said, his voice steady. "I will not live peacefully in a world that is run by Saddam Hussein."

"All right. Then I won't see you again." Hesam embraced the courageous Kurd.

"But they will be here, eh? You said that they would," Amza said.

Hesam walked east once more, again resisting the idea of sporadic public transportation. He could buy a bicycle tomorrow. Maybe. He only had perhaps two more meetings; then he would leave.

He covered the six miles to his room in less than two hours. No one paid any particular attention to him and he was not followed. There was no reason to believe that the secret police who had been at the café were looking for him, not Amza. With two of them dead in the streets of Baghdad, the hunt would be on. It would become intense. They did not know what he looked like, of course, but there was always the danger of accidentally becoming one of the thousands who were imprisoned or murdered in reprisal. Or that the café proprietor would be caught and made to talk. Any man could be made to talk sooner or later.

Hesam watched his apartment for a half hour from a distance before climbing the steps that took him to his room. He did not stay long, only long enough to gather up a worn metal salad pot and a blanket from his bed. He let himself down to ground level, but instead of using the street and sidewalk in front of the house, he walked into the rear and made his way east. At the last unpaved road that serviced his rural part of Baghdad, Hesam crossed, certain that he was unseen. Occasionally, a dog barked at the sound of his movement in the night, but after nearly a mile of traveling, the last thirty minutes of which was on the fine sand of the desert, Hesam glanced around for a landmark. A few meters from him he spotted it, five smooth stones, fifteen to twenty pounds each. One would have to look more than once to notice that they were laid in order.

Hesam fell to his knees and began digging with the salad bowl. Less than eighteen inches below the surface he struck a piece of thick plastic. He pulled and it came easily out of the hole he had just dug. He removed several items from the plastic bag which kept its contents free of weather and even free from sand. Among other items Hesam had stored an MP-5 submachine gun and several full clips of ammunition. He ignored the gun, however, and withdrew a small electronic device, which contained a keypad as well as a burst transmitter. He placed a piece of black cloth over the transmitter and the keypad to cover its glow, then began to tap English characters on the keypad. The machine would then convert the input data to a string of scrambled symbols.

He closed his eyes as he recalled the information taken from the dinars he had examined in the café. There was first the name of the facility, then the product specialization. *Badr Yousefiya,* missile casings, mobile launchers; *Qaqa'a,* missile fuel; *Al Wafa'a,* missile research; *Al Faris,* outer missile structures; *Ibn Majid,* missile structures, distilling vats, large metal parts; *Al Doura,* nuclear reactor parts, high pressure equipment for reactors; *Khawre Al Zubayr,* oxide magnesium heavy water; *Al Tajiyat,* metal conversion labs for nuclear fuel for PWR reactors; *Al Kindi,* UCL4 235 production; *Al Mansour,* laser-guidance systems; *Ibn Al Athir,* nuclear warhead assembly plant; *Bilad Al Shuheda,* R&D for missile launchers; *Al Muthanna,* the biggest factory for chemical weapons production; *Al Qadissiya,* centrifuges for U235 production; Project 710, long-range missile production.

Hesam noted that the Optical Center Jadriya lasers, located behind the Science College, was headed by Saddam's nephew, Dr. Nafa Al Tikriti. Hesam knew that the Iraqi U235 source for their PC-3 program came from the mines at Ukashat. There were seven facilities that were involved in the calutron enrichment program four of which, al-Jesira, al-Atheer, al-Rabbiyah and al-Dijjla at Zafaraniyah, had not been identified by American intelligence and had therefore not included on the strike maps now being assembled by DOD. Those secret facilities, then, had continued to do their work since 1989 and had even expanded in the process. Tarmiya, located thirty kilometers northwest of Baghdad, was now the main site for an electromagnetic isotope separation (EMIS) program for the uranium enrichment program. The Iraqis had successfully hidden the site by erecting no fences near it, laying underground power lines into the plant, all done under the cover of night, and by chemically washing the recovered uranium from rebuilt calutron components. There would be no telltale yellow tailings to alert optical satellite observations.

Hesam worked as rapidly as he could, needing to transmit the data by 0430 hours, Baghdad time. The Russian satellite, Resurs-Fl, orbiting one hundred fifty-eight to one hundred seventy miles above the earth, would have closed its window by that time. It was a coup of the current American administration that Russian President Putin allowed U.S. Special Operations units to access their most secret satellite communications system to transmit highly classified material from locations around the world. Resurs-Fl, a refinement of the ZENIT satellites series, was believed the world over to be a reconnaissance satellite that carried either radar scanning or photoimaging capabilities, which it did. But the ten-thousand-pound satellite also carried EHF (Extremely High Frequency) equipment that could receive and relay nanosecond bursts of coded information of the kind Hesam had encoded.

Hesam succeeded in finishing his work with a half hour

to spare. He replaced his materials into the protective plastic bag, including the critical dinar bills, and reburied it. If events were to go as he planned, he would return for the transmitter and documents within twenty-four hours. Then he would leave Iraq. He refused to think of the old axiom that nothing ever went according to plan.

CHAPTER 3

When the sun rose the next morning, Hesam had had no REM sleep the night before. There were times of extreme stress, on this operation as well as others, when sleep and wakefulness became indistinguishable. His body was tired, but then his body was always tired. The secret to survival was to remain alert and efficient even when both muscles and brain wanted to quit working. So he cleaned his tiny space once again before setting out for the city on foot. It was too late for him to purchase a bicycle.

He went out of his way to wash himself at a public water source that was unofficially called the People's Fountain. It was already ninety degrees before 0700, making the tepid water feel cool to his touch. He felt refreshed as he walked the remaining mile to the hotel to take up his station in its arbor area.

Business was good in the morning, but the customer Hesam most wanted to see did not arrive. Midday brought the city to a standstill, as usual, by force of the oppressive summer heat. Movement out of doors was an effort, even in the shade. Hesam allowed himself to lean against one of the columns that supported a veranda that circled the garden. He knew that he would be berated if he was seen by one of the lesser hotel staff, but he was beyond caring as his head fell forward onto his chest. The movement then woke him, while the drone of the ubiquitous flies in his ears lulled him to sleep repeatedly.

Though customer foot traffic increased again by late afternoon, Hesam's business did not. He might have walked away from his sanctioned space without being missed. There was still no sign of the army colonel when night arrived and the temperature had abated. Hesam became increasingly concerned as the tempo of the city began to increase and the population escaping from the paralyzing grasp of the day's heat. But still there was no sign of the man he expected.

Cafes and upscale restaurants were, despite their limited menus, approaching their peak dining time. Hesam had been at his station for fifteen hours. A dishwasher from the kitchen had shared with him part of a *fatayer,* a sweetened bread filled with spinach and cheese, that had been left on a customer's plate. Hesam in turn purchased a *basboosa,* a semolina tart soaked with syrup, which he and his friend devoured. That sumptuous, if less than bountiful meal, had been eight hours ago. Hesam was still thinking about it when he began to place his shoe polish and brush back inside his box preparing to leave, when the figure of an army officer stepped out of the shadows and placed a black boot on his box.

"Good evening, sir," Hesam said, immediately moving to prepare the boot for an application of wax.

"Shoe shine man, after I walk away, leave your box and run," the colonel said, slowly shifting his eyes, peering into the shadows of the huge hotel building.

Hesam did not answer aloud but continued to shine the officer's boots.

"They have arrested your friend, the café owner. He is very brave, but it will not be long before he tells them everything he knows." The colonel paused until several guests of the hotel had passed by. "Did you destroy the . . . money?"

"It is safe," Hesam said, brushing the wax he had just applied to the boots.

"Damn," the officer said. "If it is ever found . . ."

"Do not worry, Colonel, when I say it is safe, I mean that it won't be found."

The colonel licked his lips, the first outward sign of nervousness Hesam had observed in him.

"I am the man you are to meet," Hesam said.

"You?"

"Yes. If you want to get out of Iraq alive, Colonel, you must do as I tell you."

The colonel was forced to make a rapid decision though Hesam could see that it clearly pained him. "All right."

"Then it is time for us to move. Before we go, there is one thing more, eh?"

"First, I want proof that Ahlam is safe."

His mistress. The name was taken from the Arabic for dreams, visions, and fantasies. He wondered where the colonel had met the woman. He was in love, no doubt.

Hesam shook his head slowly as he continued to work on the colonel's boots. "That is not possible. Think about it."

"Then our agreement is off. Finished!" the army officer said, his muted voice forced and hoarse with fatigue.

"No, it isn't. This is not the time to lose your nerve. What good would it do for you to withhold the information I want? None at all. And if our agreement is off, you stay where you are waiting for your own arrest. No, that isn't what you want, Colonel Harun Baraniq."

Looking up, Hesam caught the flicker he was looking for in the eyes of the army officer. Of course he would know the man's real name despite the cover name to which he was referred. Knowing the colonel's true identity made it much easier to blackmail him should the defector try to change his mind. Or, as in this case, threaten to call off his bargain. Hesam would not give the man up to the Iraqi regime under any circumstances, but the colonel did not know that. His shoulders slumped in surrender.

"The man is Fahad Al-Zid. He is . . ." The Iraqi colonel hesitated, but only briefly. ". . . a captain in the Saudi Air Force."

Hesam waited a moment for the rest, but it did not come from the army officer.

"He flew an Antonov out of Kandahar?" Hesam asked.

"Yes."

Hesam waited again until a family of five passed by.

"Al Qaeda were aboard. Fighters."

"Yes. There were several hundred on each aircraft," the colonel confirmed.

"But this man, Captain Al-Zeid, had a special passenger on his aircraft. Among the first out of Afghanistan. Isn't that correct? What was his name?"

"I don't know," the colonel said, his anxiety level obvious to Hesam's educated eye.

"Are you being watched?" he asked the colonel.

"No."

Not true, Hesam thought. Everyone in Baghdad was under suspicion, especially if he was a ranking member of Iraqi Intelligence. He finished the officer's boots with a flourish; then stood, hands cupped to receive his payment.

"You're coming with me now, Colonel," he said in a hushed tone, barely audible to the officer standing before him.

"I cannot," Colonel Baraniq said, slowly counting dinars, eyes downward. "There are others to warn."

"Too late." Hesam spoke resolutely, inviting no contradiction. "You have a car?"

"Yes."

"Drive to Fasheel and Ejaili Streets in the east part of the city. There is a house on each corner. Choose the one on the southeast side. The number is 2210. If the way is clear the second number will hang upside down. Knock on the door. Tell whoever answers that you are having trouble with your car. You will be invited inside. Someone will give you a small suitcase. Change your clothes quickly and wait for me. Forget about your car.

It will be taken care of. Do you understand, Colonel? Good. Leave immediately."

As the army officer departed Hesam moved to another location in the garden, melting into the shadows of the foliage. He waited there, motionless. When he was certain he was not being watched, he placed his shoe shine box in a shrub where it would not immediately be noticed; then he exited the patio and the building by a different route than the one taken by the colonel. Three blocks from the hotel he waited for a bus. When it arrived, late, he boarded it along with several other passengers. The bus was almost full and it was bound for the approximate part of the city where he would ultimately arrive, but Hesam exited that bus and waited for still another.

After making two more transfers, Hesam stepped off a wheezing Mercedes bus and into one of the poorer sections of the city. He had been on the bus routes for more than two hours and was still more than a mile from his destination. He began to jog. The sandals he wore were a hindrance so he removed them and ran in bare feet.

Swissair Flight 51 from New Delhi en route to Bern, Switzerland, cruised at thirty-seven thousand feet, or twenty-thousand feet AGL, above ground level. At that altitude the molecules of air rushing by and over the surfaces of an aircraft are far fewer in number than those at sea level. So an airplane that is indicating five-hundred miles per hour at sea level would, at higher altitudes, be traveling over the ground at a much faster rate. To a pilot, this is called true airspeed. True airspeed is a function of knowing temperature and altitude. The two-hundred-sixty-one passengers on board the wide-body jet, those who were awake, enjoyed a late evening snack while watching a recently produced American movie. The air was very smooth; the highest mountains in the world were well behind them. There were few lights to be seen below in a part of the world that was sparsely populated. Passengers had long ago ceased looking outside the comfortable cabin. The flight crew navigated solely by instruments.

They were not aware that only a few feet below them was a United States Air Force C-117 Globemaster III, a state-of-the-art rapid strategic reaction aircraft. The Boeing-built Globemaster III was part of the 352nd Special Operations Group at RAF Mildenhall, England, attached to the 321st Special Tactics Squadron.

This was a "black" plane. Black was a euphemism for secret operations.

The mission of Major Eltron Nichols and his crew was to tuck their giant aircraft so close under the belly of the unknowing Swissair flight that ground radar, tracking Flight 51, would see the image of only one aircraft and not two. The kind of up close flying Nichols was doing made tight combat formations seem loose. Holding a three-hundred-fifteen-thousand-pound airplane traveling at five-hundred miles per hour a scant ten feet directly below another massive airplane was in itself an extraordinary feat of flying. But holding that position, in this case for over four hours, required men of zero nerves, perfect hand and eye coordination, and the strength of trained athletes. Eltron Nichols and his copilot, Captain Lee Beneda, traded off at thirty-minute intervals. Every muscle in their bodies ached from the tension of free-handing their aircraft through the black skies five miles above the surface of the earth in a precise position relative to their host.

Radar tracking stations in Pakistan, Iran, including stations around the Caspian Sea, Iraq, and Syria, constantly probed the ether for indications of unauthorized aircraft near their airspace. These countries were not friends of all Western nations. Their radar systems were tied into surface-to-air missile launching systems. One such system, in Iran, employed the Russian-built 64N6 "Tombstone" missile with a two-hundred-kilometer range. It was the latest version of the SA-10. It and a similar missile system then operating in Iraq were the highest priority on USAF's strike list.

"They're painting us, Skipper," the copilot said, calmly watching his ATA, airborne threat alert screen. Somewhere below them a search-and-tracking radar had located a target high above the Earth. The passive radio warning instruments aboard the Globemaster had sensed the ground radar. If a missile was launched below them, it would identify its homing source, probably heat seeking.

"Roger," Nichols said.

After several moments of radio interrogation the acquisition radar had a firm target and would hand it off to still another radar down the chain. This would be the "fix-and-shoot" radar that was attached directly to the missiles that would fly the instant the fire control officer gave the command. It was also possible that the FCO had placed his ADB, Air Defense Battery, on an automatic profile.

"Okay, boss, they lit us up."

Eltron Nichols acknowledged the last report with less nonchalance than previously. It was one thing to get painted—that was routine—but when they "lit you up" it meant somebody's finger was tightening on the trigger. It was the last preparation before firing. Even if the finger was a robot, things could get interesting in one hell of a hurry.

"Standby ECMs," Nichols ordered, getting his partner in the cockpit prepared to release countermeasures designed to decoy surface-to-air missiles.

The copilot flipped the safety cover from a panel box that protected three switches that would actuate the release of the electronic countermeasures.

"ECMs ready," the copilot responded.

Eltron Nichols concentrated with all of his might to keep station precisely below Swissair 51. It was most critical at this time to give the radar below a single, well-defined image of a commercial aircraft on its peaceful way across the Middle East.

After several more seconds the "hot" radar receded back to acquisition and tracking mode. It would stay with

them for approximately nine minutes until they had
passed from that air defense sector to another.

Eltron Nichols exhaled slowly. If he had allowed their
Globemaster to drift nine feet left or right or drop ten
feet lower in altitude, they would have been discovered
by the searchers below. The result would have been a
missile exploding under an engine pod or, almost as bad,
a blown mission for the Leopard team sitting in the back
of the aircraft.

The most efficient Special Warfare teams are those
that have been together the longest, whose dendritic
parts are so familiar that they function as a single organ-
ism. Their personalities mesh because if there is one
among the group who does not get along with another,
he is replaced, and that replacement is replaced until all
parts of the unit are close-knit. Before the team went
operational, they had shared dangers, rigors, and passions. They had exposed their physical limits to all the
others on the team, as well as their mental abilities. The
revelations of those strengths and weaknesses would
have raised the confidence of the team's organic whole.

Each member of the team spoke a minimum of two
languages and quite likely three, four, or more. Every
team had a medic who, after two years of specialized
medical training, could perform complex combat surgery
on the battlefield if required. He was also a skilled radio-
man just as every other man on the team was skilled at
communications and skilled at the business of combat
first aid, albeit not up to the level of the team medic.

The idea was that every man needed to be able to do
the job of every other man on the team, plus have a
highly sophisticated specialty of his own. Delta, Green
Beret, British SAS, and Leopard team members were
not fresh out of high school. Because of the incredibly
difficult and taxing nature of the missions they under-
took, these men had to maintain the athletic body of an
eighteen year old. Yet they were in their middle to late

thirties, because it took years for a soldier to acquire the knowledge and skills he needed to be a competent SpecWar man.

An exception was made for Lieutenant Ross McTaggart. Only two years out of the United States Air Force Academy, McTaggert had chosen combat control for his specialty training. He had been the mainstay of the academy's water polo team and could swim like a fish. Six-four of hard muscle, he was any coach's dream athlete. McTaggart regarded himself as only a fair student so he applied himself to every facet of academics with total dedication. His work ethic was carried by him into his schooling in parachute training, underwater combat, communications, guerilla warfare training, survival skills, interrogation, navigation, Ranger training, weapons and weapons systems, escape and evasion, and hand-to-hand combat. He had either set records in most of these extremely difficult schools or merely finished first. He had done everything a SpecWar officer could do, except combat.

When Captain Rick Blanchette was promoted to the rank of major and into battalion level command, a replacement officer was needed for Leopard Team 1. Colonel John Vass had put up McTaggart's name despite his being only twenty-five and his lack of combat experience. General Coggin did not know McTaggart, but trusted Vass's judgement implicitly. Now the brass, and more importantly the team, would find out if McTaggart was as good as his file said he was.

McTaggart had read their files, too. Petty Officer Thomas Entzion was a Navy SEAL and the team's radio man. Manny Rodriguez, U.S. Marine Corps, born in Cuba and raised in Los Angeles, was the explosives expert, though McTaggart was well aware that every man on the team was cross-trained. Pete "Quack" Taylor was an army master sergeant and the medic for Leopard-1. Lee Haggar, also a master sergeant, and a qualified Ranger, was the team's weapons expert. There was one more whom McTaggart had never met. He would take over as leader of the team, at least on this mission. Among SpecOps soldiers Joe Mears was legend.

Mears had the dusty, olive complexion of those born in the Levant. He knew their customs as well as their languages, McTaggart had been told. He had also heard that Mears could walk among any group from Malaysia to India and pass as one of them. He possessed a courage, or so the stories went, that almost bordered on a death wish. Like the insane war that they all fought, Mears was as unpredictable as a booby trap. His enemies had reason to keep distant from a man who did not fear death.

But Mears wasn't there and McTaggart was the ranking officer. Not content to let the pilots do the navigation, no matter how skilled they were at their work, McTaggart had been tracking the aircraft's progress on his GPS since they had picked up the Swissair at an intercept point over Bahrat, Pakistan. He had checked his personal gear as well as the unit's equipment a dozen times since takeoff. He was nervous. More than just a few lives were at stake. His nervousness was not born out of fear, but from the need to forget nothing, to make no error of preparation. The men of Leopard-1 knew this and respected him for it. The mission, his first real black operation, was technically demanding as well as dangerous for several reasons.

This was to be a HAHO jump—high altitude, high opening. The team would go out at whatever altitude the Swissair plane was flying. If Swissair Flight 51 maintained its present altitude and position, the Leopard team would jump into the night at thirty-four-thousand feet with the temperature at minus thirty-one degrees F. At that height the air would be so thin that special charges placed inside the canopy of each chute would be needed to blow them open. Each man would be encased within a space suit to keep his blood from boiling and to keep oxygen flowing into his system during the very long, very cold trip down.

The team would be landing in the mountain region of Iraq known as al-Jazira, just over the Turkish border. But their target LZ, a large valley at the foot of high mountains, was not chosen for safety but for its remoteness.

The most complicated part of the insertion into hostile country was bringing the equipment the team would need once they were on the ground. Fastened to the cargo deck of the Globemaster were two DPVs, Desert Patrol Vehicles. Specially built in California by Chenowyth Racing for desert warfare, the DPVs were a dune-buggy driver's wildest fantasy. They were powered by two-hundred horsepower VW engines that were capable of accelerating from zero to thirty miles per hour in only four seconds. They carried twenty-one gallons of fuel for a range of over two hundred miles, but always packed external cans of fuel, or as in this case, special rubber bladders with one-hundred-twenty-gallon capacities for long-range patrol over extremely rugged terrain.

The DPVs were well armed. Typical firepower included the AT-4 rocket launcher or Mk-60 grenade launcher. In their current configuration they were packing a low recoil 30mm cannon. Also on this mission McTaggart's Leopard team mounted the new M-240 machine gun that used 7.62mm ammunition. It was an extremely dependable gun with an estimated twenty-six-thousand mean rounds between failure (MRBF), an important characteristic for weapons to be used behind enemy lines. Leopard teams carried food and water, but mostly ammunition because capture was not an option.

No ordinary troops could hope to win a shoot-out with a special operations team whose members fired endless rounds every single day using a variety of weapons. Spec-Ops people kept firing for months and years from every conceivable position until they were absolute masters of their weapons. What made them different from their opponents was that when they pulled a trigger, somebody—out there—dropped.

Radio contact with SOCCENT was an option, but

radio transmission was to be avoided if at all possible. The intent of this Leopard team was to remain hidden, avoiding contact with the enemy. Only if there was no way out would they engage the enemy head-on, but if that happened, they had to win.

CHAPTER 4

Had it not been for the need to maintain high mission mobility requiring the use of the DPVs, the Leopard team could have used the HALO technique of insertion—high altitude, low opening. They could have dropped through space at terminal velocity until they had reached the low altitude of one-thousand feet before opening their chutes. It would have been a highly accurate way of hitting the desired landing area. But the DPVs couldn't do it that way. Their chutes had to be opened immediately after the drop and then had to be *steered* all the way to the ground. Because of this, wind effect was critical. The team spent five days longer than scheduled in England until atmospheric conditions and jet stream became favorable for the insertion jump.

Steering the DPVs to the ground was to be accomplished by special cargo parachutes built with panels that could be manipulated from a remote site, in this case a person falling through space with the cargo. The technique was similar to that of flying a model airplane, using a small transmitter to control the model's rudder and elevator surfaces. To get the DPVs on the ground where the Leopard team intended to land, they would all have to fall together, the team and the vehicles. But would they fall all the way to the ground, close enough to make a common footprint? Whoever steered the cargo chutes would have to do so not from the ground, but from the air as they fell.

McTaggart would go out of the plane behind the vehicles once the pallets had dropped. Their chutes would be open as he left the C-117 and he would delay his own opening, airfoiling until he was near the DPVs before deploying his own parachute. He would then use his radio controller to guide the cargo chutes to the ground as he fell with them. Any number of things could go wrong, of course, but McTaggart felt that the greatest risk would be exiting the cargo aircraft too late. That would drop him too far ahead of the package. Dropping too soon would leave him too far behind to fly the DPVs down. He would have to exit the plane scant seconds after the package and never lose sight of it.

"Fifty out from Gurpinar," McTaggart said to his teammates through their radio headsets as he referred once again to his GPS. The team would not jump over Gurpinar, Turkey, but would exit approximately forty miles beyond where, it was estimated, there was a gap in radar coverage between Iran and Iraq. It would then be safe for the C-117 to split off from the Swissair without being detected on a ground radar screen. At the speed the C-117 was traveling, they would cover that distance in less than two minutes.

His team watched their new young officer with great interest. They would exit the aircraft on the navigation fix provided by the plane crew, but McTaggart was determined to leave nothing to chance. Very good, if he could do it. They used their last hour of preparations for a combat jump. Condoms had been placed over gun barrels. Black electrical tape had been wrapped around every item of their kit that might clang together and make noise at the wrong time and place. Combat knives and leg pistols had also received extra taping to resist the deceleration shock that would occur in a high-speed jump. They had removed all signs of identification, personal photographs, letters, anything that could provide a potential interrogator with information with which to break them should they be captured.

Their mikes were inside their helmets, which were now part of their space suits. They had been using oxygen supplied from tanks within the C-117, but would soon disconnect from that source and go on jump bottles attached to their suits.

"Thirty seconds to red light," McTaggart said.

As the team sat uncomfortably in special bucket seats loaded with one-hundred-fifty pounds of space suit, parachutes, tethered drop bags full of weapons and ammunition, they began to do a count inside their heads. About the time the men had ticked off a half minute, the red jump light turned on.

The loadmaster appeared in the cargo section wearing warm thermal clothing and a portable oxygen mask and bottle. He also wore a radio headset so that he could assist the team when it was time to exit the aircraft. He would be primarily responsible for the unmanned cargo to slide out of the cargo bay at precisely the right time. Around his upper body was a safety harness attached to a nylon tether that would keep from accidentally falling or being sucked out of the cargo door when it was open in flight.

"Stand by jump positions," McTaggart said, trying mightily to keep nervousness out of his voice. The pilot would slow the C-117 considerably, but it was still going to be a high-speed bail out.

Static lines would not be used in this jump. McTaggart would jump first, right behind the DPVs, followed by the others. Assuming there were no updrafts or cross currents to blow them off course, the team would have a full fifteen-minute fall to earth. The cargo chutes were designed to match the speed at which the commandos would fall, slightly under twenty miles per hour.

"Thirty seconds to the green light, Lieutenant," the loadmaster informed McTaggart, and held up three fingers on one hand and a zero on the other. McTaggart nodded his understanding.

"Jump positions. Oxygen on. Twenty-five seconds to the green," McTaggart relayed to his Leopard team who, to a man, had heard the loadmaster's radio voice and had read his hand signals.

The sound inside the aircraft suddenly changed as the four, four-thousand-pound-thrust GE turbofan engines were throttled back; then came the high-pitched screech of hydraulic pumps churning the jackscrews as the flaps lowered, their blunt foil gathering up more air, slowing the aircraft still more. The pilot inside the cockpit now began to pull back on his control yoke. The nose of the giant aircraft lifted upward, creating even more drag, and reducing the mighty airship to a near stall speed, holding it "on the bubble" at one-hundred-ninety knots.

From inside the cargo hull it now sounded like the Furies as powerful hydraulic rams levered open the rear cargo doors to expose the ramp inside the cargo bay. The C-117 was showing no external or internal lights, except for faint illuminators far behind them.

"Light 'em up," McTaggart said. Each man grasped a plastic tube that was attached to the back of the man in front of him and snapped the plastic. Two chemicals then flowed together to create a diffused green light. The team would know the position of the others by the discreet glowing lights around them.

The aircraft, its cargo doors now wide open, was shaking from the asymmetric flow of air over its surfaces. The horrendous noise rendered earpieces all but useless. The team now responded only to hand signals.

McTaggart, the Leopard team, and the loadmaster, watched the red light intently. The light suddenly switched to green. Immediately, the loadmaster operated the electrical release mechanism, the metal hooks inlaid on the deck of the airplane turning as one into the open position, releasing the tie-downs. Simultaneously, the load of two DPVs was pulled backwards on rollers by a line from a fast turning winch that propelled the skids out.

Mctaggart counted to three, then went out behind the

vehicles. The other four Leopard team members stepped out behind their lieutenant.

The velocity of the bodies leaving the aircraft would initially be the speed of the plane itself, about two hundred-miles per hour. There would follow an approximately nine-second slow-down period where the bodies would reach TV—terminal velocity, around one hundred thirty-nine miles per hour. To stay with the vehicles and their steerable canopies, they all had to deploy their chutes as their bodies slowed to near TV.

The jolt McTaggart felt when his chute opened was gut-wrenching. He had jumped HAHO and HALO a number of times and several of them were night operations, but never with this much equipment strapped around his body and never at speeds this great. In the moments that it took him to recover from the feeling he had been stretched at the crotch like a bungee cord, the blood slowly returned to his head. He looked for the vehicle package. No sign of it. He tried to orient himself, turning his head left and right, but his vision was severely restricted by the air pressure suit covering his entire body.

As he settled into the total silence of the black night, more than four miles above the earth, there were two things he had to accomplish above all others. The first was that he must monitor his GPS, Global Positioning System, and steer himself down to a predetermined position on the ground. That set of precise coordinates for the landing zone had been given to him in an envelope that had been marked *Top Secret* by armed security personnel just before they boarded the C-117 in Mildenhall, England. The second most important responsibility that fell upon his broad but young shoulders was to bring the two DPVs safely with him to the same location. It would not do at all for Lieutenant McTaggart to drop with his team into a dangerous enemy country and have most of their firepower, transportation, and food land somewhere else.

He had descended over two-thousand feet without

sighting the cargo package. He was tempted to ask one of the other team members if they, by any chance, knew where the DPVs were. There was little risk of radio interception, but there was a huge risk of choking on one's pride. He was licking his lips preparatory to choosing the latter action when a large form, nearly invisible in the blackness, drifted into his eight-o'clock position, perhaps ten meters away. Had the sun been shining, the huge cargo chutes could have provided him with shade.

Without delay, McTaggart pulled the protective cover from the radio controller strapped to his belt and switched on the machine's transmitter. There was very little controlling for him to do for the next several thousand feet as the jump pallette drifted easily near them at the same rate of descent.

McTaggart was suddenly aware of the extreme cold in the limitless sky. He thought that he shivered, but under all of the weight that was strapped around his body, he wasn't sure.

Nor could he find reference points between up or down or to either side. It was as though he was suspended in a sensory-deprivation chamber with nothing but a few little green lights to keep him company. At twenty-seven-thousand feet they fell through cloud cover, the effect of which was to eliminate all external references, even the dim green lights, the DPV packages, as well as stars above. There was nothing that McTaggart could think about besides the needles of cold that poked painfully into his body, despite the protection of his space suit and the thermal underwear that hugged his body.

Then, as suddenly as they were in the opaque stuff, they were out of it again. At twenty-four-thousand feet the green lights of his comrades reappeared as did the DPV package on his left side. The DPVs were no longer as close as he would have liked, so McTaggart gave the radio controller a number of steady inputs that caused their canopy mechanisms to gently direct the apparatus slowly back toward him. McTaggart was beginning to believe that the part of the drop about which he worried most was to come off as planned, after all.

It was near the village of Az Zibar, twenty kilometers from the border of southern Turkey, in a region so remote that the only access to the location was an unpaved road that led to an Iraqi early warning radar site. It was referred to only as AHA-2122, and it was thought to have been completely destroyed by a series of previous strikes by F-15 Strike Eagles, Navy Hornets, and even U.S. Air Force A-10s, during and following the Gulf War of 1991. But the Iraqis had secretly rebuilt it. This time they had buried the site twenty feet below the mountainous terrain after adding six more feet of concrete overhead.

Further, Site 2122 was currently working on a Chinese system of radars designed to defeat stealth aircraft. Stealth planes were covered with a secret material referred to as RAM, radar absorbing material, that reflected a much smaller image to the interrogating radar than the object actually was—the size, say, of a bird. Also, stealth aircraft offered fewer reflective surfaces for the radar probes to bounce. But the Chinese had theorized that more than two radar sites that were connected in such a way that the receiver of Site A could view on its scope and hear on its digital audio, an electronic probe emitted by a radar on Site B. The distance between the two units provided the operators with *scale*. It was the scale that allowed the C-117 with the Leopard team aboard to *report* easily and clearly.

Although Site 2122 had recently gone back on line, the U.S. combined target evaluation system, CTES, still carried it in the inop category.

In the early morning hours there were eight technicians working the Iraqi air defense radar in a bunker where there were few targets to identify. Those targets were almost always American high-speed attack aircraft or their Airborne Warning and Control System (AWACS) enforcing the so-called no-fly zone in northern Iraq. In the past these targets were a great concern to the operators because if the American planes were interrogated too closely, they would use the excuse to attack that radar site as "self-defense." It was nothing of the kind, as every soldier of Saddam knew. It was wanton aggression carried out by the ungodly killers in the West. In their eyes, the new Crusades would never end until the last Muslim was dead.

The technician's attention quickly refocused to the events on his screen when one image, unquestioningly an airplane, morphed into two. The technician leaned forward in his chair. The equipment was still in the experimental stage. And there was a great deal to be learned on the operational side, as well. There. It was looming larger, flying quite independent of the first target.

"A new target, sir," the military technician reported to his officer. The technician tapped keys on his computer console. The reflection on the screen changed with each command, offering a different architecture of the target. Where there had been a single aircraft for the past several minutes, a commercial Swiss flight that traveled this route five times each week, there now appeared to be two.

The officer peered into the screen. "Thirty degrees on the azimuth," he ordered. "It should clear up." He, too, had seen the Swissair flight arrive from its usual origin in the east.

The technician typed once again on his computer keys. The image changed perspective. This time the range between the two images was slightly longer. He looked up at the officer, questioningly.

"How long has it been on the screen?" the officer asked.

"One minute. Less, sir. It . . . it seemed to grow from the other. Like a birth," the technician said, slowly shaking his head.

"Speed on the first target?"

The technician checked the running data base. "Three six zero knots, sir." Nautical miles per hour converted to six-hundred miles per hour true airspeed over the ground.

"And the second image?" the officer wanted to know.

The technician was very careful as he checked the running data on the second target.

"Three zero . . . Wait, sir. The airspeed on the second target is three four zero . . . now two five five. . . . He is slowing, sir. It must be an equipment failure. . . ." the technician said, almost to himself as he continued to select different views of the two anomalies.

The officer, his right hand stroking his beard as he looked over the shoulder of the technician, said, "It is not the device, I think. Continue to track the second target."

The technician now caused the thirty-four-inch screen before him to split in two, each now focusing on different targets, each giving out a constant stream of changing data that revealed altitude, direction, speed, and a good number of other data. A telephone rang somewhere inside the bunker.

"It is AHA-2100, sir," another technician said to the officer. "They verify our data."

"Yes?" the officer said.

The technician listened for a moment as he scanned his own iridescent tubes. He spoke into the telephone, then replaced it in its cradle. "They are the same, sir. Two targets, both hard."

The officer had made up his mind. He took up his command set, punched four numbers and waited for a moment. "2122, Captain al-Kihili. No, not a fire mission, Colonel. I think we have parachutists. . . . Yes, sir. I have seen the technique before. A second target flying under another. Yes, sir. Swissair. Flight 51. At first I was not sure but . . ."

The officer listened while the colonel on the other end of the line spoke. Then he said, "Yes. A very high rate of speed. But then it slowed. Two hundred knots. . . ." The captain waited again for the colonel to speak, then nodded. "Yes. We can give you coordinates. I would not

presume to guess at what position they would have left
the aircraft. . . . In that event, Colonel. . . ." the captain
said walking across the room with the command set still
in his hand. Then studying the data that had been recorded during the track, he said, "We can tell you where
the target achieved its slowest airspeed and we can imagine they would have left the plane soon after that." The
officer related those map coordinates to his superior on
the other end of the line; then, promising to continue to
track the targets, he hung up the telephone.

The nearest element to the northern border where a
radar operator *thought* he saw two airplanes instead of
one and therefore *assumed* it was going to drop para-
troopers, was a reconnaissance platoon of the Iraqi 47th
Infantry Division of the Republican Guard. While Major
Raboudi thought it was a military errand not likely to
produce a real live enemy, he nevertheless welcomed his
commander's orders to execute a search and destroy patrol. The 1st Reconnaissance Platoon was ideally trained
for just this kind of work.

The platoon's leader, Captain Ebi Al-Zeid, listened
patiently while Major Raboudi pointed out areas on the
map where the parachutists were likely to have landed.
Major Raboudi treated the assignment as more than just
an exercise for Al-Zeid's platoon. Tensions along all
frontiers were tight as wires. Americans or their coalition
partners were expected to attack at any time of the day
or night, even though it was believed they had not yet
amassed great enough numbers to achieve their invasion objectives.

"Remember, Ebi, your radio frequencies will be monitored. Consider very carefully when you choose to contact us at headquarters. The Americans will know
everything you say. If you have the time, get to a secure
landline. You understand?" Major Raboudi said.

"Yes, sir," the captain said, a slightly twisted smile
tilted the corners of his mouth. He had, after all, trained
in commando warfare and he was well-informed about
enemy capabilities. Because of the Americans, there

were many frustrations to deal with when planning even the simplest military operations. And frustration was the cause of rage. The lack of air power was a constant source of rage among the Iraqi military leadership. Another hated weapon was the satellites that never slept, looking over their shoulders, even in the dark.

"All right," the major said, his voice ragged with fatigue.

When Captain Al-Zeid returned to his unit the men were already preparing to move out. Their vehicles, two Russian BTR-80 APCs (armored personnel carriers), had been fueled and ammunition for their heavy machine guns and their 7.62mm machine guns put aboard. These were the newest models of the eight-wheeled fighting vehicle with a single diesel engine replacing the twin gas engines of the previous versions that were easily set ablaze in battle. Along with a commander, a gunner, and a driver, the vehicle could carry seven troops in its welded steel hull.

A young sergeant, Ehsan, saluted the captain casually. "The platoon is ready, Captain."

"You picked them yourself?" Al-Zeid asked.

"Absolutely. The others wanted to go as well, even when I told them we would probably all become martyrs."

"That is very funny, Ehsan," the captain scowled, not thinking it was funny at all. He looked at his watch. "1028 hours . . . now."

The sergeant set his watch exactly with his commander. Each man in the 1st Recon had been issued a watch, a very decent extra reward for men who courted danger. It was a source of pride with them.

The captain pulled up his operational map. His sergeant had one just like it and the men of the platoon each had smaller, crudely drawn, area maps. "You see these coordinates? They correspond here, here, and here to where we are going to look for the enemy. I want to be on station and beginning the first sweep by 1400 hours," he said.

The sergeant made marks on his map similar to those on the platoon commander's. They had four hours of very hard terrain to cover to arrive on time. The roads were little more than goat trails in many places. The troops in the bowels of the APCs would take a beating. They would not be happy men.

Between the high walls of mountains in southern Turkey there was a long valley sloping from northeast to generally southwest. McTaggart was a California boy and mountains in that part of the western United States were legendary. He had trained at the fourteen-thousand-foot level at the Marine Corps Mountain Warfare Center in the Sierra Nevadas. He had always been a lover of the outdoors and an avid hiker. His training in mountain operations was complete. Or so he thought. So intent had he been in hitting his GPS coordinates that he had forgotten an important maxim of parachuting: look down.

McTaggart landed on a reasonably flat surface as, he found out, had the other team members. As he gathered up his parachute and looked at the cargo he had flown to the ground, his heart sank. Had McTaggart been more alert he could have steered the cargo chutes to land his desert vehicles in the valley barely one-hundred meters away. Safely. But the pallets containing the DPVs had struck a narrow wash in the foothills. The wash, or wadi, gripped the pallets on either side like a vise. The vehicles were jammed nose down, the pallets smashed, and the front of the first vehicle had all but disappeared into the arid, crumbling mountain soil.

"Shit," he said to Quack, the first man to arrive at McTaggart's side.

"Could've been worse, Ross. Could've been the radios," Quack said.

McTaggart began to climb around the sixty-degree wadi. The others joined him, saying little, keeping their voices low in the dark. "How about I take a look around, Ross?" Haggar suggested.

"Right, Sarge," McTaggart said. He should have immediately sent out a pair of scouts to look over their position. If there was somebody out there, the team needed to know who they were, how many there were, and exactly where they were. Haggar's gentle reminder was welcome.

"Take Entzion with you," he said. "We'll stay here and dig."

"Password?" Haggar asked.

"Los Angeles and Lakers," McTaggart said for the entire team to hear.

"Tommy," Haggar said. "I go east, you go west."

"Roger," Entzion acknowledged.

The team had opened the padded drop bags and quickly tore off their outer thermal clothing, including their space suits. They removed ammunition, extra personal weapons, and some MREs—meals ready to eat—and stuffed the bags full of discarded gear that they would bury in the ground and leave behind. Uniforms were worn, but floppy field hats were more useful to the Leopard team than helmets. The uniforms were camouflaged for desert operations and, if taken prisoner, would identify them as something other than terrorists or criminals. The hope was that a prisoner might be spared an interrogation Saddam Hussein style, but none of the team had any illusions about that.

They were already "painted up" and ready to go. They carried the favorite weapon of Special Forces, the collapsible stock M-4 carbine with scope, laser, and night sighting gear. The Leopard team used 6X power with ambient light scopes. Each carbine had an attachable suppressor, referred to by civilians as a silencer. The M-4 was not only a rapid-fire submachine weapon, but it was also highly accurate from distances of up to eight-hundred meters. On this mission the team elected to bring the Sig-Sauer P-226 handgun, chosen by them for reliability and its fifteen-round magazine.

The team also packed a single sniping rifle. They called it "Beast." It was built by Barrett along the lines of their semi-automatic Model 82A1, but was customized for Leopard teams. The team considered it as their very own artillery. To appreciate the impact Beast had on a potential enemy, one ammunition dealer test fired the rifle at simulated wooden frame houses and found that it blew through six houses— not six walls, *six houses*. The diameter of the round was .5 inches, but the round itself could vary from three to six inches in length. It was accurate up to two-thousand yards. "Accurate," to a SpecOps team, meant that it would hit a human head over a mile away. The rifle could hit larger targets and cause massive damage up to seven-thousand five-hundred yards, or seventy-five football fields.

Haggar, Leopard-1's weapons expert, brought each man on the team to a high degree of proficiency with Beast. They fired into jeeps, tanks, personnel carriers, and other vehicles, penetrating all of them with ease. If used against a human target the shock of getting hit with one of these special rounds frequently resulted in death, no matter what part of the body was struck. Haggar believed in God, Ford Motor Company, and heavy firepower. Whenever the team went in country, he brought along Beast and as much ammo as they could carry.

"How come we have to pack an extra seventy pounds so that Haggar can play with his cannon?" Manny Rodriguez had asked the newly assigned lieutenant at Fort Benning.

While McTaggart struggled to come up with an answer, Tom Entzion, the team's commo expert, supplied it. "Because he cleans it with his dick. Personally, I just as soon he took it along."

"Is that right?" Quack asked. "Is that how you do it?"

"Sure," Haggar said.

"Is that legal? I mean, isn't that against a training manual, or something?" Quack pressed.

He shrugged. "I don't think so. I've read most of 'em. All of them, matter of fact."

"And there's no rule against sticking your dick down the barrel of your rifle?" Quack said.

"Well, yeah, if you're doing it just for fun. But not if you're cleaning it," Haggar said.

Now, in the north of Iraq, Haggar's Beast was packed somewhere inside a DPV and when he got back he would get it out. He moved quietly, quickly away toward the north, his night vision glasses casting a green hue over everything before him, turning night into eerie day. He decided that the unit would be safe with a two-hundred-meter perimeter, so he placed his M-4 rifle to his cheek and looked into the distance. He chose a large rock that his rangefinder indicated was one-hundred-four meters from the immobilized vehicles. He would work along this line, then turn east and, remaining approximately one hundred meters from where he started, he would continue walking in a semicircle. Entzion, he knew, would circumscribe the center containing the vehicles, turning west, until he had completed the other half of the one-hundred-eighty-degree arc.

The two men returned within twenty minutes.

"Los Angeles," Rodriguez had challenged as they were headed in.

"Clippers," Haggar answered.

"I know that I'm going to be sorry later that I didn't shoot your ass when I had the chance."

"Clear," Entzion said, moving into the area.

"Clear," Haggar concurred.

Good progress had been made digging out the DPVs. McTaggart had been the first man to pick up a shovel and had not slowed his digging. The team respected him for that. Rodriguez had worked on the opposite side of the skids, the least difficult of the two positions. It was getting light now and they could not afford to be seen, either by a military patrol or, for that matter, by civilians who might be in the area. The nearest village was more than twenty miles from their position and they were well away from improved roads, but people from this part of the world were travelers. Their commerce depended upon getting their goods to various markets.

While Haggar and Entzion took up their shovels and began to help in the digging, McTaggart got on his belly and stuck his head into the hole he had dug.

"What do you think, Lieutenant?" Quack asked.

There was at least another hour of digging before the first vehicle could be manhandled out of its nose-down position onto flat ground. He had to add to that the time needed to free the bindings on the DPV and to assess the damage, if any. The first vehicle might have its suspension wrecked so badly that it would be inoperable. Even then, if both machines were able to run, the mission plan was to lay up during daylight and travel at night. Even if the team started digging in right then, the sun would be fully up by the time they had finished.

"We'll put the nets over the DPVs," McTaggart said, referring to the LCSS (lightweight camouflage screen system-desert). "We'll spread it back, up the wadi, and we'll lie up here today."

As one, the team looked up the wadi. Using it, covered with camouflaged netting, would save them the time of digging even bigger, deeper holes in which to hide. But they would, in effect, be standing upon each other's heads, lying on their backs, but at angles so steep as to be almost erect. The were careful not to stretch the net too tight lest it create an unnatural contrast with the terrain.

"Lee, Tom, see any water while you were out there?" McTaggart asked.

"Negative," they responded. Water was not a problem yet. They had several liters that they jumped with, but whenever possible they would use hydro systems to filter indigenous water to make it drinkable.

They were able to remove virtually everything from the DPVs in a matter of minutes and had almost completed the last net tie-down when Rodriguez, keeping lookout for the team, adjusted his range scope. "Got some movement, Lieutenant," he said.

McTaggart moved to the Cuban's side, raising his spotting scope to his eyes.

"About five-thousand meters. The tallest peak in the east, now drop to its three o'clock. See the dust?"

McTaggart watched for several minutes. He could see

the dust and he could see vehicles that were making it. "I see two. Could there be more?"

"Yeah. Possible," Rodriguez said, watching intently.

The two soldiers continued to silently examine the progress of two vehicles, either or both of which could be civilian. Then McTaggart said, "They don't seem to be getting nearer. I think they're moving east to west."

"Agree."

"Okay, we'll watch 'em for a while," McTaggart said, glad that his vehicles were covered up and that they, whoever "they" were off in the distance, were making the dust instead of the Leopard team. He referred to his map and to his GPS, checking the satellite coordinates. He reckoned the vehicles were in Iraq, whose border was about a mile and a half away. He also knew that borders to the people out here meant exactly zip.

Back at the layup McTaggart spoke softly to Entzion and Haggar. "Two vehicles, maybe three, five-thousand meters south. They're passing east to west, maybe on an old road. Civilian or military, no way to tell yet. If they turn in this direction Manny will let us know."

Quack was on the outer perimeter on the east side of the wadi. Plenty of time to tell him if events warranted. McTaggart rolled into his position above the DPVs and closed his eyes.

CHAPTER 5

It was dangerous for Hesam to go to the rocks but he
went every night. Once he was seen a few hundred
meters from his hidden radio by a group of young men.
They approached him, yelling at him to stop when he
turned his back and hurried away. They were certainly
not police, probably doing something illegal themselves,
so he didn't worry about them. Another time he was
detained in a police sweep, but remained in the center
of others caught on the streets of east Baghdad. He did
not stand out and his latest change of identity papers,
once belonging to a deceased citizen, went unchallenged.
But the sweeps continued day after day as the forces of
Saddam intensified their hunt for the missing army colonel, the intelligence officer who could do the regime
great harm. There had been more than one attempt at a
house-to-house search, neighborhood by neighborhood,
but Baghdad was a large city and the task was more than
even the Iraqi army and police could accomplish without
specific information.

Colonel Baraniq, meanwhile, paced the floor of the
basement on Ejaili Street. There were two families living
in the house, both Arab. They were strongly anti-
Hussein, for whatever reason, but Hesam worried about

the increasing size of the reward for information leading to the arrest of Colonel Harun Baraniq, a traitor. Like torture, enough money could make any strong man or woman weak, even those of high principles. So each night Hesam continued to avoid contact with other people, slipping through the oldest and poorest section of the city and into the desert beyond, in the early morning hours.

Shivering as he moved, he was continually amazed that a place in the world that was so intensely hot in the afternoon could become so incredibly cold only a few hours later. He hoped tonight would be the night for the message he had been waiting for, and he glanced upward at the stars as though he might see it drop out of the sky.

It wasn't help from the stars that he needed, of course, but a capture of a CRYSTAL-class satellite on an orbit of 89 x 236 x 240 x 62.0. The coded message, or "toss," would be steganographic, meaning that it would be buried within or under a routine cover message. The cover message might be a weather report sent via the BBC or a radio station in Madrid, Spain, playing music. Or it might even be a military message sent from Brussels, Belgium, intended for a U.S. Army receiver in Fort Lewis, Washington. The originator would assume that every message would be intercepted by a hostile listening system. The sender, however, would attempt to trick the computerized interrogating processor into recognizing the cover transmission as benign, and miss the steganographic transmission underneath. The real message, the steganographic one, would likely be sent in a compact burst, a fraction of a second long, so that if the cover message were to be written out in longhand on a sheet of paper the burst message would look like the dot over an i.

Hesam arrived a full fifteen minutes prior to the scheduled message time. Because his message was arriving on the back of another, Hesam's passive receiver would have to listen to the broadcast in real time. When his discreet signal was received on his handheld radio, he would then be able to ignore the remainder of the transmission and decode his message. It would appear in the small window on the palm-size radio.

At 0310 Hesam switched on his transceiver. He listened. A small earphone plugged into the radio delivered a series of sounds that sounded like static, but was not. The "noise" that he heard was, he knew, scrambled numerals, representing letters, that were unique to the pre-assigned frequency he was on. He had watched the face of his radio less than two minutes when a small red light began to wink on and off very rapidly. After a moment that light stayed off. Hesam pushed a series of numeric keys on the face of the radio, then waited. Several more seconds elapsed before the first word appeared on the tiny, faintly illuminated screen. It read: *Firemen arrived Galveston today. ETA Waco plus 72.*

Firemen was a Leopard team, Hesam knew, and Waco was the predetermined code reference to Baghdad. The exact Zulu time of the landing was omitted because it might confirm a third party observation, like a radar site. That they were seventy-two hours out was all Hesam needed to know. He looked at his watch, calculating that the team would be traveling at night, over poor roads, and laid up during the day. There were any number of hazards along the way. It would be safer to assume things went sideways rather than assume they would be smooth. Hesam wished that he could have worked out a fall-back plan to get Baraniq out of Iraq independent of the Leopard team. But he could not and now it was too late. How long should he wait if the third day passed and they did not show up, he wondered? Waiting was a dangerous business. It played into the hands of the searchers.

He knew by experience that it was safer to make a deadline—then move precisely on that deadline. Hesam estimated that his should be approximately eighty hours. If the team had not arrived by then, they would be compromised. Aware of the dangerous consequences of violating guerilla warfare rules, he nevertheless postponed his decision.

* * *

McTaggart came instantly awake when he felt a nudge at his elbow.

"They're closer, Lieutenant," Entzion said, squatting with one foot anchored into the side of the wadi for balance. "And there's three of them."

"What kind?" McTaggart said, rolling out of his position. He could see that it was after midday. The team had let him sleep. He was instantly irritated with himself for not taking his turn at a post.

"BTRs," he said.

McTaggart mentally thumbed through the index of Russian-made armored personnel carriers. Iraq had been their best customer for the very efficient series of APCs. The Gulf War had given Hussein all the reason in the world to purchase the newest version, having lost so many to coalition forces. They were well armed and fast. In their present state, however, the Leopard team's DPVs couldn't outrun a dead rabbit.

"I'll take a look," he said. McTaggart kept low as he moved to the southern post position where Haggar was watching the Iraqi patrol's progress through a rangefinder. He moved aside so that McTaggart could have a clear field of vision.

"Affirm three," McTaggart said over his shoulder to Entzion and Haggar. "Any chance there's another one around? How about from the north?"

"We haven't seen any others, same from the north," Haggar said into his lip mike. "Right, Manny?"

"Affirmative," Manny said from the northern post, his voice as low and modulated as he could make it.

McTaggart turned back to the range finder for a last look. He considered. "All right. We don't want to shoot it out with these guys. They're looking for something. Maybe us. They don't know we're here or they'd come direct." Mctaggart looked at his watch; then at the sky, as though there might be some way he could move the sun to a more favorable time of day. "So here's what I think. Anybody comes up with a better idea, lay it on me. We leave the vehicles where they are under the camo net. We move out fifty meters and set up an ambush. If they don't find the vehicles or us, we all convert to Christianity. If they find them, we execute the ambush."

"We'll have to make sure we kill 'em all, Lieutenant," Entzion voiced the obvious. If any of the Iraqis got back to report what they had seen, or if they had time to send a radio message that a Special Forces team was operating on their turf, Leopard-1 would never get out alive.

"Concur. So let's talk about worst cases, then figure out how we deal with them," McTaggart said.

The team liked what they heard. Their untested leader had given his first battle order and he had done it with aplomb. He showed respect for his men while at the same time indicated a willingness to listen to other ideas that might be better than his. He was getting the most out of his team. That was what a SpecOp leader did best.

They began to run through the possibilities. First, they were outgunned. They would have to disable the APCs quickly, before the Iraqis could bring their heavy weapons to bear and, almost at the same time, the Leopard team would have to neutralize their communications. Third, while the first two objectives were being achieved, the personnel inside the armored carriers would have to be stopped cold. The survival of the team required a one-hundred-percent kill.

One of the team's DPVs mounted an AT-4 anti-armor rocket launcher. And each vehicle was equipped with an M-60 light machine gun that could do some very serious work in a short period of time. The downside was that these weapons were still fixed to the vehicles.

"We'll take the guns and the AT-4 off and set 'em up. . . ." McTaggart looked around. There was no vegetation and, except for rocks, not much in the way of natural cover. "Over there. We'll dig in the MGs there and there. And the rocket launcher will go over there." McTaggart pointed toward the eastern side of their perimeter. "Haggar?" McTaggart said, recognizing that his weapons man had something in mind.

"I want Beast to go back there, Lieutenant," he said, indicating over his shoulder toward the northwest. "I believe I can punch those motherfuckers out. The first round goes to the driver. If they try to run, I'll blow their engines up from the rear."

McTaggart as well as the other squad members assessed his proposed emplacement. It seemed solid. A man dug in, wearing a camo suit, the muzzle of his .50 pointed right down the throat of an APC. Yeah. That might work. With Beast set on semiautomatic, Haggar might even get all three drivers before they could react.

"I like it, Lee," McTaggart said.

Captain Al-Zeid kept one of his APCs well out on his right flank. It was heavily armed with a 30mm rapid-fire gun mounted on a turret above the driver. If it ran into trouble it was capable of shooting its way out—or in—until the other two vehicles could join up. It was commanded by the capable Sergeant Ehsan, a veteran of recent fighting in Afghanistan. It was Captain Al-Zeid's intention to cover the entire valley, some nine kilometers wide and twenty kilometers long, before it sloped abruptly upward into the mountains.

In thirty hours of searching the area where the northern military commander believed might have received an airborne party, Captain Al-Zeid had found nothing. No, not nothing. They had interdicted Kurdish goat herders on the east side of the valley. He had ordered his machine gunners to kill the goats. He allowed the herders, an old man and two young boys, to return to wherever they had come.

Captain Al-Zeid commanded his driver to halt while he raised his binoculars again toward the west. Sweeping slowly, he looked for any irregularities in the terrain— signs of fresh digging, trees that might give cover, indications of camouflaged netting. He referred once again to his map, looking for sources of water. If there was an airborne unit out there they would have brought water with them. But if they had reason to loiter in one area, they might look for a water hole of some kind. It might be a mountain trickle from melting snow or rain, or it could be one of the natural wells that inexplicably appear in all of these valleys.

The captain did not expect to see anything on the sides of the nearby hills. There would be no reason for any unit, either on foot or with vehicles, especially with vehicles, to linger on the sides of the mountains. To what purpose?

"Abahi 2, this is Abahi, over," the captain said into his field radio.

"Abahi 2," the sergeant's voice crackled in response.

"Anything, Ehsan?"

"Nothing, sir," the radio voice said flatly.

The captain would go two kilometers farther north. That would bring him to the base of the foothills; then he would swing east. He would meet up with Ehsan's vehicle and all three APCs would return together.

"Abahi 2, I am moving north. Turn to join us at the rocks at your ten o'clock position," he said, keying the radio mike.

"Yes, Captain," the sergeant said.

If there was nothing to be found in this sweep, Captain Al-Zeid would return with his unit to headquarters. Radar operators were wrong in their target information as often as they were right. The units of his patrol were using short-range radio signals. Captain Al-Zeid knew that his transmissions could theoretically be picked up by American listening posts around the world as well as the all but invisible satellites hovering overhead. But as a practical matter he could not bring himself to bypass the convenience of using electronics to communicate with his flank units.

Unbeknownst to Captain Al-Zeid, an E-2C Hawkeye from the *John C. Stennis* Battle Group was cruising its assigned sector in the Iraq northern no-fly zone. The

Grumman Hawkeye was probing the known Iraqi air defense system with its newest radar, the APS-145 as well as using IFF passive detection system. The crew, two pilots and three technicians behind them, had arrived on station forty minutes prior and had picked up two short radio transmissions from the ground below. The transmissions were received by the Hawkeye on 1030 MHZ; then immediately sequenced into the onboard computer, an enhanced high-speed processor that identified the type of radio that emitted the signal. Within minutes, coded information was returned to the Hawkeye technician that the intercepted message was unique to an Iraqi Republican Guard Special Reconnaissance unit.

The Hawkeye pilot altered course sixteen degrees and flew twelve minutes before it arrived at his northern-most sector.

"What've you got, Ticker?" the Hawkeye pilot, Lieutenant Arnold "Kong" King, said to Lieutenant "Ticker" Swash. Swash was verifying what his airborne electronics laboratory was showing him in real-time visual on the ground.

"Three Iraqi vehicles. They're probably detached from the 47th Guard," Swash replied over the intercom.

"Amazing," Kong mumbled.

"Say again?" Lieutenant Swash asked.

"What's your pleasure? Want to hang around or go west?" Kong asked the tech officer.

There was no immediate response from the back of the plane. The pilot was about to speak again when Swash's voice crackled over the intercom. "Ah, standby one, Kong, while I jump off-line to talk with Combat Control."

The intercom went silent again while Swash switched to one of the battle group's frequencies. Kong put his E-2C into a two-minute turn to the left that would bring him back to the same location over the ground in one-hundred-twenty seconds. His Allison turboprop engines maintained a "working" speed of two-hundred-eighty knots at ten thousand feet. He and his copilot, constantly scanning their instrument panels, noted that they had used half of their fuel from the internal tanks.

"We'll need to refuel in five-zero minutes," Kong intoned.

"Roger," the copilot said as he turned to the refueling location charts. They had slightly over six-thousand pounds of fuel on board, about half of their take-off load. Eight-hundred gallons would leave them about seven-hundred-fifty miles of range before the propellers stopped. Since they had no idea of how long they may have to loiter on station because of a possible target, the refueling operation would have to be moved up. A tanker might have to rendezvous with them more than once en route home.

"Kong," came Lieutenant Swash's voice on-line. "Looks like we have people on the ground down there. Maybe something black because they aren't giving any details, but they want us to loiter for two or relieved."

The pilot understood that they were to remain on station, watching the Iraqi ground unit for a minimum of two hours or until other friendly aircraft arrived to take over.

"Suits me, Ticker. We're gettin' paid by the hour. Do the folks below know we're here?"

"I'm dropping a dime now," the tech said. Swash punched in a call sign on an air to ground VHF radio using the ground unit's discreet identification code given him minutes before by CCC (combat control center) aboard the *Stennis*. There was no response on the other end despite repeated attempts. Swash did not continue the call lest it attract the attention of Iraqi radio monitors. They would stay on station, however, as ordered, and Swash would try again later.

Kong rolled out of his slow turn and flew straight-line in a western direction. He would lurk his aircraft over the horizon, out of sight of the potential ground targets, but not out of sight of their airborne surveillance equipment.

In the foothills McTaggart watched the progress of the

Iraqi unit as they approached. There was no doubt, now. At two-thousand meters, he could see the smallest details of their APCs. The lead vehicle was the 2S23 model containing a self-propelled 120-mm howitzer on its upper turret. This guy would be the most dangerous of the group. The flanking APCs were BTR-80s, eight wheels, each mounting machine guns that could be operated from inside the vehicle. At their present course and speed, they would arrive at the Leopard team's position within thirty minutes. It was also possible that they could pass close to the team's location and not spot the camouflage netting, but McTaggart couldn't take the chance. Staying low to the ground, he returned to the dugout area.

He switched on his radio and adjusted the headset over his ears, the microphone near his lips. The other team members, following his lead, did the same.

"Unless they change plans, they'll be here in thirty. We'll set up for ambush," McTaggart said, glancing at his watch. "Lee," he said to Haggar, "the lead vehicle packs a 120-howitzer. The driver is still priority number one, but then get right on their gun position before you go for the other drivers. Agree?"

"Yes, sir," Haggar answered.

"Radios . . ." McTaggart began.

"If they find our cars," Quack interjected, "I guarantee they're going to come piling out of their APCs. When the doors open we can put grenades right inside. No more radios."

"That's right, Lieutenant," Rodriguez said. "Soon as they come across our OP, me an' Quack will come up shooting. No more than twenty meters. Can't miss 'em."

The outer perimeter to which Rodriguez referred was moved in to thirty-five meters for purposes of the ambush. The P1 M-203 grenade launcher for the M-4 Commando Carbine was a highly accurate and very lethal weapon at that range. McTaggart knew that if they could explode a grenade inside one or more of the APCs, the battle would be short indeed.

"So, what if you can't get a shot at the back doors?" McTaggart asked Rodriguez.

"I don't have an answer for that one," the Cuban said.

Their ambush plan included a pair of layout positions dug in the ground in an area where the Iraqi APCs would have to pass if they were to get near the Leopard team's desert vehicles. Two men would lie prone, covered with netting and loose indigenous material. They would wait for the enemy to pass; then rise up and fire from the rear. McTaggart knew it was a high percentage technique for rolling up an enemy force and, like Rodriguez, he couldn't come up with a better idea for assaulting the APCs and silencing their radios. He slowly nodded his head.

"Okay. Let's do it," he said.

The plan called for Rodriguez and Quack to take the layout positions, Haggar to use his .50-caliber rifle from cover directly in front of the Iraqi patrol, while McTaggart and Entzion each took a flank to shoot targets of opportunity.

For the next several minutes the team helped cover up Rodriguez and Quack in their shallow holes. They would be extremely uncomfortable, enduring high temperatures from the sun and remaining absolutely still while Iraqi hunters roamed the area searching for prey.

There were techniques and training regimens for enduring the pain caused by muscle cramp and lack of food and water while engaged in motionless observation for hours on end. All Special Ops people were required to accept high levels of physical pain that would be caused on virtually all hostile missions.

After they were all but invisible to the most alert probing eyes, the rest of the Leopard team carefully swept the ground with shelter halves, removing all traces of footprints, then took their places surrounding the netted DPVs.

From behind a clump of rocks, McTaggart slowly raised his head toward the south. The high-pitched whine of turbodiesel engines was becoming louder with each meter of the Iraqi approach. The vehicles loomed large in his vision, and he guessed that they were one-hundred-fifty meters off, grinding relentlessly toward them. For whatever reason he did not then consciously know, McTaggart happened to look down at the small radio receiver attached to his combat harness. A red light was blinking insistently. Should he take the chance that by answering, his concentration on the imminent combat would be jeopardized? Would his voice somehow be heard by the other side? Not likely, he thought, but they were near. It took effort to remove his eyes from the advancing Iraqis to key the outside frequency. But he did.

"Frogpond," McTaggart said, whispering the team's coded identifier into the interrogating signal. "Over."

"Frogpond, this is a Hawkeye 2C with you at Angels 10. Advise you have first call on room service this frequency. Menu includes Tomcats for lunch and Hornets for dinner. Do you copy? Over."

McTaggart did not recognize the voice, but the naval aviator could not have announced himself at a better time. The Iraqi vehicles had arrived. Like metal monsters from a child's bad dream they crouched, far larger than the DPVs of Leopard-1, diesels snorting as they came to a clanking halt, turrets moving cyclopean eyes for prey. Rather than answering with his voice, McTaggart keyed his push-to-talk button on his belt twice. The rapid clicks on the radio told the listener that the last transmission was acknowledged.

It was impossible for McTaggart's Leopard team to move without discovery. They had to wait until the Iraqis either left or . . .

A hatch over the lead vehicle opened and McTaggart saw the upper half of a soldier rise from within. The soldier, an officer, scanned the area. The officer turned slowly, looking in a two-hundred-twenty-degree arc, peering carefully at the rocks and topography around him. Apparently seeing nothing of interest, the officer lowered his head slightly to speak to someone inside the

APC, probably the driver. The vehicle began to move; then it stopped again. The officer pulled himself up and out through the hatch, dropping gracefully to the ground. A second soldier emerged from within, this one to take up position at the 120-mm gun. In the second vehicle, still another man materialized behind a 7.62 machine gun, racking a round into the gun's breach.

McTaggert's heart was racing, he licked his lips, anticipating action. But the Iraqis before him seemed not fully alarmed. Instead, they appeared only to be moving warily. Nor did the rear access doors on the APCs open so that the troops, if troops there were, could get out of what must have been very hot boxes. The vehicles had to employ very effective air-conditioning systems inside, McTaggart reasoned.

The officer was now walking slowly from his machine toward the wadi over which was stretched the camouflage net. The officer paused, his head turning, his nose rising slightly as though sniffing for spoor. As his eyes drifted slowly back toward the wadi, the officer began to walk once more.

McTaggart slowly raised his M-4 to his cheek so that the officer's image filled his M-68 aimport. He was about to fire his rifle for real. Blood pounded through his body, into his ears. It felt as though the man at whom he was aiming his rifle would sense the danger, would see him before he could pull the trigger. After years of training the young lieutenant wondered if he was doing it all right. Maybe he had better wait for one of the other, more experienced men, to take the first shot.

But by now he was on autopilot, his body and brain reacting as they had been trained to do. There was no need to use laser sighting, the Iraqi being less than fifty meters. When it seemed the Iraqi officer would walk right into the netting, he halted. Then he turned slowly to his left, raising his eyes to the surrounding hills, and began to walk almost nonchalantly back toward his unit.

There was something about that walk that bothered McTaggart. The man was too casual, as though he . . .

Mr. Taggart pulled the trigger of his M-4. His fire selector had been set for a three-round burst. All three rounds caught the officer, two in the upper body and one in the head. McTaggart immediately turned toward the second vehicle, to the man at the machine gun, but Tom Entzion was already on him. Entzion's first burst took the man down, sending him over the side of his perch, half out of the armored machine.

McTaggart heard the lead APC engine gunned, ready to turn or run, when the unmistakable sound of Haggar's .50-caliber rifle barked once, then again. The vehicle's engine returned to idle as the armor-piercing round passed through the driver's narrow window slit. No doubt it penetrated through the driver and rattled around inside the vehicle, perhaps even smashing through the floor. While McTaggart could not see the effects inside the vehicle, he could see that the rear doors clanging open and two Iraqi troops springing out from inside. McTaggart gunned one of the two emerging soldiers before, from the corner of his eyes, he saw Quack and Rodriguez rise out of their ambush trenches and simultaneously fire grenades into the open rear doors of the first and second vehicles in line.

There followed violent explosions, made even more effective because of the steel containment of the armored cars. Nothing inside could have survived the blast. These actions, however, gave the third APC's gunner and driver time to react. The Iraqi gunner turned his coaxial 7.62-mm PKT machine gun toward Haggar's place of concealment and opened up. He laid down a steel hose of gunfire turning stone to dust and causing Haggar to press his nose deeply into the baked clay ground. The gunner continued to sweep to the right, seeking to pinpoint McTaggart's concealed position. The gunner must have glimpsed McTaggart at the outset of the firefight because his concentrated aim was taking him close to the mark. McTaggart had always appreciated his own size and strength, but at the moment he would have traded all of his six-four for the body of a midget. Like Haggar,

McTaggart was covered with pieces of broken rock and dust as the relentless gunner maintained a wicked stream of steel-jacketed rounds smashing and probing for living flesh. No sooner had Haggar attempted to set up the Beast for a shot at the gunner, than the Iraqi swung toward him, and Haggar once again dove for cover.

The rear doors of the third Iraqi APC were left closed, but the troops inside took full advantage of firing through the seven gun ports, three on each side and one in the rear, causing Leopard team's Rodriguez and Quack to roll to either side of their ambush positions to find better cover. Entzion was taking fire as well, but because he did not have to deal with the machine gun, he was able to place well-aimed shots through the vehicle's gun ports. He had scored two hits before the APC driver began to move his vehicle backward. Placing a round through the gun ports while the machine was on the move was almost impossible.

Suddenly, there was another roar from Haggar's rifle and the turreted machine gun suddenly fell silent. Haggar's round had penetrated the gunner's armored shield, striking the Iraqi soldier in the upper body, killing him instantly. Gunfire slowed when the Iraqi APC driver put the machine in full reverse, moving out into the flat land from whence it came. At five-hundred meters, it wheeled, paused briefly while forward gear was selected, and sped away. Haggar fired several rounds at the rapidly retreating machine, but it was concealed in its own cloud of dust. The Leopard team knew the APC would escape.

"If the fucker's radio still works, we're in a world of hurt," Rodriguez said.

McTaggart double-timed it to where their own desert vehicles were half-in and half-out of the wadi. He snatched the team's UHF backpack command radio and switched it on. He punched in the Hawkeye guard frequency.

"Hawkeye 2, this is Frogpond, over," Argel transmitted.

"Frogpond, this is Hawkeye 2. What's your pleasure?"

"We have just engaged a recon patrol with three vehicles. One of the APCs got away, heading approximately one niner zero degrees. Do you have air assets? Over," McTaggart said, his eyes searching the blue skies overhead.

"Roger, Frogpond, we have two Hornets with full ordnance. Also have visual on your running bandits. Standby one," the air combat controller said, momentarily breaking away from the lieutenant. McTaggart waited impatiently knowing that the controller was in the process of vectoring his Hornets onto the Iraqi armored personnel carrier.

Moments later he was back on McTaggart's frequency. "Yo Frogpond, estimate in one minute plus ten ticks there is gonna be a bunch of happy virgins waiting for Allah's warriors to arrive. Sit back and enjoy."

McTaggart and his team looked in the direction the APC had been traveling, by now too far away to be discerned in detail. After many very long moments there were two events, one following closely behind the first. On the distant horizon was a large flash of orange that quickly turned into a ball of black smoke roiling skyward. A deep rumble, like thunder that follows lightning, rolled across the desert to reach the Leopard team. The second event was the sound of screaming, high-performance engines pushing the vertical twin-stabilizer Hornet fighter jets through the air. The team swiveled their necks as one while the Hornets finished their dives to the deck; then pulled up, rolling into steep turns, flying over the Leopard team's position, covering the distance in a matter of seconds.

As they passed overhead the team waved their arms or held weapons overhead in salute. Then the Hornets were gone as suddenly as they appeared.

"Big-time thanks, Hawkeye," McTaggart said over the command radio.

"We are your humble servants, Frogpond," the combat controller said.

"Any chance the APC got a radio call out?" McTaggart asked.

"No guarantee, but if they did we probably would have picked it up. Nothing shows on our monitors." There followed a pause in the communications, then the Hawkeye controller came back. "Frogpond, Hawkeye."

"Go," McTaggart said.

"We're out of here soon. We continue this loiter and we'll attract more attention to you."

"Understand. Go with Allah," McTaggart said.

"Hawkeye, out."

And the connection was over.

CHAPTER 6

Hesam had watched while Harun Baraniq's nerves slowly corroded. The large-framed Iraqi ate sparingly after his arrival at the house on Ejaili Street. He prayed six times a day. As the hot, suffocating days dragged by, boredom, interrupted only by fearful escapes into the hidden basement of the house when soldiers were in the area, Baraniq began to pray more and eat less. The permanent residents of the house had been instructed not to engage in unnecessary conversation with their "guest," but even they noticed that the defecting Iraqi officer had become increasingly remote.

As Hesam looked at his charge he saw a man who could never seem to find comfort in his own body. When seated there did not seem to be a place to put one arm or another. His legs constantly crossed and recrossed. His attention span grew increasingly shorter and, despite a goodly supply of reading material, neither books nor periodicals held his interest. Hesam attempted to take the former Intel officer for walks during the night when there was less risk of being recognized, but fear or ennui prevailed and Baraniq remained inside.

They had been laid up in the safe house for more than five weeks. There had been no communication of any kind for five days since he had been advised that a Leopard team was now in country. He had envisioned any number of reasons why the team had not yet arrived in Baghdad, but none of his imagined scenarios had been comforting. Discovery and destruction of the unit was topmost on his list of horrors. His vision of their capture by Iraqi forces was among the worse. He calculated and recalculated their projected progress from their northern LZ to Baghdad. Even allowing for the inevitable, unplanned contingencies that affect all missions, the team was late. If they had somehow been taken out, killed, or captured, he surely would have received some form of revised intelligence, followed by orders to proceed on his own.

He could understand Colonel Baraniq's stressful state of mind. Hesam could feel the vise of nervous tension tightening around his own head. He felt an unusual sense of isolation, compounded by his inability to communicate with his seniors or with the Leopard team that might no longer even exist. Nor was he able to enter the city for fear that he might have been associated with Baraniq by the secret police following the colonel. Colonel Baraniq's image was in newspapers, television, and in fliers handed out everywhere to the populace.

As he pondered his next move, certain that to do nothing was courting disaster, he heard the sound of a vehicle in the street outside. The "residents" of the safe house were all at their places of work, leaving Hesam and Baraniq alone. It was now early afternoon, the torpid part of the day. For Hesam, the night brought an ease of tension. If there was an advantage he might have over an enemy, he believed it was the darkness that would allow him to prevail. That was not so for Baraniq, Hesam knew. He had witnessed the man struggle with sleep that eluded him. The slightest noise in the dark would pop open his eyes, as though evil spirits could be kept at bay only as long as he hid from them in the safety of his basement room.

Hesam walked softly to a small window, a slim, single opening from inside the house onto the street looking south. He saw at once an official vehicle parked in front of a neighbor's house. A sense of danger nearby created a tingling along Hesam's nervous system. Military or police? Coincidence?

He thought not. He was about to turn away from the window with the intention of rousing Baraniq who had drawn himself into a corner of the main living area of the house, when his attention was arrested by two uniformed men emerging from within the neighboring place. Hesam could see they were police, not soldiers.

Like most domiciles in this quarter of the city, more than one family, often several, squeezed into a small space, sharing cooking and sleeping facilities. Inside water was problematic making bathing and toilet a communal enterprise. Hesam glimpsed the neighbors in their doorway gesturing and pointing in his direction. The policemen began walking his way.

Hesam believed it was useless to hide in the basement. Worse, he realized that he had left his semiautomatic pistol there. Suddenly, there was a loud knocking on the door.

He shot a glance at Baraniq whose eyes were now wide open, his jaw slack beneath his black, untrimmed moustache. Hesam pointed his index finger theatrically toward the floor, and the Iraqi defector understood what was needed. He had only to crawl two meters to the hidden basement access under the cooking area.

The police banged loudly this time, probably with the butts of their rifles.

"Yes, yes!" Hesam responded loudly toward the door. "I am coming."

By now Baraniq had descended the wooden ladder and was pulling back into place the tile block flooring, upon which was attached a crude cutting table near the oven. Before Hesam reach the door it flew open with a crash, and two armed men stepped inside.

"Aha!" Hesam said, raising his voice at the intruders. "You are finally here! I have been calling all day and you take your time, and then when you come you kick down my door. What kind of police do we have, eh? Do you call yourselves soldiers of the mighty Saddam?"

The policemen were expecting anything but an aggressive greeting, and for a moment Hesam succeeded in confusing at least one of them.

"What? What are you saying, you donkey? You did not call us, we . . ."

"But you are wrong! Wrong, sir. Those people next door are criminals. They are thieves, you see. They have eaten my dog and they steal my chickens! I have seen them do it. Black market jewelry. People come in and out buying from them. Oh, they are terrible people. They have accosted my daughter, you know. Did you know that one of them was Kurd? Eh? In ten years I have known those cursed asses. . . ."

"Shut your mouth! They say it was they who called us. They say you are hiding someone here in this house. Who else is here? Don't lie, or you will pray to Allah that we only cut out your tongue."

"There is no one, sir. I swear it on the moustache of the our leader, the Great One!" Hesam whined, clasping his hands to his breast as he pleaded his innocence. "Allah be praised. Please come in and look. Look everywhere. It is a small, very small house. But you would do me a great honor if you would search here for whatever you are looking for. Then you will go to those evil people and arrest them, yes?"

The two policemen, becoming increasingly uninterested in following up a tip that seemed clearly between hated neighbors, stepped into the main room. One of them glanced into the cooking area, but seeing nothing of consequence, turned away, jerking his head at his partner.

The partner slung his weapon over his shoulder, stepping back across the threshold of the open front door.

"You, blabbermouth. Do I know you?" the policeman said, looking steadily at Hesam, trying to place a familiar feature. "What is your name?"

"It is Faway, sir. I was once a cook, you know, in the army of our great leader, Saddam. I have offered you nothing to taste but if you would sit down and be patient I have a haunch of Nubian goat that I can roast. . . ."

"No, no," the policeman said, holding up his hand. "We are busy with our work. My advice to you is avoid the, ah, people over there. They do not like you. Don't talk to them."

"I understand exactly, exactly, yes, sir," Hesam said. "If there is one thing I am able to do it is not talk about almost . . ."

Hesam's drivel was abruptly interrupted by the deafening report of a gunshot at close range. One of the departing policeman sagged, a hole through his uniform blouse just beginning to show traces of blood from the wound. Hesam did not waste time turning to look behind him. He knew who had fired the shot.

Hesam had to reach around the staggering man's large shoulder to get at the first policeman. Had the first officer stepped forward, away from the doorway, he would have succeeded in removing his assault weapon from its place on his shoulder. He would have been able to bring it to bear on Hesam and Baraniq. But in the reflex of the moment he had turned toward, not away, from his falling comrade and, in that elapsed moment, Hesam was able to grasp a fistful of clothing. He jerked the man toward him, the rifle falling uselessly onto the stone step in front of the door.

The policeman, however, used his momentum to twist away from Hesam's grasp. He rolled onto the floor, coming up into a combat crouch. Hesam had no wish to fight with the man and, expecting Baraniq to finish the job he had started, hesitated.

"Shoot him!" Hesam said.

Baraniq stood frozen, the pistol still in his hand pointing at nothing but a blank wall. The policeman, who one second earlier had expected to be dead, and Hesam, who expected precisely the same thing, suddenly leaped for

Baraniq. Both of them wanted the gun, but neither man willing to release his grip on Baraniq's wrist as they scratched, pounded, and bit each other.

The gun exploded again, and a super hot powder flash sent searing pain up Hesam's upper arm, almost causing him to lose his grip on the gun Baraniq still clutched. They were all on the floor, now, the Iraqi policeman opening his mouth to take a chunk out of Hesam's hand when Hesam was able to attain enough leverage to draw his right knee sharply upward into the policeman's crotch. Hesam could hear the man grunt with pain and sensed a sudden relaxation in the man's grip on the gun. Hesam used all of his strength to press the muzzle of the piece into the policeman's chest. He fumbled while he struggled to place his thumb inside the trigger guard. Suddenly, even to Hesam's surprise, the .40-caliber fired. The policeman jerked, then rolled away.

Hesam quickly went to the policeman's side and, touching the carotid artery, determined that he was still alive. Quickly covering the pistol with a small pillow, Hesam placed the pillow over the policeman's head and pulled the trigger.

This time there was no doubt. A large part of the man's skull and its contents were spread beneath him, including small pieces of gray matter. The pillow had protected Hesam from splatter and partially muffled the shot. But the other shots had to have been heard by someone outside.

"You stupid piece of camel shit!" Hesam snarled at the cringing Baraniq. Hesam knew, even as he uttered the invective at the Iraqi defector, that the colonel was not wholly responsible for his acts.

"We are trapped," Baraniq said flatly.

"No, we're not."

"There is no way out. They know where we are, now," the colonel said.

But Hesam was already going through the pockets of the policemen. He found both notepads on their persons, and he quickly read their entries. One of the pages contained the address on Ejaili Street and a pencil entry of time and date. It was, he hoped, the policeman's notation of the neighbor's complaint. This page he tore from the book, carefully returning the notebooks back in their pockets.

"It is a big country, Baraniq. Here, help me with them."

When it was dark the two dead policeman were buried in shallow graves behind the house of his neighbors on Ejaili Street. Let them do the explaining. Meanwhile, Hesam led Baraniq along his path to the desert.

Cyrille Cosette had toiled in the vineyards of the French DGSE—Directorate General for External Security—in one of its many forms since the end of his contract with the Legion thirty-two years prior. That was when the French Foreign Legion was permanently garrisoned at Djibouti. He was the very embodiment of virile manhood then. He had the kind of physique for which a uniform was designed. At the age of sixteen, Cosette felt it was his duty to spread his sperm widely about the European continent, but because he assumed *les dames* loved him instantly in return, there were times when he was careless about mutual consent prior to *l'acte.* Nor did he always take care that his "dates" left his company with at least as much money as when he had picked them up. One careless habit led to still another until the Interpol took an active interest in his every move.

The Legion had enlistment stations all about Europe, but it happened that Cosette was in his home country of France when, streaking from the back door of a Toulouse flat he was "tending" for a friend, he practically hurled himself into the arms of a khaki-clad soldier wearing a white kepi. The door was closed behind him barring the entrance of a pursuing gendarme, or so he later told the story. An accomplished liar, Cyrille Cosette told the FFL recruiter that he was eighteen years old, the minimum enlistment age for a Legionnaire recruit. The recruiter chose to accept his lie and provided him with a contract of enlistment to sign.

To his surprise, Cosette found that there was much about military life that pleased him, including the discipline imposed upon him. There were long days, weeks, and months of tedium, as well as endless training, but there were also periods of excitement so intense that he feared he might become addicted to the life.

In the end, however, Cosette completed his five-year contract with the Legion and, as a civilian with the knowledge of things military he had gained, he was able to regularly provide information to a number of intelligence agencies with interests in the Middle East. By age twenty-six he had become reasonably fluent in Arabic and passable in Farsi. He spoke English as well, a language and culture for which he had little respect. But it was a requirement for anyone who sought to make his living by selling information on a global scale. As with many independent purveyors of stories, written or spoken, secret or public, Cosette survived but did not flourish until, seeking stability of income, he became a permanent employee of the French government. He was hired by the DGSE and posted back to France where he spent a year learning the art of spycraft. Then he was once again posted to the geographical area where his affinity for the languages and his easily accessible, if not influential contacts, were located.

The quality of intelligence information gathered by Cosette over the years was never spectacular, but it was steady and, to a surprisingly degree given the industry's quality as a whole, reliable. With the cachet of the DGSE behind him, Cosette became a man to respect, someone who had a reasonable budget with which to purchase information of value. And Cosette had a thief's instinct for what was valuable and what was not. Also, with the onset of prematurely graying hair—heavily and naturally streaked before age thirty—his access to increasingly higher levels of various government officials opened sources for weightier stuff. He was the first field agent among his French colleagues, for example, to provide his senior officers at Boulevard Mortier in Paris, in the 20th Arrondissement, that Israel would react with massive force to the provocations of Egypt, Syria, and Jordan.

In March of 1967, Cosette provided the DGSE with keen insights into the Israeli general staff, short only of a complete order of battle. The Israeli military, Cosette summed up in one of his reports, was confident that it would defeat any combination of Arab armies put before it. Officials in Paris believed no part of it. It was, a senior DGSE analyst said in dismissing Cosette's report, a careless invention of a field agent who had failed to do his homework. Arrayed against the Jewish nation were an overwhelming numbers of armies, armed with the latest Soviet tanks, artillery, and planes.

Then, in June of 1967, Egypt's arrogant leader, Gamal Abdul Nasser, closed off the Strait of Tiran, Israel's important international trading link, which the Israelis considered an act of war.

As Cosette had predicted, the Israelis chose to fight on the Arab desert, rather than in Israel, and on June 5th the Israeli Air Force launched a first strike against Egyptian air facilities. In the space of only hours, the Egyptians suffered three hundred nine of three hundred forty combat aircraft destroyed, mostly on the ground. Now enjoying total air superiority, the Israelis were able to protect their armored vehicles, troops, and heavy guns. Under the relentless assault of highly trained Jewish pilots, the Egyptian military was broken in ranks and set to retreat. Without hesitation, Israel forces wheeled to take on Syria and Jordan, rolling up those armies and pushing them back across the Jordan River. The Six Day War amazed the entire world, including students of war planning everywhere. While the books of desert warfare tactics were being rewritten, the stock of Cyrille Cosette shot to the top of the sub-rosa world of spydom.

Doors that were closed to him suddenly opened. He began to gain access to leaders of nations on the African continent, the Mediterranean into Turkey, Asia Minor, and, when he chose, farther east. He was quietly recommended to powerful men who believed he could supply them with secrets from the other side which, occasionally, he did. When he ran out of the real stuff he merely made up intelligence summaries out of whole cloth. Often when he was passing on genuine Intel he garnished it with his personal estimates of next-to-worst scenarios of what could occur. He framed what-if analyses with the touch of an overworked city editor of a large newspaper.

Cyrille Cosette became the master of Ponzi intelligence. Enough of his suppositions presented as fact were eventually realized, giving the consumers of his information high value for money spent. The intelligence that was revealed to be worthless he simply shrugged off. Like any dealer in commodities with a short shelf life, there were bound to be losses.

A small but significant percentage of the DGSE's field agents worked both sides of the fence; sometimes, as in the case of Cosette, both sides of many fences. The Directorate realized that one of the techniques of effective espionage was to appear to be a double agent, sometimes a triple. It was the nature of the business that spies were seldom savory characters and, to use the old cliche of catching a thief with a thief, spies had to sometimes appear to be for sale. As long as Cosette's *real* allegiance was to France, and as long as he never lied to the Directorate, they would let him be.

Still, over a period of almost thirty years, Cosette had burned a good many contacts and he had dumped enough of his low-grade merchandise on people who once stood in line to pay for it. Life became increasingly like walking a buttered tightrope. Once the intrigue had suited Cosette's personality. He had been comfortable crossing the rope back and forth over a moat of crocodiles, assuring himself that sooner rather than later he would come down off the balancing act and settle in a country that served liquor in public and where girls could walk around in short skirts.

It was only the American intelligence system, agencies that included the CIA, NSA, Defense Intelligence Agency, Department of State, who did not know that Cyrille Cosette was something less than the most trusted name in the Middle East. Certainly not the United States Navy Intelligence service, Task Force 28-B, whose ultimate responsibility it was to provide for the extraction of Leopard-1 from Umm Qsr in the Persian Gulf. Lieutenant Commander Stockton Briggle, USN, was the liaison officer between the SEAL teams and *Les Swimmers*, the name that the French Navy had ascribed to their underwater warfare operators.

"They're the best," Commander Briggle said to Captain Daniel Unrue, his immediate superior. "You know how they launch for most missions, sir? Right out the torpedo tubes of one of their subs. No special designs. They just pack those guys inside a tube and when they get near their target, they blow 'em out."

"Jesus," Unrue said, shaking his head in admiration.

"They have a panic cord in there, but it's a matter of pride nobody ever pulls the damn thing," Briggle added.

"Talk about claustrophobia," Unrue said.

"None of our guys panicked, either, but more than one told me they got fired out just in time. Pitch black and you're touching the tube with each shoulder. It's only twenty-eight inches wide," Briggle said.

"They know the territory we're interested in?" Captain Unrue wanted to be reassured.

"Absolutely, sir. The French have been down here for a hundred years. Longer, I guess."

"Okay. What we want, Stockton," the captain said, "is to get this guy out quietly. We don't want to go in with force. We'd lose the man and we're not ready to start the war yet. We'd end up fighting the whole Middle East. We want him out of the red zone and back here before anyone figures out where he is."

Commander Briggle nodded his head in agreement. Unrue's staff were ace planners and they had all the toys in the U.S. arsenal to call on if needed. If they opted to

take him out on water wings you could bet they knew it
was the best way.

"Who's the guy?" Briggle asked.

"Iraqi defector. Colonel Harun Baraniq. Know the
name?"

"If I don't know about Baraniq then I'm in the wrong
business," Briggle said.

"All right, then, you pick the local guy. It's our passenger's and your ass from the pickup point on the beach
to a place twelve miles out to the Mark V boats," Captain Unrue said as he led Briggle to a large table upon
which was spread a detailed map of the Persian Gulf.

Briggle knew all about the Mark V boats. They were
hot, SpecOp crafts, eighty-two feet in length and could
rip through the water at fifty knots. They mounted a
variety of weapons including 25mm Mk-38s for main
guns or M-60 or Mk-19 grenade launchers or .50-caliber
MGs. They were ideal for high seas in bad weather. Captain Unrue explained where the V boats would loiter
until Briggle and his Iraq defector arrived. They would
then run twenty-four miles at high speed to meet the task
force. Captain Unrue and Commander Briggle discussed
times, places, and provided for contingency locations.

"He's coming out with a Leopard team," Captain
Unrue said.

"Ah. So there'll be eight of us aboard the Five boat,"
Briggle said.

"Right," Captain Unrue said, stepping back from
bending over the map table, "do you have a name?"

"Yes, sir. He's an old sand fly, as they call them down
here. Been with French DGSE forever. They say he
knows every inch of the Gulf and everybody who lives
within a thousand miles. Cyrille Cosette."

CHAPTER 7

There had been other American Special Operations teams as well as British and Israeli units in Iraq for several months. When the American president identified Iraq as an originator of weapons and exporter of terror, teams began preparation for a day when coalition forces, or America alone if need be, would begin an invasion designed to throw out the current government. Plans for a massive build-up had been taking place for a number of months and the SpecOps units from the United States had executed incursions in a variety of locations inside the country. It was part of U.S. intentions to launch the attack in early spring or late fall in order to avoid the killing heat of Mesopotamia that hovers around one hundred twenty degrees in the summer. Fighting a war under those conditions might become a significant factor against Western troops who had lived their lives in more moderate climes.

But Special Forces personnel were selected for their high tolerance of hostile environments and trained to function efficiently in them. SpecOps teams had ranged all the way from the north, essentially where Leopard-1 inserted in country to as far south as the oil cities of Mosul and Kirkuk, including the western desert near Syria. They fought hotly contested gun battles near the

Wadi Gowdaf and in the Shat al-Arab and Urr regions. The United States had never acknowledged that they were there, of course, nor had the Iraqis admitted that "enemy" troops were operating within their sovereign territory almost with impunity.

At 0200 hours Hesam, with a shivering Colonel Baraniq at his elbow, had dug up his satellite transceiver. He was loathe to send a signal in such totally hostile countryside, easily within range of the Iraqi RDFs, (radio direction finder), but if there was ever a time to risk discovery, this had to be it. He quickly filled in the hole before striking away to the east of the city as far as possible from police and army patrols that would surely be out in force the following day. By the time Hesam found a location he thought was temporarily safe, he halted.

"Rest here, Colonel," he said to Baraniq.

There was no argument from the defector, whose last decade behind a desk had left him exhausted from their forced nine-mile hike. He sat heavily at the base of a electrical transmission tower that had once been knocked down by a bomb, but now repaired and put upright. It was one of a long line of such poles that seemed to come from the vast ocean of sand in one direction and sailing off into the opposite direction toward a distant town. The Iraqi had no exact idea where they were located, even in his own country. After crossing a secondary highway out of the city the colonel had seen but two more, the last a narrow service road and it was several miles to their rear.

While the colonel rested and drank deeply from one of the water bottles they carried, Hesam had readied his transmission. Using his key pad he recorded the following message: *Artful Dodger dep Waco w/Griffon wait Lp1+48.* Hesam added the Zulu time, then punched in the numerals taken from his GPS, then pressed the send key. The burst transmitter would automatically scramble the letters Hesam had entered into a blur of photons which would be reconstructed at a receiver in Florida, U.S.A.

He had just informed SOCCENT that he and Griffon, the fabled bird with head and wings of an eagle but with the body of a lion, code word for Colonel Baraniq, had departed Baghdad and would rendezvous with Leopard-1 at a particular location within forty-eight hours. Hesam switched on his GPS, hardly larger than his hand, and watched the indicator that would show him that the instrument was picking up the continual signals of a constellation of satellites. Hesam waited less than half a minute until he had a firm fix on eight satellites. Now the location on any spot on the surface of the earth could be obtained simply by pressing a simple "Mark" key on the global positioning system, the GPS. The precise latitude, longitude, hours, minutes, and seconds, accurate to within ten paces, would immediately appear on the small display window. These fixes Hesam would include with his transmission to SOCCENT on one of scores of frequencies monitored by South Central Command (Special Operations). He would not send position reports to any other entity, however.

"Where are they? Your men," the colonel asked.

"They will be here," Hesam said, moving to the rucksack that had remained buried for so many months. All of their supplies, the things they would need to survive, were there. Hesam had to think for several seconds to remember where the covering was located. The whereabouts of Leopard-1 was a total mystery to him. For all he knew he and the colonel might have to walk three hundred miles to the nearest safe zone.

"That is what you say."

"They'll be here," Hesam repeated as he dug into the sack. His fingers at last touched the fine mesh that had been rolled tightly into a corner of the bag.

"Take this," Hesam said, pulling up an MRE. "Put water with it and eat." Hesam did not want the Iraqi to think about heating his food. Heating food carries a smell. Aftershave, toothpaste, even the tabasco sauce that often comes with the rations carry an odor. At night, these could lead to an early death.

"I am not hungry," the Arab said.

"Your belly is playing tricks on you. You are weak, Colonel. We may have to walk a very long way and I can't carry you."

Baraniq regarded Hesam for a long moment, his eyes unblinking. "You are not an American," he said.

"What is an American?"

"Don't play foolish with me," the colonel snapped, not used to flippancy.

"An idea. That's what an American is. We come in all shapes, Colonel," Hesam said. He could not remember when he had last taken diphen. That was a SFO's abbreviation for diphenylmethylsulfinylacetamide, the chemical that allowed a man to stay awake. It did nothing for fatigue, but the diphen maintained clarity of mind and allowed the body to repair itself while it was still on the move.

"I never should have left," the colonel said.

"You did the right thing," Hesam contradicted. He unrolled the mesh and began attaching two parts of it to the base supports of the transmission tower while allowing the outer edges to slope down to the ground. He twisted down titanium screw anchors, running them a full twenty-six inches into the sandy soil.

"What do they think of Arabs in America?" Baraniq asked.

"Arabs or Iraqis?"

Baraniq snorted. "All right. I am an Iraqi. Am I a monster, then, in America?"

"Do you know any Iraqis who live in America now, Colonel?" Hesam said, knowing the answer even before he spoke.

Baraniq had turned his head away. The night was very dark, but Hesam could easily read the man's expression.

"I did no killing, you know," he said, his voice a whisper.

"No," Hesam agreed.

"I did not approve," he insisted. He turned toward Hesam. Hesam knew what the colonel wanted. He wanted absolution. Not for pulling a trigger. Not for ordering the planes and helicopters that dropped the horrible gasses on men, women, and babies. Not for throwing the enemies of Saddam into acid vats while still alive.

Finally resting, Hesam worked to open his vacuum-packed MREs. It would have been easy to agree with the colonel that he had committed no crimes against people. Not just against his state's enemies, but his own people. But neither had many of the top Nazis actually laid hands on a Jew. Hesam had read that Adolf Eichmann had gotten along famously, on a personal level, with a good many Jews. Baraniq had been a reliable and brilliant intelligence officer. Without Baraniq and the excellent network of agents he spread around the globe, Saddam might not be alive today. Certainly his war-making capabilities would be dramatically less were it not for Baraniq. Most important, Hesam knew, the information the colonel had inside his head at this very moment was beyond price.

So Hesam said, "I know that, Colonel. You are held in the highest esteem in America."

Baraniq knew it was a lie, but drew comfort from it, anyway.

"Eat, now, Colonel. Here, let me help."

Nabil Zibri had no intention of shooting his way out of Monaco like a desperado in an American gangster film. For him, the European continent was an open road, a place that held no threat for him. And it *should* be friendly to him, Zibri thought, as he rode the train comfortably in first class accommodations en route to Paris, because he loved it. Unlike the less privileged classes in his country, Zibri was fortunate enough to have been born into a family of wealth. One of nine boys and ten sisters, Zibri and his brothers were treated to the treasures of travel beginning at a very young age. At five,

Zibri was in Switzerland sliding sideways downhill on a pair of skis, rolling over on the hard packed white stuff; then popping up again on his skis to continue his run. Years later there was rowing for his public school in England, and playing goalie on its soccer team. Later yet, were the challenging but intellectually stimulating academic requirements of Oxford. He loved them all.

He was by no means deprived of the privileges and beauty of his own lands. The magic of the Crescent was only enhanced when he studied about it from the very complete and seemingly endless rows of history books on the shelves of the schools he attended. Then, with his head filled with pride, put there by the glowing, almost lyrical histories of the Levant, he would return home to appreciate it anew. He related to other such historical truths as the brave exploits and eventual triumph of Saladin, the great Sultan of twelfth century Egypt, who captured Jerusalem and denied it to the infidels during the Third Crusade.

Zibri's doting father, Fahim, endowed Nabil and his brothers with bank accounts containing far more money than they would need to live carefree lives. Of course the father knew by virtue of his age and studied wisdom that there was no such thing as a totally free life. There were always the requirements of the Koran, the allegiance to the will of Allah, no matter how lofty one viewed one's position on earth. Allah did not require wealth, Fahim believed, but he did require obedience, and the respect of all places and things that were holy.

Zibri was fortunate enough to have never acquired the taste for alcohol that his non-Arab school friends seemed to naturally possess. There was hardly an occasion at school where an alcoholic drink of some kind was out of place. Realizing that social activity was just as important to a university education as course curriculum, Zibri tried never to miss a party. Yet he was never seriously tempted to violate the laws of Islam by using alcohol. Nor, he was pleased to experience, was he considered strange or an outcast for non-indulgence. He was still considered a "regular guy" among his friends and class-mates.

Zibri was quite aware of what caused the stirring in his loins as he began to mature as a teen and enter into manhood. There was no lack of elders to instruct him and his brothers, including his father, Mullahs of Islam, and hygiene classes in school. It was the animalistic drive to reproduce, to propagate the species, and there were even facets of love that could derive from the often heady adventure of sharing sex with a mate. But girls were separated from boys for as long as he could remember. Even as adults their faces were hidden, their bodies were covered, and they were expected to remain all but silent when men were together. So, while there might have been a fully socializing experience at university with persons of the opposite sex, Zibri did nothing to remove the artificial curtain that was required of him through the dictates of the Koran.

Strangely, he found himself drawn toward other men in ways that could not be explained by a simple need to be comradely. Often, while in the company of healthy young men of his age, he felt the familiar urge in his crotch. He would always shake it off, knowing the conse-quences that would befall him if he were to give into sinister passions. As his sexual desires began to take more acute shape in his mind, he became all the more determined to resist them, to remain clean and true to Allah and to the men and women who carried out the proscriptions of life under the True God.

By the time Zibri had graduated from Oxford, aca-demically undistinguished, he had begun to resent the lack of personal discipline he found in others, first no-ticed in individuals, later in considering the leaders of nations whence they derived. After experiencing the ex-hilaration of America's breathtaking pace, loud, colorful, almost riotous quest for personal wealth, world hege-mony, personal freedom, and literally free sex, his fasci-nation had worn off. Zibri's attitude changed.

American women wore scanty clothing and often went

all but naked in public—and not only at beaches, spas, and swimming pools. They painted their faces, colored their eyes and lips so that they would attract the attention of men. And for what purpose? To seduce them. To weaken men by pitting them against Allah and the Prophet Mohammed. They, who were without shame, were the whores of which the Koran warned. And American women were doing nothing more or less than the rest of the society and that was to make believers into infidels. Who was it, at base, who gained by creating infidels? It was he who had always sought to defeat Allah. Satan.

Quite simply, America was a metaphor for sin. To live the life of an American was sinning and tolerance for America was to embrace evil. Zibri's transformation from a carefree young student to a man consumed with rage was not overnight, but his hatred for the enemy of Islam was implacable. There was no accommodation for Satan. Satan either ruled or he was defied. America, like Satan's whore, and Israel, her handmaiden, never rested. And if a war for men's souls was at stake, then the war must be carried to the enemy.

The American president had said, and lied even as he uttered the words, that the war was not against Islam. But there *was* a war and it *was* against Islam. And if you were a Muslim, you were against the Americans. The president was right—it was about good against evil. And when Zibri had reduced the equation to its simplest components, he enlisted at once in the army. Not in the army of Saud. No, it was to the army of al Qaeda that he gave himself.

For five months he trained in one of the hundreds of camps operated in Lebanon. He became familiar with all forms of weapons, including assault rifles, mortars, machine guns, and grenade launchers. There were courses in explosives and guerilla operations where one learned the most vulnerable parts of electrical generating plants, railroads, and the setting of booby-traps. Zibri was then sent to Afghanistan to do combat against Soviet forces.

For more than two years, he endured the hardships found in the incredibly energy-taxing high mountains of that country, its tortuous cold, and, of course, the heat of the summer.

He had learned to fight on an empty stomach, and how to carry on while short of ammunition, vehicles, and manpower. The vaunted Soviets, a ruthless, unbending enemy who never surrendered, began to weaken. Despite their superior numbers of aircraft, vehicles, and equipment of every description, the mujahidin had the force of Allah behind them. Nothing could defeat them. Certainly not the infidels.

Zibri was aware of the irony that America was supporting the mujahidin against the Soviet Union. He and his brethren, one of whom was Osama bin Laden, soaked up American military largesse like gluttons, but without the slightest notion of gratitude. It was a case of killing a common enemy. Later, of course, the American president and the Russian president became brothers in collusion against Islam.

After the Soviet aggressors put their tails between their legs and ran from Afghanistan, Zibri understood that the war was only beginning. He also vowed that never again would he fight against any foe as a surrogate for America. From now on, Satan could do its own dying.

Zibri felt compelled to make a brief appearance in Saudi Arabia to visit with his family. As he was chauffeured by his father's personal driver to Fahim Zibri's main compound outside of Jiddah, he was uncertain about the reception he might get. He had not seen his father in almost two years, although they had written and talked on the telephone. But their dialogues were superficial. Very little was given to political conversation, a subject that made his father distinctly uncomfortable. Zibri tried to recall Fahim's attitude about the House of Saud. He was, by any measure, a grand recipient of the ruling royalty's good graces. With the support of the House of Saud, Fahim Zibri had built a supermarket chain patterned after Western models, founded an insurance company, which was now the second largest domestic insurer in the kingdom, and started a bank and its branches, which was among the top-five largest such enterprises in the Gulf states. So, Nabil Zibri reasoned, his father must hold the royal prince and his family in the highest esteem, shouldn't he?

Zibri's idle thoughts drifted toward his brothers and sisters. Most were employed in their father's businesses, but two of the brothers lived in America. No danger of seeing either of them at Jiddah. He had thought of them only fleetingly in recent years but now, he believed, he should make contact with them, force them to make the decision that would save their lives and the lives of their families by leaving America. The great Satan was collapsing. It was even now beginning its death throes.

The Zibri estate was a cluster of buildings that encompassed the larger manor house. Those outbuildings included a garage with room for ten cars and a twin-engine aircraft, an equipment building for maintaining the grounds, housing for security personnel of whom there were more than a dozen, household staff, with the women on an opposite side of the complex from the men even if they were husband and wife. No children were permitted among Zibri's household employees. The entire estate, consisting of nearly one thousand acres, was surrounded by a beige, flagstone wall with electronic sensor systems to detect motion, sound, and touch. Hidden cameras swept every inch of the wall, while mounted patrols circled the perimeter of the compound at varied intervals.

One of the outbuildings housed a desalinization plant that drew water forty miles away by aqueduct from the Red Sea, then sweetened it for irrigating the compound's entire area. Inside the walls were palm trees, thousands of square yards of neatly trimmed grass and flowers, two small artificial lakes, and three swimming pools, two of them indoors.

To Nabil's surprise only two of his sisters were at the

Jiddah home when he arrived, and only one of his brothers. The brother, Omar, was several years his junior, and because of the difference in their ages there had been little closeness between them. They all felt a bit awkward, with the exception of his mother, Nura bin Ahmet bin Saleh Al-Fulani, who retained her family name with no connection to her husband's, as was the Arab custom. She pulled him to her bosom and held on with all of her strength. His father had only three wives, but could have afforded many more. Even while enjoying newer, younger ones, his father seemed to choose Nura with whom to spend his leisure time. Inexplicable, Nabil thought, but since he had no wife of his own it was not a phenomenon upon which he dwelt.

With the serving of the evening meal nervousness eased considerably, but politics and world events were treated topically if not ignored altogether. Nabil Zibri's mouth watered with his first bite of baba ghanoush, a grilled eggplant cooked in olive oil, lemon juice, and garlic, and served as a dip. There was falafel, the highly spiced fried patties of chickpeas. The hamour, a Red Sea fish, spiced and grilled in foil wrap, melted in his mouth. His mother beamed at the ecstasy written all over his face. Zibri ate so fully that he could hardly finish his banana mutabak, a sweet pastry turnover. He took kahwa, the rich dark Arabian coffee that was never black enough to suit him. Except for this night. It was perfect.

"You look very well, Nabil," his father said when the two were alone.

His father looked good, too, Zibri thought. Serene. "And you, Father. Business must be very good," he said politely.

"Good, yes. It could be better," Fahim Zibri said.

"Is that so?" Zibri said, his question framed rhetorically because if there was any business at all done in the kingdom, his father would be doing it. "Are you down to your last airbus?" he teased, referring to his father's European built aircraft.

"Are you now opposed to private capital? I thought I had succeeded in making my sons at least as greedy as their father," the elder Zibri chided back.

Nabil Zibri smiled, beginning to relax despite his father's stern presence. "No. That is not what I meant."

"I think I know what you meant, Nabil. While you are off fighting a war to save my generation from spiritual corruption, your ungrateful father, the blood-sucker, is continuing to do business with the enemies of Allah. Something like that, yes?"

"No, I . . ." Nabil began, then stopped. He was a grown man, a soldier of God. Why should he stoop to deceiving his father even if in so doing he intended only to spare the aging man's feelings? Besides, Nabil realized that it was long past time when his father's institutions needed to be shaken to its roots. "You are not a blood-sucker, father. . . ."

"Thank you, son," Fahim Zibri said dryly.

"You know what I mean," Nabil Zibri said.

"I think I do. I believe there is still a viable place on this Earth for men like me. Whether you care to acknowledge it or not, the money that I and my industries produce makes it possible for all of us to live, not just the wealthy ones, and unfortunately not just the poor ones, but everyone in the middle, as well," the senior Zibri said.

"Is that what you think? That I'm fighting the enemies of our culture because of money? That is ridiculous, Father, and I am disappointed if you think so little of me."

"Is that what you were doing in Afghanistan? Fighting against the enemies of our culture? And who, pray, are these enemies? Although I must admit that I am not an adoring supporter of the Russian bear," Fahim said. "And why must we have a war? We have our share of madmen, Nabil. That terrible man, Saddam Hussein. He is nothing but a disgrace. He is almost as bad as the J͏͏͏s, if that is possible. But a war that goes on forever ͏͏͏ the answer."

"How do you know what I did in Afghanistan?" Nabil Zibri asked his father.

"Oh, please. It is not necessary for me to spy on my children. Not even you. Tongues wag throughout the days and the months, all of them too eager to inform me that my son has taken to war against the world," the father said, despairingly.

"We did not start this war," Nabil Zibri said, his eyes meeting his father's. "They are not exchanging commerce. They are looting our nation's riches and . . ."

"Indeed! Our riches? Are they stealing our sand? Nabil, do you know how much arable land exists in the Kingdom of Kuwait? None. Zero. They grow nothing. No crops, no trees. It has no minerals. No ores. It manufactures nothing. What riches are there in Kuwait to steal? If Kuwait had no oil to sell, how would its people live?"

"The Americans started this war and they pay for it. If it were not for America the Jews would still be haunting the streets of Europe and New York gathering up still more money and power. Now they are here, among us, on our holy land, and their cancer is spreading as America takes our oil to fuel its war against us Arabs through the Zionists!"

Nabil had risen from the cushioned floor to stand at full height. He paced the room while his father sat silently, touched by certain truths uttered by his son. After a prolonged period of quiet in the room, Fahim Zibri cleared his throat.

"Yes, the Jews have displaced our fellow . . ."

"Displaced?" Nabil Zibri blanched at his father's understatement. "Father, we are talking about sacred Arab ground. And the Americans have sent tens of thousands of troops into our country, here, to the land of the Prophet Mohammed, while your indolent fat Saudi friends . . ."

"That is enough!" the senior Zibri said, his voice rising in volume. "They *are* my friends and I will not have

them insulted in my house! Whatever they have done in
their good and just rule has been done for the citizens
of the Kingdom."

"You don't believe that for a minute, Father. Not at
all. They are corrupt, the Sauds. They have turned their
back on Islam. They wallow in vulgarism of the flesh.
They put on a front for the world to see them as pious
men but the reverse is true. They should step aside and
allow the mullahs to rule," Nabil said, also raising his
voice.

"Like Iran? As the mullahs did there? Allah save us,"
Fahim Zibri said, dramatically closing his eyes as he
looked upward to the heavens.

Neither man spoke for long minutes.

Nabil leaned against the cool plaster wall, reaching for
highly filtered cold water that ran out of a tap into a
small stainless steel service sink. He filled an eight-ounce
glass and started to drink before stopping to look toward
his father. He raised his glass in respect, a silent gesture
acknowledging the senior Zibri. The older man shook his
head at the offer. Fahim Zibri inhaled deeply before
slowly letting the air in his lungs escape.

"I love you more than my own life, Nabil," he said.

The son bowed his head at his father's simple elegance.

"I do not want you to die. I lack the courage of others
who seem willing, anxious, even, to give their children
to martyrdom. Anyone can die. Dying is not difficult.
Anyone can do it, Nabil. It seems to me that a man's
higher calling is to solve our problems while we are still
alive. So I am selfish. I want you to live and I even
believe we can deal with our difficulties with
America. . . ."

"With Satan?" Nabil said softly.

His father's eyes drifted away again, frustrated.

"That is what she is. America. She is the embodiment
of Satan who seeks to destroy us by seduction," Nabil
Zibri said, still speaking in an undertone.

"I confess I am a skeptic," Fahim Zibri said.

"What? What did you say, Father?"

"I have, shall we say, reservations about. . . ." Fahim waved his hand, airily.

"I don't believe you," Nabil almost whispered the unthinkable. "You are only upset. Confused about the war."

The older Zibri slowly shook his head. "I sometimes wish it was so easy."

The next morning Nabil's mother rose earlier than usual, happier than she could remember being for years. She wanted to supervise a special breakfast for Nabil who was the source of her uplifted spirits. But a servant she sent to look in on her son returned to say that he was gone.

CHAPTER 8

Hesam let Baraniq snore lightly through the night. He was relieved that the Iraqi defector had finished the MREs that Hesam had kept pushing toward him. They were reasonably tasty, Hesam thought, but more importantly they were very high in concentrated nutrients. It was possible that if the team did not arrive by sundown they would have to begin a very long trek. There could be no stopping, no reconsideration, inside Saddam's Iraq. Falling back into the hands of the secret police, alive, was unthinkable, so the fact that Baraniq was eating again gave Hesam some measure of comfort.

He thought they were well enough concealed to continue their lay up through the day, but of course that depended upon what kind of forces were out looking for them. They had to remain exactly where they were for at least twelve more hours to allow the Leopard team to reach them. He could only hope they were still operational. Hesam had not properly slept for several days, yet the feeling of fatigue was minimal. He allowed himself to nod off for short periods before opening his eyes again to observe his surroundings. His waking hours were filled with absolute clarity. He went from a state of sleep to a state of full wakefulness instantly, with all of his senses operating at high efficiency.

A change in the air brought him alert.

He sensed, rather than saw, a movement in the time between night and light, the period when dawn was little more than a suggestion. Hesam felt they were not alone. There was another man, someone other than his fleeing Iraqi colonel, who was close and getting closer. Hesam's hand closed very slowly around the stock of his MP-5, his compact submachine gun. He allowed his eyes to open just slightly, enough for him to see while they still appeared to be closed in sleep.

The man was closer now, but the smallest puff of air now obliterated the odor of a human body. Unmoving, Hesam strained to sense motion. He cursed the slumbering Iraqi defector whose light snoring made sound discrimination difficult. Hesam could feel his pulse quicken as his adrenal gland pumped larger amounts of the action-oriented chemical into his bloodstream. Whoever was out there, closing on them, was good.

Not exactly a sound, not a breaking twig or a dislodged rock, but *something* told Hesam that his stalker was at his ten o'clock. In less than a second, Hesam would have squeezed off a six-round burst, then lobbed a grenade. He knew he could get the first man. Were there others?

"Hey, shithead. If you want to go back to sleep I promise I won't hurt you," the voice came out of the gloom.

"I smelled you a hundred yards away, Rodriguez. No wonder these people fall in love with camels, they smell better."

Rodriguez rose from the sand, arms wide as the two men embraced.

"God damn, Joe, good to see you, man. Damn!" the Cuban-born soldier received a heartfelt set of arms around him in response.

Then Joe Mears, until that moment known as Hesam, extricated himself from Manny Rodriguez. "All right, let go of me. I'm trying to turn on to girls. Where's the unit?"

Manny gave a hand signal, which he knew, even before

he lowered his hand, was unneeded. Other figures nearby rose from their prone positions and advanced.

"Hey, Joe!" Lee Haggar said, his arm going around Joe's neck, kissing him on the cheek. "Damn, you look just like one of the homies."

"Glad you finally showed up, Lee. Hey, Quack," Mears said to Pete Taylor, shaking his hand, then exchanging embraces. "Tommy! How's it going?" he greeted Entzion as he did the others. It had been more than a year since their last operation, the one that Mears intended would be his last. Then he had spent another six months surviving inside Iraq, communicating with members of the Iraqi Freedom Front (IFF), attempting to sort out friends of America from all others. He had inserted in country at one-hundred-eighty pounds but had lost twenty-five in the first sixty days, partly because food was not plentiful, but also because the threat of capture, torture, and death peeled it off with great efficiency.

"I'm Ross McTaggart, Colonel Mears," the last man said, extending a hand that could cover a big city phone book. Joe looked up at the young team leader.

"Joe Mears," he said. "How many men did you lose getting here, Lieutenant?"

"I don't know, sir. I didn't think it was all that important," McTaggart said.

"Right on, McTaggart. The vital part is to enjoy yourself while you're on these trips. Just think of all the people in the world who would cut their nuts off to be in your place," Joe said.

"Yes, sir, and we did see a lot of the sights," McTaggart said.

Mears glanced around once more looking at each man. "Nobody looks beat-up."

"Wasn't my fault, sir," McTaggart said. "I led us right into an ambush outside of Kirkuk. Lucky any of us got out of there, let alone in one piece," McTaggart said.

"Lieutenant McTaggart's not being very honest, Joe," Haggar said. "We had to cross the main highway running east from the city. They had armor all along there. We got through it at night, but a company of Guards fired on us. Manny did a forward recce and he didn't see 'em either. Hey . . . shit happens."

McTaggart's face remained earnest. "They were looking for us, no question, but I think they might have been using some kind of field heat sensors, then fired along that line. They were pretty damn good."

"One side?" Mears asked.

"Sir?" McTaggart asked.

"Enemy fire. Did it come from one flank or more?"

"One. From the southeast," McTaggart answered.

"Then it wasn't an ambush. If they knew you were coming they would have had concentrations on each side," Mears said. "Want some tea?"

"Sure," McTaggart said, indicating to the men to help themselves. "Got your package?"

Mears jerked his head toward Harun Baraniq, late of the Great Leader's army. "His code name is Griffon. What's inside his head is important mojo for our intel people. People, places, and things. He gets through even if we all go down. *Comprendé?*"

"Understand," McTaggart nodded emphatically.

"Colonel Baraniq," Mears said, bringing the tall American lieutenant to meet the defector, "I'd like to present Lieutenant Ross McTaggart, United States Army, Special Operations Command."

McTaggart brought himself fully erect and raised his right hand in salute. "It's an honor to meet you, Colonel Baraniq," he said, looking down upon the Iraqi despite the man's height of six feet.

Baraniq, visibly impressed with the correct young American officer, arched an eyebrow as he returned McTaggart's salute. "Well," he said approvingly, "I am relieved to know the Americans have sent a fine officer for me."

The Iraqi's inference was that Mears had been dealt to him below the table in the international spy game and that he, the colonel, deserved much better. Mears had never revealed to Baraniq that he was a lieutenant colonel. It suited his purpose that Baraniq remain in the dark about such details in the event, down the road, things went sideways. Mears caught McTaggart's sidelong glance and winked, remaining silent, hands clasped behind his back. His deference was McTaggart's signal to continue as the OIC—officer in charge.

"We're going to lay up here for the day, Colonel Baraniq. My men are dug in fifty meters from here. Tonight we'll travel south. We have vehicles and we can make good time at night with any luck at all. My orders are to get you safely out of Iraq and into American hands at all costs," McTaggart smoothly explained.

Mears thought McTaggart sounded like a vacuum cleaner salesman extending a money-back guarantee on his product while he folded the customer's check and put it into his pocket. The military academies were producing a fine crop of resourceful fighting men these days, it seemed.

Mears and McTaggart took the first perimeter watch while the men finished their morning tea. It would give the officers an opportunity to talk, to bring each other up to date on previous action and to plan for the journey home.

"You can bet your next promotion that Saddam has every unit in his army circling Baghdad," Mears said, moving his index finger around the map indicating a wide area. "He knows we can't fly out and we don't have submarines that operate in sand, so he'll have everything from armored units to gravel pounders out here."

"Any chance of getting an air unit to take our man out?" McTaggart asked.

Mears shook his head. "We thought about that. To send in a helo this far takes an air package to support it. What the Iraqis have here in their sandbox is a damn good EW radar system and it gets better every day, especially down here in the south where we're going."

"And just where is that, Joe?"

"Here. Top of the Persian Gulf, Kuwait area. They'll have a liaison officer name of Briggle to meet us. He's a Navy lieutenant commander attached to a battle group out in the gulf. I don't know the details, but he does," Mears said, pulling an energy bar from his pocket.

"Three-hundred miles if you were flying a jet," Mears pointed out on his map, while McTaggart made mental notations. He would place no pencil or pen marks on the map lest he be killed or captured and it fell into enemy hands.

"It'll be a whole lot longer by the time we get through shuckin' and weaving. Whether we like it or not, and I don't, we're going to have to travel on the west side of the country. Over here is a hundred miles of mud and bogs," Mears said.

"No way to get the DPVs through?" McTaggart asked.

"Nope. Doesn't hurt to think about it, though. So here's where I figure we have to go. If you don't agree, come up with a better idea that I can fall in love with and we'll do it your way." Mears referred to his map once again while McTaggart followed along. "We cross the Tigris and 6 Highway somewhere between Ali ash Sharqi and Al' Amarah, then we run southwest toward An Nasiriyah, cross 7 Highway, cross the Euphrates, and break out west of Suq ash Shuyukh. Then south, entering Kuwait about here."

"What kind of time do you figure we can make?" McTaggart asked.

"Four days would be wonderful. Five days very good. Six days means we're getting beat up. After that I think the navy would be ready to write us off," Mears said.

"How about you, Joe?" the younger officer wanted to know.

"I'm never writing us off," Mears said and winked.

The two men sat in silence for several minutes while Mears chewed on his energy bar. Finally, he turned toward the junior officer. "When you got your mission briefing did they tell you who you were bringing out?"

"You mean Baraniq? By name? No, just that he was very important," McTaggart said, waiting for Mears to continue.

"They tell you what has to be done if we go down?"

"You mean putting a bullet into his head? Yeah, I got that order."

"Any problems with it?" Mears wanted to know.

"I don't think so. Can't say I like it, though," McTaggart said, but did not drop his gaze from Mears.

"Okay," Mears said, allowing his eyes to drift, unfocused, into the vast distance of the desert. "If I'm alive when it has to be done, I'll do it. I've made a career out of chickenshit killings."

The team devoted two hours to sleep, then turned to work on the DPVs. Sand gets into every pore of the machines and, if not removed sooner rather than later, the vehicles will stop running. Air filters were removed, cleaned and replaced, and the specially built oil filters were also removed and replaced. Fuel filters and caps were checked and cleaned. All wheels were removed from their hubs and inspected. One grease seal was found to be penetrated, so it was removed, cleaned, and treated with a liquid that covered the crack and bonded with the metal. The crew of that vehicle could only hope it would hold.

The guns were stripped completely, cleaned carefully, and put back together. The sand, blown by desert winds, had penetrated even into sealed ammunition boxes, so all of the ammo belts had to be removed, cleaned with brushes with the same care one treats one's teeth, then folded and reseated in their metal boxes. The Mk-60 grenades and their launcher were stripped as well and those rounds meticulously cleaned of sand.

Also given close attention were the animals of the desert, including a highly toxic scorpion species that was indigenous to the region. One had set up housekeeping inside Entzion's rucksack as he reached inside. The crablike animal was pulled outward as the radio man jerked his hand in painful reflex. Too late to prevent the injection of the animal's toxin into his flesh.

"Hot damn," he murmured almost to himself. "Quack," he said to Taylor, "what've you got for scorpion stings?" The team medic looked quickly at Entzion's hand to see how close to a major blood site the animal had struck; then looked down at the scorpion, its tail still up and ready to continue its fight.

"You got a nasty one, cowboy," Quack said to Entzion. "The small, skinny ones have the baddest mojo. Standby."

Quack opened one of his medical bags, rummaged through it for a brief time, then returned to Tommy Entzion's hand which was even now turning fiery red.

"This stuff is Bioclan antivenom," Quack said, rubbing Entzion's arm with an antiseptic skin prep before stabbing a disposable needle into it. "Might work and it might not, partner."

"I didn't sign up to save the world just to die from an overgrown spider bite, Quack," Entzion said sarcastically.

"Well, just in case the venom stops your heart can I have your Corvair?" Quack asked.

"I'm taking that baby with me," Entzion said with certainty.

Iraq had more than its share of venomous snakes. The blunt-nosed viper that ranged along the river drainage in the northern part of the country imparted a hemorrhagic venom. The Kurdistan viper and the saw-scaled viper in southern Iraq and elsewhere in the Arabian peninsula were man killers, especially the saw-scaled variety. This was very deadly even if its bite was treated promptly with one of the many viperine antivenoms Quack carried with him. And there were times, as Quack learned in his two-year medical course at Fort Sam Houston, as well as other operations, that nothing short of whole blood products had any effect on the bite.

Iraq also hosted the desert black snake. Its fangs were

large and fixed into position, administering a highly potent neurotoxin. The treatment required was sedation, intubation, placement on a mechanical respirator, and careful observation. That was not possible where the team was operating. In fact, few victims survived that snake's bite even under the best of conditions. The fact that the snake was literally everywhere in Iraq, even in the open desert with no vegetation for miles around, added to its deadly threat. That, plus the fact that the desert black snake looked almost identical to the equally ubiquitous but harmless species known as *abrid* or *urbid*, was even more confusing. The team was not only briefed on specific threats in Iraq, they were thoroughly drilled on all forms of running, crawling, leaping, and slithering animal life that could succeed in killing or putting a good soldier out of action where an enemy had failed.

The wind began to blow. The daily prevailing southerly and southeasterly *Sharqi*, a dry, dusty wind with occasional gusts of eighty km an hour, could become very large sandstorms, some lasting for days. Depending on conditions, the winds could reach hurricane velocity, and its blowing sands could strip the paint from vehicles and buildings.

The hottest part of the day reached one hundred seventeen degrees. The wind slowly accelerated. The men kept themselves hydrated, knowing that if they failed to do so enemy search patrols would not have much to worry about. They tried to sleep again in the late afternoon hours, but it was hard while water was sucked from their brows by the wind and painfully drying the tissue inside their noses and mouths. Throughout the day they heard the sounds of armored units clanking up and down roads only a few hundred meters away. They watched foot patrols walking in files, looking at the ground, seeking some spoor that the Leopard team fervently hoped they had not left behind. Twice, a small aircraft had flown over, probably artillery spotters turned to the work of searching for Leopard-1.

The team was not concerned about their lay-up position being spotted from Iraqi aircraft unless they had infrared equipment on board, but given the sorry state of Iraqi's air forces, it wasn't likely that a light aircraft would be carrying anything so sophisticated. They were quiet on the ground with equipment and weapons taped to eliminate sound.

Their collective hearts almost stopped, however, when an Iraqi patrol vehicle transited a small hill directly behind them. When the vehicle stopped, an Iraqi officer stepped up from his passenger's seat into a gun swivel, his upper body coming completely out of the armored machine. He raised his binoculars and began slowly to sweep around his location. Obviously, the Iraqi was attempting to take advantage of the nearby elevation to look out over the valley that lay directly into the east side of Baghdad. The Leopard team pressed their bodies harder into the sand, knowing that if the Iraqi were to lower his field glasses just a few meters into the ground directly in front of him, he would have seen their camouflaged position. While the Iraqi officer surveyed his assigned search area, Haggar had the man in the center of his sniper scope. It would have been a can't-miss shot, but it would have set off a major firefight which the Leopard team would have lost.

Mobility and darkness were their only friends.

CHAPTER 9

"Joe," Lee Haggar whispered softly.

Immediately awake, Mears could hear the sound of heavy duty engines, like those of tanks and trucks. They were not only loud in volume, they were many in number. Mears followed Haggar as the weapons man crawled on his belly to a location four meters from the vehicles. Haggar put a finger straight into the air and made a complete circle, meaning "Look all around" or "there is something all around us." Mears did as directed. The two Leopard troopers were atop a small berm, but it was high enough to view the terrain for several kilometers around. Mears turned slowly, his eyes awash with a unit commander's worst dream. All around them was the better part of an armored army division.

He counted either one or two tank brigades, depending upon if there was another unit just like it in their rear, three mechanized infantry battalions, a rocket launcher battery, three or four self-propelled artillery battalions that appeared to be 152mm. There were other units scattered about, which Mears had to assume included a recon battalion and combat engineers. He could not be sure, their well-maintained equipment and well-organized formations led him to believe that he was looking at the entire 24th Republican Guard.

The division-strength army was entirely around them and, by the looks of their activities, they were planning to stay awhile. While he was not certain, it was possible that most of Saddam's Baghdad military units were assigned just to locate Baraniq. If he were Saddam, that's exactly what he would do. Slowly pulling his head down, Mears made a "follow me" motion and began to crawl back toward their lay-up position.

The word among the team was passed quickly and quietly, the men silently girding for combat. In this case, each man knew, the combat was not going to last long. But they also knew that while it lasted it would be very bloody on both sides. All eyes turned toward Mears. Their best hope was continued silence, hoping that the night would arrive and find them still alive. Mears made the motion of a finger over his lips, and a palm down motion to stay low.

In the early afternoon, in the crushing heat of the day, the winds began to blow. Although the team had already covered every conceivable equipment aperture and gun mechanism, they went through it all again while their movements were obscured by the blowing sand.

As they continued to lie perfectly still there was a movement nearby, a kind of shadow, that was not one of them. The nearest Leopard trooper to the shadow was McTaggart. The young lieutenant looked toward Mears who nodded, indicating that McTaggart was to be ready. Though the volume of the wind had increased, there was no blocking out the smell of an uninvited visitor emptying his bowels nearby. As desert winds will do, the air swirled into a two-second twisting spin, leaving a momentary tunnel of almost perfectly clear air between Mears and an Iraqi soldier caught, literally, with his pants down. In less than the blink of an eye the following blast of wind pulled close the sandy curtain that had been open for a millisecond.

The Iraqi's brief sight of a totally unexpected stranger sealed his doom. McTaggart's strong arm caught the man's head in the crook of his elbow, pulling the head back, preventing any sound as the KB knife sliced deeply across the soldier's throat. As blood spewed forth, McTaggart tried to avoid as much of it as possible, but the bottom part of his battle blouse and his multi-pocketed trousers became covered with the crimson stuff.

Without being told, Entzion used his entrenching tool to dispose of the man's body waste, covering it quickly, lest his comrades in arms follow the stench that would lead them to the team. When the man did not return they would soon come looking for him. All eyes again turned to Mears.

There was no choice now. They had to move. As he considered their options, the wind continued to build in volume and the sand began turning day into twilight. The team waited patiently, nobody getting excited. They had already wrapped pieces of field tarps, blankets, even spare items of uniform clothing over gun breaches, barrels, ammo containers, and engine intakes despite the fact that the vehicles were specially designed with desert sand in mind. Then they used three-inch-wide khaki-colored duct tape to secure them.

Still Mears sat, assessing the weather and, no doubt, trying to imagine the mind-sets of the officers and men who were halted and blinded by the same storm that was obscuring them. He estimated that the wind was now at forty knots with gusts to fifty-five or sixty. Rather than diminish, it seemed to be steadily increasing its speed. This area was famous for its frequent and fierce winds that blew sand and dust into unimaginable places, effectively bringing an entire region to an absolute halt. Vehicles could not move, aircraft could not take off or land, and people walked at their own risk because visibility was now down to six meters.

Mears motioned the men to gather round. It was necessary to raise his voice, almost shouting, to be heard above the wind. The enemy was within a hundred meters, perhaps less, but the howling of the hurricane forces around them provided safety. Mears removed his rubberized mask and filter, quickly replacing it with a scarf tied over his nose and mouth so that he could be heard among the team.

"We can't see but they can't, either," he began. "So we're moving. I'll ride in Frogpond 1, McTaggart has Frogpond 2. We're going to get separated, can't be helped." Mears paused to look around, making sure everyone understood. "McTaggart, I'm probably going to get me and my men killed, but I expect better out of you."

"Yes, sir," the still-bloody junior officer said, calm given the recent violence. "You'll have Griffon."

Mears nodded affirmation. "If we get through we'll meet up at this fix: railroad bridge over Adabah Wadi. Easy to find." Mears wrote two map coordinates on two pieces of paper. He kept one and gave the other to McTaggart. He didn't like the idea of putting the map coordinates in writing, but under the circumstances it couldn't be helped. "Swallow it if you have to," he said quite seriously. Both men were aware of what conditions would have to exist should swallowing the rendezvous location become necessary.

"McTaggart, forty-eight hours. We're not there, you go. You're not there. . . ."

"Gotcha, Joe," McTaggart shouted through the screaming wind.

The team touched hands, patted shoulders, hooked arms around necks, wishing good luck while saving their voices.

Hot sand savaged any exposed piece of skin, getting into noses and mouths, even when goggles and face masks were left in place. And to keep them in place was another kind of acute discomfort. Unable to see beyond six meters and sucking hot air through neoprene filtering systems was like being buried alive. It took great willpower to resist the temptation to rip away the mask and gulp fresh air. But fresh air was nothing more than a memory.

Operating like blind men, the Leopard team took down their LCSS netting, rolled it up, and secured it with bungee cord. They searched for and picked up every

telltale sign that they had been there. Some they stowed
on the vehicles, other items they buried in the sand and
carefully concealed the excavation. Then they checked it
all again. Every movement in the screaming storm was
difficult, challenging their abilities to concentrate. They
hydrated themselves by drinking all that they could hold
knowing that it could be a long while until they found
new water supplies. The combination of wind and heat
drew water from their bodies even when they were not
exerting themselves. They could not touch metal with
their bare hands, the sun having heated it to cooking
temperatures, so they wore gloves while they silently
packed up.

As Rodriguez started the engine of Frogpond 1—as
the DPVs were now designated—he passed within a few
feet of a scrub tree. Beneath it was one dead bird and
another on the ground nearby, both caught in the grips
of the sandstorm and dashed to the ground. Their eyes
and beaks quickly filled with heated dust and silicon.

The DPV carried very large loads, all of it lashed to
the frame with strong nylon lines. On either side of the
machines were specially built baskets into which could
be stowed more gear or, in emergencies, a casualty. On
top of the steel-bar frame was perched a main gun and
the gunner to operate it. Secured to either side of the
upper frame was an extra wheel. There were three men
assigned to each vehicle, four in Mears's machine with
the addition of Colonel Baraniq.

Seated to Rodriguez's right, Mears looked at the compass he—as well as the others—wore on his wrist, then
pointed in a particular direction. GPS receivers would
not pick up reliable satellite signals inside the swirling
sand. Rodriguez peered ahead, but despite his crawling
speed of less than twelve kilometers per hour, visibility
was still six meters and the wind was still increasing.

In the backseat was Baraniq. Sitting high in the main
gun position was Quack. In Frogpond 2 with McTaggart
was Tom Entzion and Lee Haggar on the main gun. For
the first several minutes the DPVs maintained contact.

Then, when Mears turned his head to check his six o'clock, they were gone.

Every eye was strained, peering into the distance that was all but impenetrable. Mears kept a careful watch on their compass heading, frequently giving Rodriguez hand signals, while the driver looked sharp for what lay ahead in the blowing sand.

Suddenly, Rodriguez let off on the accelerator, braking the DPV to a full stop. Dead ahead of them was an Iraqi tank. It was a forty-four-ton, Russian-built T-72 main battle tank, and it was squatting, deadly, less than ten meters from the DPV. There was no one outside of the tank. Rodriguez turned the wheel sharply, dropped the DPV into a lower gear, and drove off. By the time Mears had turned in his seat to look at their rear, the tank was no longer visible. No one aboard the DPV had said a word.

Rodriguez kept the DPV moving according to Mears's hand directions, watching for riverbanks, wadis, pits, and traps of all kinds ahead. He slowed; then braked again, the vehicle stopping entirely. To their two o'clock were two more tanks, again of the same kind they had just passed, T-72s. They were powered by eight hundred forty hp V-12 engines that ran on kerosene fuel, and could maintain a good speed over any terrain. They were not as fast as the DPVs but in this kind of visibility, or lack of it, top end speed became moot. For a very long moment the Leopard team was sitting at the receiving end of a pair of smoothbore tank guns. This time they were spotted.

An Iraqi tanker had just opened his hatch to look outside. He must have first seen them from his periscope inside the tank before he popped up to verify for himself the strange looking vehicle. Two more soldiers, very likely members of the motorized infantry battalion assigned to the tank division, peeked from around the body of the tank where they, no doubt, had been taking shelter.

Again Rodriguez turned the wheel hard, giving the

DPV all the power it would take, quickly leaving the
tank and gawking Iraqi soldiers behind, lost in the blowing curtain of sand. Then there was a tremendous blast,
illuminating the windswept sand in an orange flash, as
though lightning had struck from within a storm cloud.
Immediately following was a second explosion as the
tank round hit—something. Another roar, then another,
and another as a flurry of heavy gunfire joined by automatic weapons resonated above the howl of the wind.
Then it all stopped as suddenly as it had begun in the
confusion of the first report. Rodriguez continued to
drive the DPV toward the southwest.

Mears and Rodriguez exchanged glances. The tank
commander who started it all had no chance of hitting
his target. Indeed, if his rangefinder had acquired the
DPV target at all. Worse, the gunner was totally surrounded by vehicles and personnel of his own units,
sprawled about a vast area large enough to support an
entire armor division. If he had not hit one of his own
it would have been a miracle.

Mears craned his head around toward Quack. The
team's medic gave the okay sign with his fingers. Mears
then looked below Quack's gun position at Baraniq. Like
the others, Baraniq was covered from head to toe, his
leg and arm cuffs taped tightly closed to keep out sand,
his brown Arab eyes looking out from behind the team's
special desert goggles. Mears thought that Baraniq must
have seen hundreds of sandstorms growing up in this
region, and had very probably done military operations
just as they were doing now. He seemed strangely detached from the discomfort and danger around him.

Mears was considering a number of operational imper-
atives simultaneously. First, was obliterating their trail.
It was true that desert winds would cover their tracks
with deposits of sand, but it was also true that the winds
would also blow the sand back out, leaving a straight
path in whatever direction they were heading. Somehow,
Mears had to figure out how to obscure the trail. Second,
he had to guide the DPV to a southern location that was

inside the UN imposed no-fly zone. If he could do that, they could avoid the great threat of being spotted from the air, and even being attacked by helos. Finally, and this was equally vital, was locating water. The team had comprehensive map notations for access to water that included rivers, lakes, wells, and even inhabited areas which could provide water. But some of it was easier to get to than others and their water supply was just about depleted.

They pounded along for hours, every kilometer an agonizing gain as they dodged from shadows in the swirling sand that could be threats. Nerves straining, muscles cramping, they were already beginning to feel the effects of dehydration as the torrid heat continued to extract moisture through their pores, mouths, and noses. The problem of leaving an easy to follow trail in the sand constantly worried Mears. If the storm suddenly stopped, and sooner or later it would, they would be spotted.

By the end of four hours, the sun was beginning to slip behind the mountains in the east, toward Iran, and there was a noticeable cooling in temperature. The wind had not dissipated, and visibility had worsened, but Mears took comfort in the knowledge that what was difficult navigation for them was equally bad for the Iraqi forces who were looking for them.

For several months Cyrille Cosette had not done business inside the French embassy in Kuwait, or any other Middle Eastern nation for that matter, even though the DGSE had extensive staff and communications support there. There were certain elements in the *Le Service* that had become unfriendly toward him. Lines of communications that had always been open had become erratic, and people upon whom he could always rely were either transferred to other directorates or seemed distant when he was able to get through to them. At first he had hardly noticed that his work was becoming more difficult than it had always been. Any government bureaucracy was, by definition, reactionary and tedious, even the intelligence arms of a nation. Perhaps *especially* the intelligence services. It might someday make an interesting academic challenge for a university graduate student to measure the procedural viscosities of various branches of government; then rank each by the potential catastrophic effects that might ensue should it collapse under its own political inertia.

But lately Cosette had come to believe that there was a plot afoot to undercut his importance within the ranks of the DGSE. In point of fact, he had always preferred to do most of his work in the privacy of his apartment. In Kuwait he leased a spacious apartment overlooking the beach in the Persian Gulf. His was a corner location looking north, and by leaning forward on his balcony he could see Emir Al-Ahmadi's Sief Palace. Despite the two thousand square feet of space inside the apartment, the furnishings were austere, not because of Cosette's conservative tastes, but because he could not move his furniture out of his last apartment in Cairo until he had paid the ten months arrears on his lease there.

Now he was in danger of falling a full two months behind in Kuwait City because most of his government check had been attached by *Soficom*, the French stock exchange, and the vultures who did their work. He had been shamelessly ill-advised about certain American investments in electronics, and his effort to recoup money lost on the roulette wheel and racetracks of Europe had failed utterly. At almost the same moment he had transferred borrowed funds to pay for the new shares, America's global Internet stocks had fallen off the edge of the world, taking Cosette with them.

He could have made a strong argument for the ironic justice of recouping his small but important financial fortune from the same country that had caused him to lose it in the first place, but the fact was that Cosette had no love for Americans anyway. He was, however, prepared to swallow his considerable pride, hoping to parlay an expected small request from the American navy, whatever the request might turn out to be, into perhaps a permanent retainer as "their man" in Kuwait. They were rich enough, trusting enough, and desperate enough to hire an experienced man like him to gain a pipeline into more than one Gulf state regime.

He rehearsed various approaches designed to convince the American officer that his government could not possibly do without the permanent services of such a well-qualified and highly regarded agent in the Middle East, one who was at least part of the answer to America's Intelligence shortfall in the Muslim world. As the footfalls of his pacing echoed through the near empty walls of his new home, he wondered if he should have a drink before the American liaison arrived. He had no idea what was keeping the man who had called nearly an hour before and said to expect him within thirty minutes. Cosette could only pray that nothing the American navy officer might have learned between that phone call and now would cause the deal to fall through. Cosette would take that very seriously, indeed. He was an extremely busy man, he hoped the American realized, and it was with no small risk that he had extended himself to help.

He recapped the bottle of Spanish cognac at the sound of a knock at his front door. The speech of mild indignation that had been forming in his head only moments ago suddenly vanished. Forcing himself not to hurry—important men never hurried—Cosette measured his steps from his kitchenette, the Arab euphemism for a wet bar, across the main living room, and down a short hallway to the door.

"Monsieur Cosette?" the man in the doorway asked.

He was a bit shorter than Cosette, with reddish hair that the English would call sandy, and freckles on his forehead as well as the backs of his hands. It was a genetically unfortunate protection against the sun of the Middle East. The fact that he remained unburned revealed to Cosette that the man spent most of his days indoors or covered with sunscreen or both. He appeared to be in his early thirties, at least twenty years younger than Cosette, a fact that made the Frenchman a bit more relaxed. A two decade advantage in the world of espionage afforded Cosette a generous psychological edge he was glad to have. Americans, renowned for their naivete in international intrigue, had proved that well-deserved attribution by sending to him this green-eyed tyro.

"*Commandant Briggle, je présume?*" Cosette said, pleasantly. Then, switching to English, he said, "Come in, please." Cosette stepped aside, ushering the American naval officer inside where the apparent temperature dropped thirty degrees.

"Ah," Briggle said, following Cosette down the hall into the apartment, "feels good. It's hot out there. Don't know how you stand it. Stockton Briggle," he said, offering his hand.

"One gets used to the heat in this part of the world," Cosette said. "During the winter months it is very pleasant. How did you arrive, *Commandant?* An agreeable trip, I hope?"

"Oh, sure. We have courier aircraft every day from all over the Gulf to places like Riyadh and Cairo. That's how I came, from the ship to Riyadh, then commercial to here so I wouldn't attract attention."

Kuwait International Airport was sixteen kilometers from Kuwait City, a complex that represented state-of-the-art airport architecture. It was a high-volume travel hub, central to the massive amount of oil and petrochemical business that was done throughout the Middle East. Commander Briggle would not have appeared out of place among the uninterrupted stream of businessmen who pursued every facet of that trade. No doubt Briggle would carry proper credentials indicating that he was in the country for that purpose and was prepared to confirm that he had not been in or was planning to go to Israel. Travel around the Middle East, always monitored closely, was made even more difficult if one's interests were political rather than commercial.

"Something to drink, Commander?"

"Call me Stockton. And I'll call you Cyrille, if that's okay. No alcohol for me." Briggle hesitated, then quickly put in, "Not that I'm, you know, religious about it. I like wine and cocktails. Just not right now."

"Good thinking, Stockton. Clear head while we're about this business, *non?* I, ah, am having my furniture shipped here from Egypt," the Frenchman said, sweeping his arm widely to indicate where the stuff might go when it arrived. "Held up there, red tape. I could cut through it, of course, but I would rather not use my, shall we say influence, for so trivial a cause. Would you not agree, Stockton?"

"Hell, yes. You must be gone most of the time, anyway," Briggle agreed.

"Yes. That is so. Perrier?" the Frenchman suggested, correctly guessing that the American would not refuse the offer of something so obviously healthy as water.

"Yeah. I could probably drink a couple of them. Okay," Briggle said, following Cosette into the kitchen area where the Frenchman withdrew bottled water and ice cubes from the refrigerator, "let's talk a little bit about who you are and who I am; then maybe we can make a deal." The American ignored a glass in favor of drinking directly from the bottle.

"But of course, Stockton. I am sure I have been recommended to you by sources that you respect, *non?* You will forgive me if I do not offer a resumé," Cosette smiled fraternally.

"For sure. You worked with Jerry Piscuss. Canadian MI," Briggle said, opening the conversation while drinking more of his water.

Cosette thought for a moment. "Military Intelligence? Piscuss, if it is the same man I know, is Canadian Security Intelligence."

"So? Same thing, isn't it?" Briggle said, seeming genuinely surprised.

"Jerald Piscuss. From Ontario. Amateur astronomer. We met in Tehran. I helped him in a very small way, only because I speak Farsi. I was nothing more than a tour guide for him," Cosette said, modestly.

"Yeah, that's the guy. He said he met you in Iran,

somewhere. Stay in touch with him at all?" Briggle asked.

Cosette began to get an uneasy feeling about the American. Was he brighter than he let on? It would do to take time to think before answering. "Sorry, no. Should I?"

"Nope. Except Piscuss is a rising star these days in the United States. I'm not even sure what he does. Someone else speaks highly of you. Gary Tieso, CIA. I had to run your name through those folks just as a matter of form and I wound up talking to Tieso. He gave you a really big thumbs up."

"Is Tieso still active?" Cosette asked.

"Well, he's doing contract work for them now, but I doubt that he had to move his desk across the room," Briggle said, his eyes unblinking, regarding Cosette sincerely.

Cosette was feeling a chill, but did not allow the American officer to see it. He knew Gary Tieso very well indeed. Ten years ago the American CIA case officer worked out of the Cairo embassy. It was natural that the two of them would meet. The two men, Tieso and Cosette, had at least two things in common: the need for additional money beyond their government salaries and expense accounts, and the willingness to "help" those in need, whatever the need might be. One such need arose when a Budapest arms merchant had difficulty finding an employee who had suddenly left Hungary and disappeared with a large amount of money that belonged to the merchant. Tieso was easily able to locate the dishonest employee who was en route to America via EgyptAir. With Cosette taking care of the technical details, Tieso, a physically large and capable man, met the fleeing employee as he was leaving his hotel and detained him. After three days of very probing conversation, the money that the man had stolen miraculously appeared while, virtually at the same time, the employee disappeared never to be seen again.

There was no way the American officer could have the

slightest knowledge of the event in Cairo a decade ago.
A trap? Cosette leaned ever so slightly toward the navy
commander. As he considered his words he was now
certain that he had been wrong about Briggle. There
was something intangible about the young man's self-
possession that was unnerving.

"Stockton," Cosette began, choosing his words with
care, "what I am about to say, it is with regret." Cosette
paused for dramatic effect, head down, inspecting his interlaced fingers. "If my association with the United
States is to be predicated upon the recommendation of
Mr. Tieso, even in part, then I shall very respectfully
have to decline that honor."

"What? How come? I don't get it," Briggle said, sitting
bolt upright in his chair.

The roller coaster Cosette had put himself aboard suddenly took a snap turn to one side. Had he miscalcu-
lated? Had he just removed himself from a position he
desperately needed? He resisted swallowing the lump
that had lodged in his throat.

"I am afraid I cannot say more." Cosette forced his
suddenly watery knees to support him as he rose, signal-
ing, with genuine regret to the American, that they had
nothing further to discuss.

But Briggle did not stand. Instead he held his hand
out, palm down. "Sit down, Cyrille. Please. I hear what
you're saying. Fact is that Tieso's got his tit in a wringer
with the Company. I don't know what it's all about and
I don't want to know. It's also a fact Tieso said that you
were a hell of a resourceful guy. No reason to think he's
lying about that. Okay? Can we talk business, now?"

CHAPTER 10

Cosette paid a Kuwaiti pickpocket fifty American dollars for the papers of Roulon Bartholoma, an independent Danish petroleum engineer. Mr. Bartholoma was fifty-two years old, with brown hair turning to gray, and nearsighted. Mr. Bartholoma was considerate enough to own an international driver's license whose photograph, as with his passport, was sealed in the thin plastic that covered most important documents. It took Cosette less than two hours, using a razor blade and a jeweler's loupe for the fine work, to cut out photographs of Bartholoma and insert his own. He then applied the same chemically based plastic compound around the edges of the cuts, and heated them with the tip of an ordinary Teflon-coated laundry iron.

He held the freshly improved laminates to inspection under strong lights, viewed them from various angles, and pronounced them good. He had accomplished this operation more times in his life than he could remember and took pride in the fact that he had never allowed himself to become careless or overconfident. Cosette's pickpocket assured him that Mr. Bartholoma had "lost" his wallet and its contents only the evening before. Given the time it would take the Dane to replace his necessary papers and for a general warning to be issued throughout the Middle East, Cosette could feel quite comfortable on his brief planned trip. He fingered the credit cards that came with his recent purchase. There were three, including an American Express Card, a Platinum MasterCard, and a bank transaction card issued through Barclays of London. Cosette had no pin number for the Barclay card and rejected the temptation to find it out by circumventing the bank's security. But the American Express Card was another, easier, matter.

He would have no trouble paying for the entire trip via the American Express, including moderate cash advances at, as the company advertised, any one of the many locations throughout the world. An agent of Cosette's experience would never, at least in ordinary times, jeopardize his mission by using stolen credit cards. But by the time Cosette arrived at the ticket counter of Syrian Airlines to pay for his fare to Beirut, he had convinced himself that these times were anything but ordinary.

He traveled with a very light, easy to search overnight bag containing little more than bathroom articles, a change of socks, and underwear. His new papers were examined three times before arriving at the departure gate and he noticed that his photograph was taken by an automated security camera. His image would be immediately processed at a distance location where a computer base would compare his face with thousands of others. The fact that he would be allowed to board his flight did not necessarily mean he would be free at the other end if his papers or photo were to arouse the interest of Lebanon Security Police. As it happened, he was passed through customs at Beirut's International Airport with hardly a flicker of attention by the officers and soldiers on duty.

He taxied to the Sheraton Coral Beach on Jnah Avenue, less than ten minutes from the airport. It was a hotel of convenience, favored by international businessmen who were in a hurry to conduct their affairs under conditions of high quality, if not wasteful luxury. Rooms ranged from $150 to $225 for deluxe accommodations, although one could spend as much as $1200 per night for a suite. Cosette briefly considered such a room as he pushed Roulon Bartholoma's American Express Card across the counter to the desk clerk, but the notion was instantly rejected. He had already violated enough basic rules of his craft without attracting unnecessary attention to himself by acting like a minor rajah. Obscurity was a spy's best friend and the good ones would not include opulence in their m.o. Still, the top end of the deluxe room selection seemed to Cosette as perfectly deserving of a—let us admit it, middle-aged—public servant who was respected for his years of dedication.

He appreciated Lebanon's secular understanding of the world outside the Levant, necessitated by the country's fundamental driving need to conduct commerce in all of its forms. It was unlike his current host, Kuwait, and other Muslim states which did business only in oil and only on their terms. And those terms were noticeably devoid of creature comforts, like alcohol. Cosette tipped his bellboy generously while ordering a bottle of good French cognac. He also asked the man to bring mezze, a salad, a bowl of assorted nuts, and marcook, a thin bread baked on a domed dish over fire.

He showered while waiting for his food and liquor, lingering under a lukewarm stream of water, enjoying the rich liquid soap and bath oils provided with the room. He even found a perfume intended for a lady, but Cosette judged it good enough to use on his own flesh, splashing it generously on his neck, arms, and the top of his head. Part of the luxe in the deluxe advertised for the room was a soft terry cloth lounge robe, which was Cosette deemed, an improvement over his well-traveled suit that should have been cleaned weeks ago. He ambled to the balcony that overlooked the beautiful Mediterranean. The city lights of Beirut cast a romantic glow onto the waters below. At moments such as these Cosette almost wished he could share his life with a special woman other than the prostitutes he had used for so long.

He was pleased with the way his interview had gone with the American. His instincts for self-preservation were, as usual, right on the mark. He replayed in his mind his carefully couched disclaimer of Tieso, avoiding the snare set by Commander Briggle. He had handled himself just right, not too condemnatory, but appearing to be wise, as though he understood Tieso on one level, but was unwilling to support his subtle character deficiencies.

He glanced at his watch, mildly irritated that his cognac had not yet arrived. In fact, he was about to call room service when there was a knock on the door. Ah. This would be it. He had not eaten since early morning and his mouth was beginning to moisten at the thought of food. He was surprised at the sight of two men standing in his doorway, neither of whom were bearers of food or drink.

"Mr. Bartholoma?" one of them asked. The men were swarthy, typical of Lebanese, and mustachioed. And they were unsmiling. The first man had a streak of white running through the center of his otherwise black hair. Cosette thought it was caused not by genetics, but by the skillful application of a hair dresser's hand. The second man had a large, black mole growing from the side of his nose. It was difficult for Cosette not to stare at it.

"Yes. And who are you?" Cosette demanded without asking them into his room. He sensed, however, that he knew who the men were, or at least who they represented, because Cosette had been involved with such men for almost as long as he could remember.

"ISF," one of the men said, languidly holding open an identification card in a leather wallet. The man closed it and dropped it back into his pocket before Cosette had a chance to look at the picture, much less read the print. Neither of the two were broad in the shoulder, but they looked to Cosette more than fit. He was quite familiar

with the Internal Security Forces of Lebanon. A good
part of their personnel were uniform, and they possessed
all of the sophisticated fighting equipment that a small
army would need to wage war. They also regulated traffic
and, like most police agencies, issued tickets for infrac-
tions of all social laws. But there was a darker part of
the ISF, no doubt represented by these men, that operated below the surface of Lebanon's overt police.

"Yes, and your names?" he asked, cautious not to
sound threatening.

Ignoring his question, the uninvited policemen walked
through the door, the first one shouldering his way indif-
ferently passed Cosette, the second policeman pushing
the Frenchman ahead of him. The police glanced carelessly about the room, one of them strolling into one of
the two bedrooms and began tossing Cosette's clothing
out of his bag as he spoke. He let the items fall where
they might, mostly on the floor. Then he opened a
drawer of the nightstand and removed Cosette's freshly
stolen papers.

"What is your real name?" the Mole asked Cosette,
thumbing through the wallet.

"I believe I asked you first," Cosette said, somewhat
truculently.

The Mole turned toward Cosette as though he could
not believe the Frenchman could be so unawed. Stupid,
perhaps. The blow to the side of Cosette's head came
powerfully and without warning. Cosette's ear stung
where gloved fingers had delivered the warning clout.

"Your real name," the Mole said again, his eyes rising
from the stolen documents to meet Cosette's.

Cosette hesitated but only for a moment. "It is Cosette. Cyrille Cosette," he said, attempting to regain his
dignity. His bathrobe had become untied and his soft
belly protruded from within its open folds. "I am a citizen of France."

"You are a thief," the Mole said. "Come with us."
The Mole and his partner with the white stripe took him
by the arms and propelled him toward the door.

"Let me get dressed," Cosette said, as the policemen snapped handcuffs onto his wrists.

"He smells like a French whore," the Mole remarked to his partner.

The ISF men pushed him roughly toward the exit so that he slammed into the door and bounced back. Then they opened it for him and led him unceremoniously down the hotel hallway. Cosette managed to retie his robe as the men propelled him into an elevator. At the lobby level they maintained their hold on his arms, marching him across the lobby and out through the revolving doors of the hotel. An unmarked police car was waiting for them. White Stripe opened a rear door and Cosette was thrust into the seat. The Mole slid in next to him while the French spy sat uncomfortably with his arms and hands locked awkwardly behind his back. White Stripe drove.

"I know what you are thinking. . . ." Cosette began, but gulped in pain as the Mole delivered a fist into his unprotected rib cage.

"Ah, Kahlil, we have mistakenly arrested a mind reader," the Mole said. Kahlil, with the white stripe, laughed in appreciation of his partner's humor. Then, to Cosette the Mole said, "I am liking your game, Cyrille Cosette. What else am I thinking about?"

Cosette struggled to regain his breath against the sharp pain in his side. He was certain that his rib was broken. "I am a professional. Like you. I . . ."

Another blow from the Mole's gloved hand exploded not only against Cosette's rib cage, but detonated inside his head bringing flashes of light before his eyes. His stomach heaved, but he swallowed hard to keep down its negligible contents.

"Wrong. That is not what I was thinking. Go ahead, I am ready for the next answer."

The policeman waited while Cosette continued to gasp. "Well? I said I am ready."

As the man called Kahlil drove through the streets of Beirut, Cosette sensed that they were not going to any of the police stations that he was familiar with. They turned off of Damascus Street, where one of the Internal Security Detachments was located, and wove through traffic, speeding toward the outskirts of the city.

The Mole pretended to direct a blow into the same area of Cosette's side causing the Frenchman to flinch, which, in turn, caused more pain. "You had better say something of interest, Cosette, if that is your name. But how are we to know, eh? You have not provided us with proof. The man whose identity you stole, why did you kill him? Only for his papers? Or did you kill him for another reason and take his papers because it was convenient?"

Cosette managed to register genuine surprise. "Kill him? But I did not!"

This time the blow to his ribs robbed Cosette entirely of air to breathe. He did not remember passing out until the car in which he was riding had stopped and he was dragged out of it. It was now parked behind a large stone building along with two other vehicles on a dimly lit cobblestone street. He was virtually dragged, stumbling, toward a steel-plated door, which the Mole unlocked with a key. Cosette was pushed inside, his shattered ribs making him hunch forward and over to one side. Then they continued down a cement corridor past several cell doors. Kahlil opened one of the doors with a key and Cosette was forced roughly inside.

It was an interrogation room. Cosette had seen many like it before and he harbored no illusions about what was in store for him unless he could become inventive in some way that escaped him now. Only the Mole entered the room with Cosette. Kahlil remained on the other side, closing the door behind them.

"Water," Cosette said.

His questioner, experience manifesting itself in the knowledge that prisoners who were deprived of the basic requirements of the human body would tell him nothing, brought him water in a plastic cup. When Cosette had gulped it all, the cup was refilled and put before him again. He drank all of that, as well.

The Mole took one of the three chairs in the room surrounding a steel table. All of the room's furnishings were permanently fastened to the floor.

"You were having a little well-earned vacation from Kuwait on your victim's credit cards here in Beirut," the Mole began, mildly. "Or you are here for another reason that is not so obvious. Tell me which. Cyrille? Is that what you wish to be called? Cyrille?"

"If you like. That is my name. Cyrille Cosette," the Frenchman said.

"And what is it that you do, Cyrille, when you are not murdering innocent businessmen, eh?" the policeman asked.

"I did not kill the man. No, no. . . ." Cosette said, drawing himself away from a blow he feared was coming to his ribs. "I bought the papers from a thief. Foolish, but I had no way to know he had been killed."

"Yes? And why?" the Mole said.

Cosette considered. Obviously he could not reveal his purpose in traveling to Beirut. To say the name of his "business" associate would ruin everything. Gaining an agreement with the right man from Baghdad was imperative. To disclose his name or to say the nature of his hoped-for deal would end it all before it had begun.

"I am French and I am employed by the French government. The DGSE," Cosette spoke with effort. "*Vous trouverez la référence moi dans vos dossiers.*"

The Lebanese policeman leaned back in his chair to regard Cosette more fully. After several moments he rose to his feet and exited the room, leaving Cosette handcuffed to the metal arms of his chair. Cosette was certain that he was bleeding internally, that he needed proper medical attention. He cursed himself for the stupidity of using the credit cards. No doubt the number was automatically transmitted from the computer terminal in the airport to either Interpol or to one of the several cooperative Arabic security systems that had been put in place recently. Sloppy. Careless. He chastised himself for using a common thief who, in retrospect, he never trusted anyway. Bartholoma had probably been dead for a week or more when Cosette had paid good money for a bad cover. He tried to imagine how he could extricate himself from a murder charge under the present circumstances. He was certain that in the end he could accomplish it, but at what cost in time and in money? Not to mention the blown deal with the Americans. He shook his head in despair.

The constant and worsening pain he experienced in his side caused Cosette to lose track of time. His head was swimming, but he was awake when both of the policemen entered the room once again. The Mole sat at Cosette's side while Kahlil took the remaining empty chair across the table. The Mole pursed his lips, theatrically conveying that he was near a decision.

"Cyrille," the Lebanese policeman began in a tone that might have been directed toward a child, "what should we do with you? Eh? Even if you did not kill this man, Bartholoma, whose papers you stole, you have committed crimes that are punishable by twenty years in Lebanese prisons." The policeman paused as though expecting a reply from his prisoner that would make sense to him. "But I think you know that. We have verified that you were once an employee of the DGSE, but they have no knowledge of your present whereabouts or your current business activities."

Cosette experienced more than a mild shock at this news, assuming that the policeman was not playing games. *Was* an employee? Why would they say such a thing? It was very unlikely that the DGSE would fail to verify his status when a bonafide police agency such as Lebanon's ISF asked for it.

"We are going to let you go, but only temporarily, Cyrille. You may return to your hotel, but you had better make other arrangements to pay the room bill, you silly bastard. And you are not to leave the country without permission. Here," the Mole said, scribbling on a piece of paper. "Call this number tomorrow at 7:00 P.M. and every day. If you fail to call, you will be arrested. We will tell you when you may leave. Do you understand this, Cyrille?" the Mole asked.

Cosette, humiliated, as it was the policeman's intention, nodded his head despondently.

The next morning Cosette painfully pulled himself from his hotel bed, cleaned up, then took a taxi to the French embassy. He was among the first waiting to pass through the guarded iron gates. Because he had no means of identification, he was reduced to explaining to several lesser ranking guards that he needed to get inside. Once inside, he had to explain all over again to more minor officials that he had lost his papers to thievery and needed replacements in order to return to Kuwait. He persevered, however, and was given the necessary replacement papers without resorting to contacts within the French Intelligence community of which he had been a part for so many years. He would look into his current employment status at a later time. For the present, he could not allow himself to consider, or others to know, that he was no longer a part of his government abroad.

There was a message waiting for him when he arrived back at his room at 6:00 P.M. Mr. Mohammed Fahdi had called, leaving a number for him to call in the city. Cosette found a public telephone in a street near the hotel and dialed the number.

"Yes?" a woman's voice answered at the other end.

Cosette gave the number of the telephone he was using and hung up. As he waited impatiently on the street he patted his pockets, but did not find cigarettes. He had left them in his room. A Beirut citizen moved toward the public telephone with the intention of using it, but Cosette blocked the man's way. The telephone was out of order, he said. Suspicious of the veracity of the infor-

mation he had just received, the citizen nevertheless
moved on, glancing over his shoulder just in time to see
Cosette answer the telephone as it rang.

"Cosette," he said into the mouthpiece.

"There is a café in El-Chebback called Boulos. Do
you know it?"

"No."

"Take a taxi. Twelve o'clock. Are you followed?"

"No," Cosette said.

He heard a soft chuckle at the other end, then a click
as the connection was cut.

Cosette allowed himself only one cognac as he waited
for the hands of the clock to move imperceptibly through
the late afternoon and into the evening. He decided that
in spite of his unrelenting pain he would eat an early
dinner in one of the hotel's restaurants. He ordered
Kabsa, a common Arab dish of meat with rice, but only
after instructing his waiter that the meat had to be
minced no larger than pieces of rice. He also ordered a
cold, dry wine which he quickly drained and ordered
another. He drank the second glass more slowly, dipping
a piece of bread into hummus.

Cosette struggled between enjoying the cold wine, the
almost sensuous taste of the food, and the gut-churning
pain that threatened to obliterate every other sense in
his brain. He left half of his plate unfinished in a rush
to return to his room and the bottle of pain relief capsules he had purchased at a chemist's shop near the
hotel. He doubled the dosage, pouring pills generously
into the palm of his hand and washing them down with
large gulps of water before falling onto his bed. He
closed his eyes and when he opened them again it was
dark in his room. He looked at his wrist, but the watch
that had been there for so many years was missing. He
painfully raised himself out of the bed in his luxury
suite—which he still occupied despite the fact that it was
now he and not Roulon Bartholoma paying the bill.
After he located a light switch and turned it on, the clock
on his nightstand, provided by the hotel, told him that

he still had one hour to make his appointment across town. He called the concierge and ordered a cab to pick him up promptly in twenty minutes. That done, Cosette hobbled toward the bathroom where he was determined to soak in a hot tub of water until it was time to leave.

He arrived at Boulos with minutes to spare. He gave his name to the maitre d' and was shown to a reserved table located against the east wall that provided a modicum of privacy. While he waited for his guest to arrive, the waiter appeared at the table to provide menus. Cosette snatched up the water glass even as the waiter was pouring it, eagerly washing down yet another handful of painkillers. He allowed his body to arch back ever so slowly, leaning to one side, in his never ending search for a position of comfort.

Cosette was totally uninterested in the café's decor, but could not help noticing that it seemed to be an Arab restaurant trying garishly to create an Arab atmosphere. Murals depicted desert scenes such as camel trains, ancient traders, and oases. Faux gas torches were used for illumination, while the entire interior was meant to feel like a Bedouin tent. It was the kind of place that would appeal to tourists from the West. Cosette acknowledged to himself that it was an ideal location to meet Fahdi.

"You seem to be in pain, Monsieur Cosette," an Arabian-looking man said, taking a chair beside the Frenchman rather than sit across the table.

"I am in pain. How did you know who I was?" Cosette grimaced. What hair he had left was dark, as was his moustache, although now flecked with gray. But Cosette had always been able to pass for Arab or Egyptian without question. And he had never before met Mohammed Fahdi.

"It was easy. I followed those two ISF people who are following you. There are probably Interpol following all of you, but in fact I am not entertained by any of that. Cigarette? They beat you at their little hideaway on Jeersmar Street, eh?"

Cosette waved away the cigarette, unable to imagine

that he had enough lung capacity to keep one lit. Instead, he motioned to the waiter. When he arrived, Cosette asked for cognac. Fahdi shook his head at the offer of alcohol, but ordered sweet tea.

"So," the Iraqi *Jihaz al-Himaya al-Khas* (Special Secret Service) officer began, "you have something important for us? I hope that is the case, Monsieur Cosette. My superior is a very impatient man these days. It would have been much easier for all concerned if you had traveled to Baghdad."

"No offense, *mon nouveau ami,* but I am aware that it is often far easier to enter Baghdad than to leave it for people in our business," Cosette said, uncaring at this point whether the man was amused or insulted.

By his unchanging expression, Mohammed Fahdi was neither. A good sign, Cosette thought. Professional. Maybe this business could be accomplished after all.

"I have something of value that you people have lost and wish to get back. Its return will make your trip to Beirut worthwhile. You might even get yourself a medal for it," Cosette added carelessly.

"I'm not aware that we have lost anything," the SSS officer said, allowing his eyes to wander. It was a practiced attempt at nonchalance that was wasted on Cosette.

"My mistake. I thought you had most of your armed forces and all of your police out looking for a certain individual who is on his way to meet the Americans. Sorry to have put you to the trouble," Cosette said.

There was never any mistaking body language if one knew how to watch for it, Cosette knew. While the Iraqi officer attempted to sit back easily in his chair the effort turned out to appear stiff. His blink rate increased rapidly, while his eyes shifted from left to right as his brain processed and discarded various possibilities, which Cosette had long ago determined, returned to only one.

"And that person is?" the Iraqi officer asked.

"He is the defector, of course. Colonel Harun Baraniq," Cosette said.

"Is he hiding in the closet of your hotel room?"

Fahdi's attempt at sarcasm was weak. Cosette had a momentary feeling of comfort, for a change. He would not respond until the SSS officer changed his arrogant demeanor.

"Well," the Iraqi said, mashing his cigarette impatiently in an ashtray, "there is more, I am sure."

"*Certainement,* there is more. I have been approached by the Americans to arrange Colonel Baraniq's transportation out of . . . wherever he is, into the safety of their hands."

"Out of where? You were about to say where he was now," Fahdi said, unsuccessful in concealing his eagerness for more precise information.

"We need to discuss the reward—" Cosette began, totally ignorant of where Baraniq was. Or would be, for that matter.

"Reward?" Fahdi interjected. "Well, maybe some kind of consideration could be paid for information that returned the traitor Baraniq to answer for his crimes." Fahdi shrugged, as though money was of no consequence.

"That would be wonderful, Mr. Fahdi. Wonderful, that is, if the consideration that we agree to is not less than five-million American dollars." Cosette motioned to the waiter for more wine. He could feel the fire in his ribs begin to ease.

"Ridiculous," the Iraqi snorted, tossing his head as he turned away from Cosette.

"Really? Out of the question, would you say, Mr. Fahdi?" Cosette asked, rhetorically, teasingly. Cosette clucked his tongue. "Silly me. I seem to be getting everything wrong tonight. First, I thought you said you had lost nothing, now you seem to say that you have lost something after all, but that it is hardly worth getting back. At least not worth very much money, I now hear you say. Well, I tried, didn't I?" Cosette, making a humorous face, turned the palms of his hands upward.

"Five million! That is absurd! We are a nation under siege. Our people are starving—"

"Please. Spare me," Cosette said. "You sell a million barrels of oil every day. With the money you make selling oil you buy weapons and war technology. Who is responsible for your people starving? Eh? You heard my price, Fahdi. I won't quibble."

Mohammed Fahdi rubbed his chin under his full moustache. "It is not so easy."

"Yes, it is so easy. Call General Hrokanen and ask him if $5 million is not a bargain for the return of Baraniq. He would pay ten times that amount. And he would be grateful. You might think of that, too, Fahdi. How grateful the Great One will feel toward you if you bring the pig back to him lashed to a pole."

The Iraqi Intelligence officer drummed his fingers on the table, pausing only long enough to flick away the waiter who tried for the second time to take their order. "How much time do we have?" he snapped at Cosette.

"I have all the time in the world, Fahdi, but you have only until midnight," Cosette pressed, not because he had to but because he could.

"Impossible!" Fahdi snapped.

"Impossible seems to be your favorite word. No wonder the Americans threw you out of Kuwait so easily," the Frenchman said.

The Iraqi looked him squarely in the eyes, a grave social offense in the Arab world. "Be careful, Frenchman. Praise flows into every river, but an insult etches itself in steel."

"Then I will see that you get more time," Cosette said, feigning contrition. He pushed a slip of paper across the table. "Tomorrow at noon I will call my bank and ask if $3 million has been deposited to this account. If it has, you will recover your lost treasure and pay the balance of $2 million. If it has not there—"

The Frenchman shrugged.

CHAPTER 11

It was totally dark when there was a tremendous explosion and a flash of light off McTaggart's five o'clock. The storm had not abated. If anything, it had increased its devilish ferocity; gusts threatened to rip supplies and equipment from the sides of the DPV.

"Hold it!" McTaggart shouted into the ear of Entzion. The DPV, already crawling, ground to a full stop at McTaggart's command. They had heard and seen other explosions earlier in the day as they passed through the concentration of Iraqi armor. Some of the 120-mm guns had hurled rounds just over their heads and there had been sporadic machine-gunning into the void of the storm from nervous tank crews, but this explosion was different. "Mine!" McTaggart said into Entzion's ear. He swivelled his head backward to see Haggar, still sitting at the top gun position despite its brutal exposure to the wind and sand. Haggar nodded his agreement at McTaggart's hand signal that a mine had exploded.

Who had exploded it? Mears and his DPV? The Iraqis? Would the Iraqi armed units blunder into their own minefield? McTaggart thought the answer was probably yes—if they were in determined pursuit and if they had been blinded by the storm. Their navigation would be no better than McTaggart's. Dead reckoning an compass.

If they were to continue punching through the impene trable darkness and driving wind, and if they were amids a minefield as McTaggart was beginning to suspect, thei chances of hitting one of the powerful anti-tank mine was high. On the other hand, to sit still until mornin would not put desperately needed distance between ther and the pursuing Iraqi forces.

"What kind of mine?" McTaggart shouted into the ea of the team's weapons expert.

"Anti-tank," Haggar shouted back. "Mi-101 or some thing like it."

"Can we see them?" the lieutenant shouted at Hagga while indicating with his hand the area in front of th DPV.

Haggar nodded his head. "Maybe. Close to the sur face. Y-fuse."

Haggar climbed down from his gun mount and, pullin McTaggart with him, snapped on a flashlight and bega walking in front of the tracks of the vehicle. He kep his flashlight pointed almost directly down as he walked Taking his cue from Haggar, McTaggart took up a posi tion to his left and kept pace. He looked down himsel for the telltale sign of an Mi-101. In order to maintain . proper space where the wheels of the DPV would go McTaggart extended his arm toward Haggar and Haggar quickly realizing what the young officer was doing, ex tended his arm and they locked them together, thu keeping a measured space between them. After walkin several minutes, with Entzion grinding behind them ir the DPV, Haggar stopped. McTaggart froze with hin and looked down.

This type of mine was placed a few inches below th surface of the sand, as Haggar knew it would be, so tha its Y-shaped fuse head would protrude just above. Th driving wind was now making the task of spotting th fuse heads possible. They were moving slow, close in and the illumination of flashlights should show then where the mines were buried. Haggar stopped and knelt in the sand. He expertly used his K-bar knife to scribe a circle in the sand from which he exposed a mine. He easily lifted it up, holding it so that McTaggart could see it more clearly.

It had a hard, molded outer surface covering a hexatol explosive interior. The fuse, below the Y, was screwed into the well of the mine and would have exploded had the three-pronged Y been pressured at about one hundred sixty pounds from the side or three hundred pounds from directly above. After Haggar had wordlessly pointed out the salient points of the explosive device, he walked the thing to the side of their course line and dropped it like a rock. McTaggart flinched, but there was no explosion. It was Haggar's way of demonstrating that the mine was a killer, but not delicate.

Returning to the DPV, McTaggart put his head next to Haggar's and Entzion's.

"We'll go with the lights on," he shouted. "Turn them down," he said while indicating with his hands that the running lights on their desert vehicle could be adjusted downward as well us up. "I'll ride out front."

With the engine in the rear there was no hood on the front of the DPV, but there was space enough between the front wheels where one could perch.

"Me, too," Haggar shouted back.

McTaggart shook his head. "Negative. Stay on the gun. We'll switch every hour."

Within minutes they had repositioned the running lights downward so that they would attract less attention from afar and also would focus on the area that was of most concern, the track in front. As McTaggart prepared to take his position he turned his thumb up for his comrades to see. "Let the fuckers follow us now," he said.

In forty minutes Colonel John Vass, SOCCENT, was due to fly out from MacDill AFB, Tampa. The two C-141s were loaded with special mountain assault troops, resupply equipment, including ammunition, vehicle re-

placement parts, and two SpecOps Intel teams that were
scheduled for delivery in Kandahar. Colonel Vass's aide
wanted his boss to make that airplane because they said
they wouldn't hold it for anyone, not even the man who
was about to assume the assignment of Deputy Commander SFs in Afghanistan. Dressed in battle camos,
Vass paced outside Lieutenant General Bruce Coggin's
office door.

"Goddamnit, sergeant—" Vass was speaking directly
at the bald head of Sergeant Eddie Hall who, not looking
up from his paperwork, or removing the cigar from his
mouth as the colonel raved, was shaking his head while
Vass's lips moved.

"He knows you're here, Colonel."

"Well, punch that telephone and tell him again!"

"Colonel Vass, sir, the general is trying to change his
tee time for Saturday morning and he won't delegate
that job to anyone, not even me," Sergeant Hall said.

Vass stopped pacing to lean forward on the sergeant's
desk. "Is that supposed to be funny, sergeant? Is that
one of your tired-ass jokes?"

Sergeant Hall, who wore badges of the Airborne,
Rangers, Special Forces, had a chestful of battle ribbons,
including purple hearts and decorations for bravery second to few men in the entire U.S. Army, leaned back in
his chair and regarded Colonel Vass.

"Yes, sir, I guess that's what I was trying to do. I was
trying to cheer you up. And I apologize." Eddie Hall
allowed his eyes to drop back to the work on his desk,
sucked hard on his cigar and allowed a huge cloud of
blue smoke to permeate the entire room.

Colonel Vass shook his head. "Christ. I'm sorry,
Sarge."

Sergeant Hall did not look up or acknowledge the colonel's apology.

"I said I'm sorry."

Hall did not raise his eyes from the papers on his desk.
Vass looked at his watch in frustration while momentarily catching the eye of his aide, Lieutenant Keel.

"What's that you're doing, Eddie?" Colonel Vass asked the sergeant.

"Stock market."

"Yeah?" Colonel Vass said, arching an eyebrow. "What looks good?"

"Well, sir, ever since my wife left me six years ago cheerleaders look good to me. I like the idea of having one of those University of Texas co-eds sit right on my face."

Sergeant Hall's attention was momentarily distracted by a light appearing on his desk communications set. He picked it up, listened for a moment, then replaced it.

"General Coggin can see you now, sir," Hall said to Colonel Vass.

Vass moved quickly to the general's door, closing it behind him as he entered. Sergeant Hall picked up his telephone and dialed a number. "Operations," he said into the mouthpiece and waited. Then he said, "This is Sergeant Hall, SOCCENT. Hold the big birds on the ramp until Colonel Vass arrives."

Hall listened to the voice on the other end. "Yes, sir, Major. I am Sergeant Edward Hall, CO/SOCCENT." Sergeant Hall listened patiently to the voice at the other end of the line. Then he said, "I will certainly tell General Coggin that you do not agree with his wishes, Major. Have a good day, sir." Hall moved the phone several inches from his ear while, at the other end, he could hear the operations officer shouting, trying to regain the sergeant's attention before he hung up. Hall put the phone back to his ear.

"I'm sorry? What's that, sir? Yes, sir, that would be Lieutenant General Bruce Coggin. I'm sure the missed communication was my fault, Major. No, sir, I'm not exactly sure how long the delay will be, but if I had to guess I'd say about one hour. Matter of fact, Major, those C-141 pilots can make up the difference if they power all the way to the ground instead of throttling back and floating down at two hundred feet a minute like a goddamn Chinese kid flying his kite! Sittin' in the back of

one of those things waiting for a stinger missile to fly up
your asshole over a hot LZ will make you think that
way."

Sergeant Hall listened for a moment. "The pleasure
was mine, Major. I'll be sure to pass your kind words on
to the general, sir."

General Bruce Coggin was a man always in a controlled rage. He tried not to show it and unless one knew
the general very well it was hard to tell that nothing
ever worked fast enough or good enough to make Bruce
Coggin happy. But he smiled anyway. Colonel Vass had
worked more or less directly for the general for almost
two years and had a deep and abiding respect for the
man's courage and judgement.

"I want Joe Mears out of there with his package when
they go, general," Vass said to Coggin as the general
drank a glass of cold milk.

"Joe's got another job to do after they get him out,"
Coggin responded, flatly.

"He's been in country too long. They know who he
is. His face is all over the Middle East," Vass pressed.

"How do you know that?"

"Mossad gave us that one. And he's hotter yet because
of the defector. They want that guy and they want Joe,
too," Vass said.

"We knew they would. That's why Mears got the job
instead of your cousin Louie," Coggin said, naming a
non-existent character as the alternate.

"We pull teams out of those zones all the time. Why
not Mears? What's the hot deal he has to attend to after
the delivery? Can't somebody else do that one?" Vass
asked, totally ignorant of Mears's secondary assignment,
but he was under no illusion that the general would tell
him. It was none of his business.

"Anything else before your plane leaves without you,
John?'

"All right, sir, let me drop him some support," Vass
said.

"Couple more Leopard teams?" the general asked, finishing his glass of milk.

Vass knew that all of the Leopard teams were already out of the U.S. on other assignments.

"Maybe not Leopard teams. We could tap SEALs and we could check with the Brits for SAS or even Special Boat people to—"

"John," General Coggin interrupted, "I've been over this fifty times with people whose planning abilities rival even yours. We've thought about Mears, the man he's bringing out, his team, and everybody else's team, too. We can't just start dropping people in there for reasons you can't even imagine."

But Vass could imagine. The balloon was about to go up in Iraq and every man in SpecOps was mission assigned. All the teams were stretched. Even the Iraqis knew it was coming. They just didn't know when or where.

"It isn't like Mears is a write-off," the general said. "He isn't being sacrificed. We want him back and we want him back alive, but he and Leopard-1 have to get the defector out of Iraq. You know who it is, John?" General Coggin asked.

"Iraqi Intel type is all I know," Vass admitted.

"Deputy Commander over there. What he has inside his head could turn around the T-war for us. He knows where everybody is all around the world. Who the cells are, who the leaders are, where they're operating, who funds them, what their missions are, who the sleepers are. Everything."

Vass nodded, accepting a higher wisdom. He drew himself into attention and said, "Understand, sir. Appreciate you letting me speak frankly."

General Coggin came around from behind his desk and put his arm over Vass's shoulder.

"You're one of the best field SpecWar guys in the business, John. I don't worry about that. I only worry about your chip shots. They're erratic. Of course I'll miss you while you're in country over there because I'll have to find another pigeon to pluck on the golf course until you get back."

"I think it's time you learned to live within the means of a lieutenant general, anyway, sir," Vass said, saluting. It occurred to Vass as he strode from the general's office that he should figure out a way to deduct his golf bets from his income tax. It would still hurt, but not as bad.

"Have a good trip over there, Colonel," Sergeant Hall said.

Vass turned. "Wish to hell you were going with me, Eddie."

"So do I," Eddie Hall said, and winked.

Mears studied his map. Again. The most difficult part of his deductive navigation was not having any idea how many miles they had traveled. Their speed had varied, they had zigzagged, they had made any number of ninety-degree turns to avoid danger. There was no way to spot a landmark in the extraordinarily limited visibility caused by the blowing sand and dark night. Nor would their GPSs pick up even one satellite when they needed at least two and preferably six to nine to gain an accurate fix. Mears was thinking of finding a road and using it. It was a course of action that he wasn't in love with, but they could make up a lot of time if it worked. Or they could get killed.

Quack was now at the wheel of the DPV while Rodriguez manned the gun above. They were out of water, their last drink given to Colonel Baraniq more than three hours ago. The wind continued to snatch moisture from their bodies although the temperature had dropped to the low fifties, and they would have to find something to drink soon.

Mears leaned over to shout in Taylor's ear. "Drive zero-six-zero. If you get to a road, turn south!"

Quack gave Mears the briefest look, but unhesitatingly turned the wheel of the DPV and drove as ordered.

Though the wind was spinning in various directions, its main track seemed to be west and it might have been Mears's imagination but the impact on his face and hands from blowing sand seemed to be less than before they made the turn. They had not seen a piece of armor in two hours. That did not mean that they were past the armored division or beyond any of the enemy forces that had encircled the city of Baghdad, but in this case no news was good news to Mears.

Mears kept one eye on the odometer and the other eye on the outside of the vehicle. Every gun was either on a lap or, in the case of Rodriguez, mounted inches away. It was not yet midnight when Mears calculated that they had to be near the highway he was looking for. He peered ahead, squinting through his desert goggles in the distance, which was, frustratingly, still only a few meters. Then another hour of grinding through sand, up one dune and down another, and still no road.

"Hold it, Manny," Mears shouted to Rodriguez. The driver halted as ordered while he referred to the map again. He would recalculate. Damn, it had to be close. He turned again to Rodriguez and said, "Turn the lights on!"

Rodriguez obliged. After several long seconds of nothing more than illuminated, blowing sand, there was another flash. Virtually dead ahead a second set of vehicle lights came on. There was no way for Mears to estimate how far away the vehicle was, but it could not have been more than twenty meters. By the time Mears clicked off the safety on his M-4 and snapped the shoulder stock into firing position, he heard the very loud *thump, thump, thump* of the belt-fed 30mm low-recoil cannon firing above his head.

Straight ahead the lights went out. But everything else got brighter. Pieces of a vehicle were blown straight up and out. Then a gas tank was lit off and Mears could clearly see bodies flying sideways, thrown away from the vehicle by the armor penetrating rounds that Quack was putting out from his gun. Every fifth round was incendiary. Soldiers outside of the vehicle but standing near it simply disappeared.

Gunfire erupted from their ten o'clock, small arms and light machine gun. Rodriguez fired back at the source of those flashes, but it was impossible to tell if he hit anything or anyone. More gunfire from approximately the same direction, but a different source. Rodriguez answered, but this time Quack had the 30mm on that sector and laid down effective counterfire. A round struck one of the DPV's cage bars, but it was, literally, a blind lucky shot.

"Go!" Mears shouted to Rodriguez who hardly needed the command to jam his foot hard on the accelerator. In a matter of seconds they were beyond the burning vehicle and in a half minute its flames could no longer be seen through the sandstorm.

Mears's heart was pounding. He looked to all sides and to the rear for more targets, as Quack and Rodriguez were also doing. But there was nothing left to shoot. They continued on for several minutes in what was, considering the circumstances, high-speed driving, probably forty miles per hour with the risk that if they could run themselves over a cliff or smash into a stone wall before they could see it.

"Shut it down, Manny!" Mears shouted. Rodriguez stopped the DPV and they sat, looking, trying to listen. But nothing could be seen or heard above the shrieking blast of hurricane-like wind and horizontally moving sand. Breathing was a chore. Mears forced himself to inhale slowly, but deeply. After a moment of trying to see and hear, Mears raised his hand to signal Rodriguez to start the engine when he changed his mind. He stepped out of the DPV, walked several paces looking down, turned on his flashlight to illuminate whatever it was he was looking at, and returned to the DPV.

"We're on the road, Manny," he said. "Turn on your lights and drive."

Rodriguez snapped on the vehicle's travel lights and sure enough, if he looked hard, he could see that the front of the DPV was on a hard surface. He turned the wheels to the right and, according to his compass, they were again headed south.

"Who do you think we killed?" he shouted out of the side of his mouth to Mears. Mears shrugged.

They periodically encountered traffic moving in the opposite direction. It was always military, always running with lights on, which gave the Leopard team, running with lights off, time to veer off the side of the road and remain motionless and unseen in the blinding storm.

At 0315 hours they were passing through a small village. There were no lights showing anywhere, the result of either a power outage or perhaps the townspeople were all abed. Cautiously they pulled off the road, concealing the DPV as best they could behind what appeared to be a seldom used shed or garage. Rodriguez relieved Quack at the light machine gun mount while Quack and Mears reconnoitered the area. In a country whose arable land was only twelve percent, the people who lived here were lucky. There was water, probably from an underground source, because the community was able to stock water. There was a modest herd of goats in a well tended corral, all crowded together against the side of a building to ward off the worst effects of the storm. Mears moved carefully toward the goat enclosure until he spotted a watering trough supplied by a spigot that emerged from within the building. Gingerly he turned the spigot handle. A trickle of water emerged from the old pipe, a stream that was sufficient to fill their water containers. Quack jogged back fifty meters to the DPV. There was little danger that the well-muffled engine would be heard in the raging wind, so he started the vehicle and pulled it forward where water could be transferred more easily.

The team set to work filling their water bags and bottles, a process that was made maddening from lack of water pressure. When the first bottle was filled, Quack immediately processed it through their water purifying system, making the stuff potable for the team.

"How are you feeling?" Mears shouted to Baraniq who sat quite still in the rear seat of the DPV. He nodded his head. "You sure? Want to walk about for a minute?" Mears glanced around again, making out the shapes of the few buildings in the tiny village. But the Iraqi colonel shook his head. Mears felt a rush of sympathy for the man. He sat, shoulders hunched, huddled from not only a raging storm but from the storm that must be rending his life, ripping away what was once security for him, and even his loved ones. He could not now return to what was his home, but only hope that promises made to him by the American military would prove to be somehow better than what he had left.

"Mears!"

Rodriguez, sighting down the barrel of his mounted machine gun, pointed. Following Rodriguez's indication, among swirling wind and sand, Mears could see chalk white figures. Their faces and necks were entirely shrouded in rags to shield them from sand and dust. They more resembled ghost-like apparitions than people. Mears advanced carefully toward them. There were two men and a boy, not yet old enough to grow a beard. Mears could dimly make out the shape of a woman standing in a window, a child in her arms. The men were not armed and did not seem to Mears to be aggressive. Curious, perhaps. He looked for a sign that might tell the name of the place, but saw nothing. He thought the people might be Shi'a Muslims who had inhabited this area for thousands of years, though their lot in life was much fairer before the state government diverted feeder streams and rivers, killing off habitats and supplies of potable water. Mears did not know what it was they wanted, if anything, nor did he know whether these peasants recognized that the Leopard team was not an Iraqi unit. He moved easily near them, making no threatening gesture, trying to allay their suspicions.

"We are lost from our comrades," he said in a perfect Iraqi dialect.

The men spoke among themselves. In the howling

wind Mears could not hear. Finished conferring with each other, the men nevertheless did not respond to Mears, but continued to eye him suspiciously as well as the DPV. Mears looked over at Quack who returned his questioning look. The people could be passively hostile. If they were left alive they would eventually give the information to the Iraqi army that the Leopard team had passed this way. Mears must have subconsciously moved his M-4 menacingly, raising its barrel as he considered his options, because Colonel Baraniq stepped forward, pushing his way past Mears to the villagers.

He spoke to them, gesturing with his hand, placing his head near theirs, and while Mears could not hear what was said he saw one of the men pull the boy from behind him, moving the youngster so that Baraniq could see. Mears could see, too. The boy walked on thin wooden pegs instead of feet. And he had no arms.

Baraniq and the men exchanged more dialogue; then the men turned toward their shelter, bringing the hobbling boy with them.

"They have told us where we are," Baraniq said simply to Mears.

They retreated to the DPV where they could examine Mears's folded map. Once Mears was shown the tiny village, he could measure their exact coordinates for radio transmission to the task force.

"Who are they?" Mears asked.

For a moment it seemed the Iraqi defector would not answer. Then he said, "They were poisoned from the air." He looked away from Mears, and said, "We did not just murder the Kurds, you know."

It was becoming light and traffic on the road was more frequent. The danger of being spotted was increasing by the minute. According to Mears' operational map there was a bridge that crossed a wadi approximately three kilometers ahead. It seemed to him that the velocity of the wind was decreasing, the dust and sand not so opaque as an hour ago. Mears made a circular motion with his finger to Quack to speed up. Quack obliged, the

DPV rocketing along at nearly forty miles per hour, their discomfort increasing with the DPV's increased speed. Also increasing was the potential danger of hitting something solid in front of them.

After several minutes, Mears signaled Quack to slow down. The driver did as he was told until he and Mears could make out a bridge ahead. Mears pointed to the southwest, off the road they were traveling.

"Follow the wadi," he spoke into Quack's ear.

The terrain in the wadi was strewn with rocks, large and small. It was like riding on a giant, corrugated washboard, and, despite being strapped in, it shook their guts until they hurt. But Mears wanted to be far enough from the bridge to avoid being seen from the road after they had dug in.

He had a good enough position fix to transmit to their SOCCENT liaison with the task force.

CHAPTER 12

Mr. Briggle, Cosette was informed by the operator at the Sheraton Hotel in Kuwait City, was working on an offshore rig today, but said he was looking forward to meeting with Mr. Cosette tonight. Mr. Briggle would return to his room no later than 8:30 P.M. Cosette thanked the operator and hung up, privately amused at the American officer's cover story of the day.

Much had been accomplished in the past sixty hours. It had been a roller coaster for all concerned. Briggle had disappeared from his room at the Sheraton and remained gone until yesterday evening when he called Cosette from an undisclosed location. They agreed to meet on the beach near Briggle's hotel.

"Sorry," Briggle had said in response to Cosette's prompting for improved coordination, "but something unexpected came up."

"I trust all is now well?" Cosette said, hoping that he did not betray the anxiety he felt.

"Yeah. More or less. Shit happens in the oil business, as you know," Briggle had said. "How about your end?"

"We are ready when you are, Commander. I have located a boat and a man we can trust who will sail her," Cosette had assured the American naval officer.

"A poor but honest fisherman," Briggle said, dryly.

"As a matter of fact that is correct. Fishing does not make one rich in the sea of oil," Cosette nodded toward the waters of the Persian Gulf, seeming to be filled with as many oil platforms as fish.

Stockton Briggle grunted. "Okay. Call me tomorrow, we'll lay it out."

"Tomorrow?" the French spy was surprised at yet another delay that the American once seemed so eager to avoid. "Communication problems?"

Briggle turned from their solitary walk near the beachfront to regard the Frenchman. "That and some other things. How did you know?"

Cosette shrugged. "There has been a giant storm in Iraq for three days. All kinds of electronics have problems then. Vehicles, too. I have been here more than thirty years, *mon ami*. The storms are the curse of the desert."

Briggle accepted the DGSE man's educated guess. They had heard nothing for six days from the Leopard team that was bringing out Griffon. They were more than three days late arriving in the south of Iraq. When CDR SPECOPS finally received the Extremely High Frequency message burst from the Leopard-1 leader it gave a SITREP (situation report) from near the Dijlah area. The team had been engaged by Iraqi forces and they had lost time in the zero visibility of a very large sandstorm. The weather had now cleared over Iraq and the team could move again. Briggle was ready to receive the team's ETA in southern Iraq. He would then transmit the rendezvous location and security identifiers here.

Now, still another day later, Cosette was a wealthy man. It was easier to wait because Cosette's time was now filled with dreams of how he would spend his fortune. From the moment the banker at Credit Suisse confirmed a deposit of $3 million in his account, Cosette had at first been stunned. It had happened. His legs were unsteady as he moved slowly from one of the multiple public telephones in the Kuwait national telephone offices into the street. He had leaned against the outside of the building until his heart slowed and his breathing caught up with his body's need for oxygen.

He was rich!

Even if the Iraqis failed to pay him the balance of his $5 million demand after the Americans were turned over, it wouldn't matter. Without question he would quit this wretched part of the world and return to civilization, this time as a gentleman. He would buy an apartment in Paris, and another in the south of France. He would live conservatively, within the means of a successful business-man. He would give some thought to a cover story that would explain what business he had retired from. A bond trader, perhaps. No, he despised the market machina-tions as well as the larcenists who operated it. Well, it wasn't important, now.

There was a minor consideration. "You will never live to spend a penny of it should the Americans get out of Iraq," Mohammed Fahdi had solemnly promised.

Cosette shuddered at the memory of the slightly built Iraqi officer's threat. They were all fanatics. They were destructive compared to the French. Even, Cosette was forced to admit, worse than the Americans. The Fahdis of the world lived to kill, to tear down what others had built up. For the first time that he could remember, Co-sette found himself longing for the grace and beauty of his own civilization, the wondrous architecture and lan-guage so uniquely French. The so-called social contracts that had changed the way men governed themselves, that had guaranteed freedom to all souls, had been refined in his country. Where once he regarded the Western justice system to be a major thorn in his side, Cosette now viewed it with new understanding, even admiration. He could now afford to survey his heritage in the cosmic sense. Only another day, two at the most, and the whole business would be finished. He would be shed of people he did not like in principle, the Americans and the Mo-hammed Fahdis of the world, and their broiling place on the planet Earth.

*   *   *

The telephone in Stockton Briggle's room rang that night at exactly 8:35. The man was nothing if not prompt, Briggle thought, as he picked it up. "Yes?"

"Cyrille here, *mon ami*." Cosette's voice was easy for Briggle to identify. "I am in the lobby of your hotel. Shall I—"

"I'm on my way down," Briggle said, interrupting. He judged that the Frenchman was more than a little eager to ingratiate himself with the American military presence in the Gulf. Briggle scooped up a lightweight linen jacket that he pulled over a cotton shirt on the way out of the door to his room. As he waited for the elevator to arrive at his floor, Briggle considered stopping by the American embassy to pick up a weapon. After all, he had no way of knowing where he and the Frenchman were going, only that they were to look at a boat. But the notion of arming himself with a gun was fleeting. Handguns were still rare in this part of the kingdom and it could easily cause him more trouble than it was worth. Even though American citizens were not loved in the Muslim world it was still much safer to walk the streets anywhere in Kuwait than almost any city in the United States. And he would be in the company of Cyrille Cosette, a man who knew the people of this region as well as anyone. If protection was needed Briggle was sure that Cosette would see to it.

Briggle had hardly stepped out of the elevator in the lobby when Cosette magically appeared at his side. "*Bon soir, mon ami*," the Frenchman said, smiling like a clothing salesman.

"Good evening, Cyrille," Briggle said, finding that he was anxious to complete the final leg of the team's egress from Iraq. "So? Where are we going?"

Cosette led the way through the lobby, ensuring that he did not outpace the American who fell into stride. "We are going to look at a boat," he said.

"Good," Briggle said, not without relief. He wanted to take a damn good look at the thing that would carry the Leopard team and their package out to the Mark V boats. It had to be seaworthy. He shuddered to imagine what would happen if some old scow sank two miles offshore with everyone on board, long before they reached their rendezvous point. If there was even a suggestion that the boat didn't support his confidence, Briggle would nix the deal at once. In fact he had an alternate plan if the Frenchman failed him. "Where is it?"

"The north side of the bay," Cosette said, meaning the Bay of Kuwait. "Near As Sabiyah."

Briggle had a fair understanding of the region, though not an intimate one. He knew that As Sabiyah was about one-hundred-fifty kilometers by automobile. It was a jumping off place for ships passing through the Strait of Hormuz in both directions. An ancient delta into which the sacred rivers of Mesopotamia once emptied, the north Persian Gulf provided natural inlets for small craft as well as giant, engineered piers for supertankers.

"All right," Briggle said. "Got a flashlight?"

"But of course," Cosette said, gently touching the American officer's arm as he guided him to a rental car parked near the hotel's main doors.

The road was first-rate, as good as anything in America, Briggle thought, as Cosette pushed the Mercedes at a steady one-hundred kilometers per hour in light traffic. Of course, all automobile traffic outside the Kennedy Freeway in Chicago, Briggle regarded as light. The scenery along this part of the gulf, if one could call it that, was almost mesmerizing in its brilliance. On his passenger side of the car, Briggle was transfixed by the incredible light show produced by the mile after mile of oil processing plants, natural gas containers, and pumping platforms. Flames were burning off the fumes at the top of gas pipes. He reminded himself that he was looking at the very heart of the world's main source of energy, and this long strip of real estate could be its throbbing aorta.

If Briggle had not been so preoccupied with his odyssey of oil he might have noticed that Cosette was sweating heavily despite the ample output from the car's air

conditioner. Briggle glanced toward the Frenchman as
Cosette slowed the car and turned off onto a service road
that inclined slightly down as they neared the dock area.

"You all right?" he asked of Cosette whose collar was
drenched with perspiration.

Cosette nodded his head vigorously but said nothing,
preferring to concentrate on making several turns among
commercial buildings and, finally, into a dock area where
there were a number of small boats, some of them fishing
boats and most of them dhows.

"You sure?"

"Yes. I am perfectly fine," Cosette said without meeting the American's eyes. "A touch of dengue fever. It
comes once in a year."

There were all kinds of bugs in the world, Briggle reminded himself.

"There. There is the boat," Cosette said, pointing
ahead. It was fifteen meters in length, Briggle estimated,
larger than most dhows, which could explain why it occupied a rather distant berth from the others. The wharf
was deserted of people, in any case. Like traditional
dhows that were so common in this part of the world
and in the Persian Gulf in particular, this one had the
distinctive raised prow and high stern castle. When Briggle was preparing for this tour of duty in the Middle
East he had familiarized himself with the dhow, a gener-
alized term for the most ubiquitous form of watercraft
in the Arabian Gulf, and he recognized that the one he
was looking at now was a *sambuq,* a name applied more
commonly to the tapered-stern fishing craft as opposed to
the square-stern trading vessels that plied the coastlines.

"Well, shall we see it?" Cosette nervously asked as he
opened the driver's side door.

"Sure as hell will," Briggle said, exiting the Mercedes.
As he approached the boat he was not dissatisfied with
what he saw. Ordinarily, looking at night at anything to
buy, rent, or even steal, was not the best choice. But in
this case there was no alternative. Mears and his people

were on their way and he had to secure their safe passage on the final leg. Danger was still all around them.

The dhow was not a well kept vessel, but it was more than big enough for their purposes. If its power plant was up to snuff and if the skipper had a regular pulse rate, Cosette would have done well.

"Where's the captain?" he asked Cosette. Briggle had in his hand the flashlight that Cosette had brought along, but there was enough light radiating from commercial working wharves and from strong building flood lamps for the American to get a good enough view of the dhow, at least from the outside. As he spoke he stepped from the pier onto the deck of the boat.

"He is on board, Commander," Cosette responded.

"Ask him to come up. What's his name? And what do you know about him?" Briggle began walking the deck of the fishing boat. She was dirty and her nets had rot, but she appeared to be sturdy enough to do the job he had in mind. He would have to look below decks, of course, and look at the engine compartment to determine whether or not it would get them there. The engine was the most critical piece of equipment on board, as far as the mission was concerned. On the other hand, he didn't want to be too fussy. Hell, they only had fifteen miles of water to navigate. They could damn near swim if they had to.

"He is Mohammed al-Ammal. His reputation among other fishermen is good, a hard worker. As you can see," Cosette said, indicating the boat with a sweep of his arm, "he has worked his way up to this fine large dhow."

"Yeah? So why is he willing to risk his boat and his life to help us? I mean besides the money?" Briggle wanted to know.

Cosette smiled broadly. "There is no 'besides,' Commander. It is only money and I have promised him a sizable bonus when he returns. Ten thousand American dollars."

Briggle turned to regard the Frenchman. He had been

assured the price was to be $4,000, plus the replacement of the man's boat if it should be sunk or confiscated. Now, without any consultation, the DGSE agent had more than doubled the agreed price. Was Cosette helping himself to a little rake-off? Briggle didn't like it but it wasn't unheard of among international agents. Besides, if Cosette was putting something into his own pocket, it would be easy to find out. When it came time to make the payment, Briggle would handle that part personally. Also, Briggle rationalized, he had hired Cosette because of the man's experience. If the French agent felt that the welfare of the American team would be improved by a higher payment than what was first discussed, it was still a bargain.

"Okay. Next time, if there is a next time, I want to be consulted on the change of plans. Understand?" Briggle said.

"Absolutely. We had little time, you know—" Cosette felt a rush of resentment. The American navy man was a beginner in the business of espionage, and he lectures to his teacher. So American.

"Yeah, I got it. I said okay. Now let's go see the head fisherman."

As Briggle made his way to the aft of the dhow he noticed at the helm station that the boat had a Fathometer and a large compass. It would have been a bonus to have a radar aboard, something that would be found on virtually all modern fishing boats and many pleasure craft in America. But, Briggle reminded himself, this was the Gulf.

Iraqi Intelligence officer Mohammed Fahdi, the man now posing as the fisherman al-Ammal, emerged from below decks just as Stockton Briggle was about to descend the ladder.

"Ah," Cosette said, "Mohammed. This is the American—"

"Jones," Briggle said, interrupting the Frenchman.

"An honor, Mr. Jones. Is that what I am to call you, sir? Only Jones?"

"Yeah, that'll do just fine, Mohammed. Serviceable boat you have here. Want to show me the power plant?" Briggle said.

"The—?"

"Engine."

"Yes, Jones, of course," Fahdi said deferentially, leading the way back down the ladder.

The ladder had a half-dozen steps to the cabin deck. On the immediate left, or port side, was a food preparation area containing a cutting board, food stowage compartments, a spigot running from a gravity fed fifty-gallon water tank, and a crude sink. On the starboard side of the cabin was a UHF radio transceiver and a small area where charts could be read. There were two bunks on each side of the main cabin but they were bereft of mattresses or blankets, probably a good thing, Briggle thought. Someone, probably the owner, Mohammed, had left a large, zippered, athletic bag on one of them. There was a stout, wooden table that swung down from the top bulkhead to feed as many as six men, two on each side and one at either end.

As Briggle took in the boat's accommodations quickly, assessing them to be more than adequate for the purposes of transporting a dozen men, including the fishing boat's crew, he turned to see that Mohammed had hardly moved after setting foot below decks.

"So?" Briggle cocked his head, waiting for the skipper to discuss the dhow's power. It had a single mast on deck and while a sail may help lower the fuel bill over a period of time for the fisherman, they were going to use max engine power from the minute they shoved off from this pier, the navy officer thought.

Mohammed bowed slightly at the waist, but did not move toward the engine.

"Diesel?" Briggle asked.

"Yes," Mohammed nodded cautiously, but remained where he stood, shifting his eyes quickly to Cosette then back to Briggle.

Briggle waited, anticipating that the owner of this boat

would be eager to show off what he had below decks. Unless . . . The navy officer took a harder look at the fisherman. The man's moustache was neatly trimmed as was his hair. He had a light beard, but for a Muslim, Briggle thought it was a very recent growth. When the fisherman had first appeared Briggle had noticed his hands. They were dirty, but not from ground-in soil, the kind that permeates every pore of one's skin when one makes his livelihood from machinery and the grime that goes with manual labor.

"What kind is it? The Japanese are making very good marine diesels," Briggle said, casting his bait. The flush-ring handle that would open up the engine hatch cover was at his feet, but the Arab never looked down. Like he didn't know it was there.

Mohammed hesitated only momentarily before responding. "Jones, I have only now bought this boat and I am embarrassed that I cannot give you answers to all that you ask. You will forgive me, I hope?" Fahdi asked, submissively.

Briggle hesitated only for a moment before turning on what he hoped was a warm smile. "Sure. Not a problem. She's a damn nice boat and she's just what we were looking for, eh, Cyrille?"

Cosette's eyes shifted quickly from Fahdi and back to Briggle, a fleeting signal but one that Briggle did not misinterpret. He waved a hand nonchalantly, as though the whole affair was a done deal and all was well.

"Good," Briggle said, turning toward the ladder. "Then we'll be back first thing in the morning and—"

The blow with a lead cudgel to the back of Briggle's head was delivered with the measured force born of practice. Mohammad Fahdi could ill-afford to kill the American before he could be made to talk.

"*Zut la chance!*" Cosette blurted, knowing even as he spoke that bad luck had nothing to do with it.

"It would happen in any case. Help me," Fahdi said after he had lowered the cabin eating table to the deck and dropped its supporting legs. He grasped Briggle under the arms and heaved. Fahdi's spare frame provided too little mass to raise the two-hundred-pound navy officer to the table. "I said *help*," the Iraqi Intelligence officer hissed at the Frenchman. Cosette quickly lent a hand and between them they managed to heft the American onto his back on the table. Fahdi placed his fingers roughly on the American's eye and opened it, shining a flashlight directly into the pupil, then did the same to the other.

He grunted. "Well, he will be able to tell us what we need to know." Fahdi moved with deliberation as he pulled the athletic bag from a bunk. He dropped the leather blackjack into the bag and began removing other pieces of equipment that were the distinguishing tools of his trade. Handcuffs and leg irons were first. Fahdi snapped them onto the prostrate American quickly, making sure that they were tight. A man could generate enormous power under the stress of great pain. Fahdi had seen hardened steel chains broken by men while being tortured. He had even once witnessed a man cut off his own hand to escape. Escape in that case took the form of suicide. It was always a net loss to the state when a prisoner upset the questioner's timetable. Fahdi could not, under any conditions, allow that to happen here.

Fahdi dipped into his bag to come up with a proper gag. One had to be very careful of the kind of scream reduction device one applied. Crudely stuffing rags, sponges, tennis balls, and other objects into the subject's mouth, and taping it closed, could very easily lead to death. Fahdi had seen that occur more than once. He took pride in the device he now fixed over the American's mouth. It resembled a respirator except that it did not cover the nose. The device allowed air in through the open mouth. It was sufficiently latticed with small membranes to suppress almost any scream, but remained open, allowing perfectly clear words to be heard, when they were spoken in a normal voice.

The nasal passages needed to be kept open and functioning without undue amounts of blood running into the prone subject's trachea. That might cause drowning. So Fahdi rummaged through a smaller zippered bag, about the size that would contain shaving gear, until he found the inserts he was looking for. They were made of semi-rigid silicone, about two inches long. Even though the American officer was beginning to regain consciousness, Fahdi was ready to insert the passageway protectors, and he proceeded. There was clearly no need to spare the American pain so the Intelligence officer merely jammed in the devices, one by one, deep into Briggle's sinus cavities, using the palm of his hand to generate enough force. He then ran rubber tubes through them into the trachea guaranteeing an uninterrupted flow of air into the lungs. The extreme pain catapulted Briggle into instant awareness, but fortunately for Fahdi, the previously fitted respirator spared his ears.

And, of course, the ears of Cosette who looked on in utter fascination while Fahdi prepped his subject. Fahdi had no time to hold the hand of his co-conspirator. He could only hope that Cosette would reflect the sturdy values of his countrymen. French means of interrogation were legendary in North Africa and elsewhere.

"Commander Briggle, can you hear me?" Fahdi asked his captive. "Answer, please."

"Yes," came the subdued but clear response from Briggle.

"Good. In the interest of all concerned it will be best if you continue to answer my questions without hesitation. Fully and truthfully. Do you understand that, Commander?"

Briggle hesitated to consider his answer. In the heartbeat that he waited, even as he was formulating his reply, he had taken too long. Using a pressure spray can, Fahdi placed the nozzle of the can into the rubber tube and squirted a chemical into one of the American's nostrils. Cosette heard the beginning of a scream from Briggle, but it was quickly dampened by the respirator over his nose and mouth. The body convulsed and Briggle pulled mightily against the chains that held his body.

"I asked you to answer my questions fully and honestly. Do you understand, Commander?"

Without hesitation Briggle nodded his head vigorously.

"Better," the Iraqi said. "We know what you call your new Special Operations teams. They are Leopard teams. Yes?"

Briggle hesitated slightly, but spoke before Fahdi was able to administer another burst of—what? Acid? "Yes," he said, nodding for emphasis.

"Good. And you are in contact with them by radio," Fahdi said, posing the question in the form of a statement to be confirmed or denied.

"Yes," Briggle said again through the mask.

"And where are they now?" Fahdi asked, calmly, expecting total cooperation by his tone.

"Don't know," Briggle said.

Fahdi frowned. He raised the chemical spray to the rubber nasal hose once more.

"No," Briggle said, "they are moving. We don't know where yet."

Fahdi let loose another, longer, spray into the tube.

Cosette winced, closing his eyes and turning away from the writhing agony that gripped the American officer. A pathetic scream barely escaping from the fiendish mask.

"You are lying," Fahdi said, maintaining his calm. "We have sophisticated radio intercept capabilities and we know that your Leopard team was east of Baghdad three days ago. Commander? Can you hear me?"

Briggle was still writhing in pain, straining to clear his head enough to respond. He nodded.

"That is yes?" Fahdi asked.

Briggle nodded again, and croaked, "Yes."

"I do not pretend that we have decoded their signal, but there is no question where they were when they sent it. They were surrounded by our forces at the time and they murdered one of our soldiers. Only a sandstorm saved them. My question is, where are they now?"

Anticipating the next administration of the chemical Briggle began to shake, straining against the chains that held him. Fahdi raised the can once again to the rubber tube. He stopped at the sound of Cosette's interjection.

"He could be telling the truth, Fahdi. All that is left to know is when they expect to arrive here. They will want our directions to the rendezvous. We can make it anywhere."

Fahdi hesitated. He looked first to the Frenchman, then down to his American captive. Fahdi, in fact, knew that most of what Cosette was saying was true. There had to be at least one more message from Briggle to the Leopard team to inform them when and where to meet. Briggle's chest was heaving from the terrible pain the acid had caused to his entire respiratory system.

"All right, Briggle, I will give you a chance to live," Fahdi lied. "I only want the return of the traitor who deserted our country. If you tell me what I wish to know, there is no reason to kill you. I give you my word. Truth for mercy. Are we agreed, then?"

Briggle nodded quickly. "Yes," he managed to say.

"Very well. We need the frequencies on which to contact your teams. We need to know the passwords, and we need the code word for Colonel Baraniq. And we need your password to identify you to the Leopard team leader. What is his name?"

Briggle again began to thrash nervously, pulling at his steel tethers, though weaker. Fahdi watched for a moment. "Well?" Then he leaned menacingly closer to the American navy officer and bared his teeth. "You will tell me, Briggle. You will tell me because I will cut you open and slice you into fish bait very slowly so that you feel each slice of the knife."

For emphasis Fahdi went to his black bag and came up with a scalpel and a surgical saw and held them in front of Briggle's eyes. "You see? You will take a very long time to die and, to you, it will seem forever. Now, Briggle, let us begin."

Cosette rushed to the upper deck of the boat, his hand over his mouth.

CHAPTER 13

Frogpond 2 had lost its chance to cross the Tigris bridge during the sandstorm. The bridges would be watched and not even the cover of darkness could get them over. They would have to find another way. They would have to float the DPV with the equipment they had lashed to the vehicle. The team's GPS's were working again, the satellite clusters being received perfectly. There was a location six kilometers to their south that was sufficiently deserted and the river narrow enough for a safe crossing. But they were running out of darkness. McTaggart was taking his turn behind the wheel while Entzion manned the gun mount and Haggar was strapped in to McTaggart's right. Night vision glasses allowed the team to travel more than forty miles per hour and to detect Iraqi units that were out looking for them. Twice since the sandstorm passed they had spotted elements of what could have been the Republican 26th Division before they could see or hear the DPV. With that advantage, McTaggart was able to detour well around their location.

"Tommy," McTaggart called to Entzion. With the end of the sandstorm they could now keep receivers in place in their ears. The lieutenant felt that at night, with the ever present threat of enemy action coming from any direction, the radio earpieces should be worn.

"Yes, sir," Entzion's voice came back.

"Both guns operating?" he asked.

"I put a poncho over the 240 last time I cleaned it. She'll go, Ross," he said. McTaggart was not worried about the team keeping their weapons operable, but he knew that breach blocks, the moving parts of an automatic weapon, were extremely susceptible to sand and dust. Didn't hurt to ask.

"We're coming up on the Tigris. We have to cross, so stay sharp," he said into his lip mike.

"Someone's about to let the shade up," Haggar said with respect to the coming dawn. Sunlight, like an implacable enemy, loomed closer.

Then, suddenly, there was the river, impossible to see until they topped a sand dune and dropped onto its muddy shore. The night vision glasses cast a greenish hue upon the water, with just enough moonlight above to give it an otherworldly glow. Without pausing, McTaggart turned the wheels and began running the DPV along the bank of the river. They arrived at an area that afforded reasonable cover with a small growth of reeds and a sizable rock nearby. They could halt the vehicle long enough to put on the float.

After turning off the ignition, the men remained motionless for several long minutes while they listened and looked about them. They seemed to be alone. They couldn't hear even a distant sound such as an engine running or voices talking. Eventually satisfied, McTaggart said, "Let's get it done."

Within less than five minutes, the three Leopard team men had broken out a synthetic fabric camouflage cover and laid it partially in the water. McTaggart then started the engine and slowly pulled the DPV onto the cover, again shutting down the engine. By now two of the men, McTaggart and Haggar, had removed their night vision glasses while they hurriedly raised the cover up around the vehicle and fastened it to the upper frame that circled the vehicle. They laced the eyelets with parachute cord and tied it firmly. The upper part of the boatlike vehicle was left open to accommodate the top gunner who had to remain in place during the most vulnerable part: the crossing.

"Want me to take the gun, Tom?" Haggar asked Entzion.

"I like it up here," Entzion said.

McTaggart looked closely at Entzion. His eyes were red. All of them had bloodshot eyes from the long hours in irritating sand, but Entzion's were different. They were ablaze. It was now cool in the very early morning hours, but the Leopard team man was sweating heavily.

"Here," McTaggart said, never taking his eyes from Entzion, "drink some water." He presented the water bag to Entzion's left hand, but Entzion placed his M-4 against the wrapped DPV and accepted the water bottle with his now free right hand.

"Take your glove off, Tommy," McTaggart said. "The left one. I want to see how your hand is doing."

"It's okay, Skipper," he said, haphazardly fingering his glove.

"Can't you get it off?" McTaggart asked.

Entzion did not answer.

"Here, let me help," Haggar said, gently taking the hand and carefully cutting the glove from his comrade's hand.

As the glove peeled back, the red, swollen hand and fingers of Entzion's hand popped out like cooked sausages.

"Holy shit," McTaggart said. "Sit down, Tommy."

He and Haggar helped Entzion to the ground. McTaggart leaned toward the trooper.

"Did the Quack give you something for this?" he asked, referring to the wound caused from the scorpion sting.

"Antivenom," Entzion said. "Sometimes it works—" Entzion shrugged his shoulders. This time, it appeared to McTaggart, it wasn't working.

"Got any left?" he asked Entzion.

"Took it all, Lieutenant."

They should take Entzion's temperature, medicate him somehow, and get him some rest. The problem was they didn't have time. They were exposed with the sun almost full. McTaggart took one more look at the trooper's arm. Was that a red line he saw beginning up the arm? The light wasn't good enough to know for sure.

"Tom, we can't stop now. Get inside the vehicle and we'll paddle, me and Lee," McTaggart said, lifting Entzion off the bank of the river even as he spoke. They helped the stricken team member up the side of the wrapped DPV and let him settle inside. McTaggart and Haggar put their shoulders to the vehicle and slowly pushed the machine off the soft sand of the river's edge and into the flowing water. The lieutenant and Haggar jumped aboard and, taking up paddles they had laid out, began stroking hard for the distant shore.

McTaggart had estimated the distance to the far side at two hundred meters. And he had tossed floating items onto the water, timing their progress over a measured distance to assess the speed of the current. At five to six miles per hour, Taggart estimated that they would make it across less than seven hundred feet downstream. Now, halfway across the river, he wished he had driven the DPV downstream to recce the river at that position. He glanced next to him to see Haggar, no doubt thinking along with him, pulling hard on his short paddle. Both men were extremely anxious to reach a place where they could get at their weapons and, even more important, to get the tarpaulin off their vehicle so they could run.

They were perhaps fifty feet from shore when a vehicle appeared atop a sand dune that ran parallel with the river's bank. McTaggart and Haggar involuntarily ducked their heads as the machine stopped. It was light enough now to clearly make out that the vehicle was military, a light personnel carrier of some kind, though McTaggart could not catagorize it. Unlike their own DPV, however, the Iraqi machine had no gun mount that he could see, nor did he believe it had armored plating. McTaggart and Haggar had stopped rowing, keeping their heads down to present the lowest possible profile.

A soldier stepped out of the car and peered through binoculars in a wide arc, turning his body as he did so. As he looked up and down the river his eyes settled upon Frogpond 2. The man leaned forward as though he could not quite make out what he was seeing, then dropped down the side of the sand dune, moving toward the water's edge, to see more clearly.

"Fuck it, Ross, we shoot him," Haggar said urgently.

"Right," McTaggart replied. As he turned toward the mounted gun Entzion, anticipating the order, had opened up with two short bursts. The soldier was caught in mid-step. He was blown first backwards, then he pitched forward and began rolling head over heels down the side of the river bank, stopping only when his body was touching the water.

McTaggart and Haggar paddled hard to reach the bank. When the DPV touched the muddy shore they leaped over the side, already slicing through the tarpaulin bindings, letting them fall where they were.

"Leave it," McTaggart snapped. He jumped behind the wheel, started the engine, and drove the DPV out of the soft sand. With Haggar still pulling himself aboard, he had the pedal on the floorboard, grinding through the gears in pursuit of the Iraqi machine. They could not let it escape.

As they shot over the lip of the river bank they were surprised to see that the Iraqi car was not running away but was heading directly for them. Entzion opened up with the machine gun from above while Haggar used his M-4, firing from the shoulder. The combination of penetrating rounds from the DPV at almost point-blank range was shattering to the Iraqi machine and its men.

The windscreen literally disintegrated, tires were shredded, and soldiers riding in the back of the car were struck with rounds from both the M-240 and Haggar's M-4. Entzion then depressed the barrel of the M-240 and raked the target again, this time the tracer incendiary rounds igniting fuel spewing from the Iraqi gas tank. It all happened so fast that none of the Iraqi's had a chance to exit the machine when it erupted. Two were ejected, sent flying through the air by the force of the explosion. When McTaggart stopped the DPV the machines were parallel to each other, less than ten meters apart.

The Americans, Haggar and McTaggart, immediately went to the Iraqis who had been injured, but were still alive. McTaggart looked down at the first man he came to. It was difficult to see where he was wounded, but in the end he knew it didn't matter. The second Iraqi who was still alive was stunned, burned, and struggling to regain his footing, unaware that he was covered by the Americans. Even as he was turning around Haggar put a round through the man's forehead, then turned toward McTaggart.

Young as he was, McTaggart had been trained so thoroughly that he had anticipated a moment like this. There was no doubt in his mind about what he had to do. There was absolutely no way they could support a prisoner, wounded or not. It was equally certain that the Iraqi soldier could not be left alive to report their position and strength to his superiors. The lieutenant and his two teammates would never make it out of the desert alive. Indeed, the entire mission would have failed. As he raised his M-4 and pointed it at the Iraqi, the man showed no fear. His eyes were steady and he had almost finished intoning, that "Allah is great" when the burst took him in the heart.

It was fully daylight when they picked up their tarpaulin, covered their tracks in the sand, and returned to the scene of the firefight. They discussed their situation quickly and rationally. They could dig as fast as they possibly could, but they would need a large hole to hide the evidence of an entire vehicle and its crew. With Entzion's hand swollen to more than twice its normal size and in his weakened condition he could handle a gun but not a shovel. The chances were good that elements of the Iraqi detachment to which the car belonged would eventually come looking for them. That being so, the Leopard team would almost certainly be found as well, even if they were well camouflaged.

The alternative was to put as much distance as possible from the action site and hope they were not seen crossing an expanse of vast desert. They would raise a cloud of dust, to be sure, and traveling fast there would be no way to obscure their tracks in the sand. But running had a couple of advantages. It would not be obvious to Iraqi elements that the tracks were not made by one of their own vehicles. The second advantage was that traveling at high speed they would either make the rendezvous with Frogpond 1 or come upon a natural layup where they could safely hide until night.

"That's it, then. We make a high-speed run. You get on the gun, Lee," McTaggart said to Haggar. Like all Leopard team members, Entzion was good on the MG and every other weapon, but he was visibly losing strength and was fighting to hold his concentration despite his fever. McTaggart approached the communication specialist and began moving him carefully into the DPV.

"Drink some water, Tommy. A lot of it. Go on." McTaggart stayed with Entzion until he was satisfied that he was drinking all of the water he could hold. "Here," he said, giving him two capsules of high-strength ibuprofen to reduce the pain and counteract some of the infection.

"I don't need 'em, Skipper," he said, his eyes fluttering.

"Take both of them, anyway." McTaggart wished that Quack was there. He pulled Entzion's sleeve up. He could now see a red line beginning to form above Entzion's wrist. He put a pack behind the radio man's head, then strapped him into the back seat.

Haggar was standing behind McTaggart, waiting for an appraisal. "I don't like the red line," the lieutenant said.

"Nope. I don't either," Haggar said.

"I think we've got to get him to the Quack ASAP," McTaggart said. It meant that they would be forced to travel in daylight, with no protection, but it was the only way. "If we get locked into a pursuit, Lee, I'm not going to the railroad bridge."

McTaggart meant that he would not lead the Iraqis to the Frogpond 1 rendezvous location. If they were caught out in the open, they would fight their way out or they would die where they stood.

"Understand, Ross. Let it rip."

The meeting took place in Bushehr, Iran. It was a convenient location for all concerned. The two were Fayed al-Barzun, an Iraqi army parachute officer, and Moammar Rumallye of the Hizballah, or Party of God, and assassin Nabil Zibri, a name rising ever higher on the list of Allah's purifying agents. The Hizballah, founded by Shi'ites in Lebanon in 1983, had been supported, nurtured, and lavishly funded from its very beginnings by the state of Iran. The organization had grown defiantly in size and lethality despite the intelligence agencies and military hardware focused upon it by the Israel Defense Force and the Mossad, not to mention the United States intelligence organizations and many of those of Europe. Its training locations were everywhere in the Bekka Valley of Lebanon, and those became the targets of Israeli air force and ground units who flew bombing sorties and armored incursions into Lebanon almost nonstop for twenty years. As fast as Israel, and later the United States, could knock out a terrorist training camp another would be built in its place. The Hizballah never experienced a shortage of volunteers who would gladly pick up a gun for the chance to attack the "godless West." The arch villain opposing Allah the Good was America, the living embodiment of Satan here on Earth and the fount of all social ills.

The Hizballah operated on two levels, the "political" one, that often appeared in telephone books around the world. Maintaining a public address facilitated the collec-

tion of money to support their "charitable" activities.
The second arm of the Hizballah was geared to extreme
guerilla warfare directed specifically against Israel and,
whenever possible, America and American citizens wherever they could be found. Hizballah targets were not
necessarily military. It operated on the belief that civilians, including men, women, and children, were legiti-
mate targets for Hizballah assassins.

There was never a shortage of funding for their enterprises that included buying and distributing arms, and
using weapons of terror, including chemical and biological agents. A number of splinter groups had been
spawned by the Hizballah and they had been handsomely
subsidized by Iran who openly listed Hizballah and assorted terror groups in their published national budget.
Other nations of Islam and wealthy Muslims spent hundreds of millions on their favorite terrorist groups, but
usually less openly. There had been for almost two decades close, albeit informal, connections among Islamic
nations that included shared intelligence as well as shared
personnel. And it was personnel that occasioned the
meeting in Bushehr.

"The traitor Baraniq was clever," Fayed al-Barzun
said as he daintily chose for himself another *kunafi*, a
pastry stuffed with sweet white cheese, nuts, and syrup.
"He was able to move his family out of Iraq without the
slightest knowledge of the *Jihaz al-Himaya al-Khas*.
There are three sons, you see."

"But he had two wives and several daughters—"
Zibri began.

"I hardly think he would return for their sake," al-
Barzun said as though he were discussing laundry that
had been left behind.

"Is that so? Then what makes you believe that he is
not in America even as we speak?" Zibri asked.

"Because he was still in Baghdad two weeks ago. We
know this. He was met by an American desert specialist
team. We believe they parachuted into Iran from the
north, in the Dahuk region. We had three vehicles de-

stroyed from one of the reconnaissance patrols who
searched for them."

"Yes? And how large was the American unit?"

"They had two vehicles. How many men, we are not
sure. Perhaps eight. Even one or two more," al-Barzun
answered.

"I understand there are many units like them in Iraq.
American, British." Moammar Rumallye said to the
Iraqi officer.

Al-Barzun grudgingly nodded his head. It was an ongoing embarrassment for the Iraqi military that belliger-
ent foreign army units could operate within their
country's national boundaries, even fighting battles, with
impunity. There were, as well, Israeli units there. Zibri
had heard that Unit 217 of the Sayeret Duvdevan was
in the Anbar desert. Zibri again looked at Fayed for
information about the Israeli special forces team.

"Yes," he sighed deeply. "They are very good. Well
armed. We don't know that they are 217, but they are
Sayeret, no doubt," he admitted.

"Well, they are only Jews," Zibri said, dryly, knowing
that the Iraqi was discomforted again. Frankly, Zibri did
not care. He did not have the highest regard for the Iraqi
army, even for their so-called special units.

"Please, Nabil," Rumallye said, softly. "They will catch
them. Even now Fayed's soldiers have set an ambush for
them that will bring the traitor to justice, but they need
our help."

Zibri had not been kindly disposed toward Iraqis for
as long as he could remember. They were arrogant. And
they were thieves. He very clearly remembered their
march into Kuwait, thumbing their noses at their neighbors, even eyeing still another peaceful nation, Saudi
Arabia, as their next conquest. Nor did Zibri have any
use at all for Saddam Hussein. Still, when Muslims were
forced to choose sides against the Americans and the
Jews, there could be no personal animosity involved in
the decision.

"What kind of help?" he asked. Even though his question sounded conditional he had already made up his mind that he would do everything in his power to move against an American special operations team. He knew all about them. He had studied their manuals, watched news film about them, and read everything he could get his hands on that was written by men who were on the teams.

"We will trap them as they pass west of Al Basrah, here, in the Olmām Anas wadi. They expect to be received by their own people, then to be taken to a boat in Umm Qsr," al-Barzun said.

"And to the American navy," Zibri interrupted, immediately seeing the obvious.

"That is so. They will be met not by other Americans but by one of ours," the Iraqi said.

"And you will have an overwhelming force to deal with them," Zibri suggested.

"Yes. Look here," al-Barzun invited Zibri's attention to a map of the area in question, southern Iraq and northern Kuwait, the Al Faw inlet that reached all the way to Umm Qsr. Oil tankers and merchant ships were loaded there. "This is where we want to trap them, between Basrah and Ar Rumaylah," the Iraqi said, using his finger to point to a location on the map. "This wadi is spanned by a bridge, here, and the pipeline. Our forces are moving into positions on either side of the pipeline on the near banks of the wadi. Almost impossible for the Americans to see them," al-Barzun said, expansively.

Zibri bent over to look at the scale more closely. The distance between Ar Rumaylah and Umm Qsr looked to be about fifty kilometers. There was a highway linking the two towns, running south along the east side of the Zubayr oil fields for the first ten kilometers. Paralleling the highway was a railroad that originated in Baghdad and terminated at Umm Qsr. The port city of Umm Qsr was situated astride Kuwait and Iraq. The shipping facilities, docks, pump heads, and road systems were used by both countries by necessity without much concern for borderlines.

"How do you know that is the way they will choose?" Zibri asked, skeptically.

"Because that is the rendezvous, you see. It is we who are directing the extraction of their team. It is perfect. The American ships have placed this phase of the operation into our hands and the so-called Leopard team has been so instructed," al-Barzun beamed as he admired his own plan.

Zibri had to admit that he was impressed. It was simple, with few things to go wrong, but it took tireless and detailed preparation. It appeared the Iraqi army might redeem itself in this case.

"So. What do you want from us?" Zibri asked, nodding toward Moammar Rumallye.

"I am aware of your specialty, and I admire it," the Iraqi said. "We would be very grateful if you would be our, ah, insurance in this deployment. Should any of the Americans get away."

"Especially, if by some miracle, Colonel Harun Baraniq escapes," Zibri added.

"Exactly so. We would like to have experts in civilian clothing on the Kuwait side of the border to cut off any possible escape," al-Barzun said, his statement actually forming a question.

It was precisely the kind of operation for which he and his snipers had trained for so many months, Zibri thought, as he continued to look at the map. He could easily do the task with ten men. Probably fewer.

"For the greater glory of Allah, and in the interest of helping our brothers, we would be honored to support your action against the enemy, Fayed. Isn't that so, Moammar?" Zibri said.

"Our commitment is total, brother," Rumallye said, embracing the Iraqi soldier, kissing each cheek of his face.

"Not that you will need our help," Zibri suggested.

"You are good to say so, brother," al-Barzun said, kissing Zibri in his turn.

CHAPTER 14

They had dug deep into the bed of the wadi, looking to find water. During the rainy season the wadi could be a raging torrent of water, sweeping down from the higher elevation of the Euphrates River in the An Najaf province. At six feet they found it, beginning with mud; then augered deeper until they could run a tap down and come up with mostly water. They could then pump the liquid through their portable hydrosystems and into their collapsible water bags. They added water purification tablets to eliminate giardia, bacteria, and even viruses.

The work was carried out while Frogpond 1 was laid up under their camouflage netting. They had placed their DPV tightly under the approach to the railroad bridge as possible; then placed the netting over the top of that. They had meticulously erased any sign of tracks the night they had arrived at a location eighteen kilometers south of the town of As Samawah through which the Euphrates flowed. Unless a patrol approached along the wadi rather than along the railroad tracks their position would have been extremely hard to detect. They were well into the no-fly zone set up by the United Nations and enforced by United States air power so they had little fear of being spotted by air. They had neither seen nor heard any sign

of aircraft for the past sixteen hours waiting for Frogpond 2. But ground unit hunting parties were intense.

Trains containing military troops and weapons system
had passed over the railroad bridge no less than four
times during the day, and desert vehicles had come as
close as ninety meters of their layup position. The closer
the Leopard team got to the south of the country, the
greater number of Iraqi elements were nearby looking
for them. The south of Iraq narrowed near the sea creating a military venturi effect.

Frogpond 2 was overdue. And it was getting dark; time
to go. Mears had received a three message group from
their US Navy liaison that would provide them with
transportation to a task force in the Persian Gulf. The
code name for the navy liaison was *Limoges*. Mears was
familiar with the French town of that name. It was well
known for fine chinaware, hence the challenge was *Teacup* and the countersign was *Porcelain*.

"Take down the nets, Joe?" Rodriguez asked his boss.

"Negative," Mears said, once more sweeping the limitless expanse of desert to the north and to the west,
most likely directions from which McTaggart would
come. When he lowered the binoculars he could feel the
eyes of his team upon him. "How's Griffon?" Mears
asked Quack, using Baraniq's mythical bird code name.

"Good. He's drinking water like a fish. Eating, too,"
Quack said.

"We have to take good care of him," Mears said, still
watching the horizon for a telltale sign of dust in the
setting sun.

"That's just what we're doing, Joe," Quack said,
soothingly.

Mears moved slightly under the camouflage netting
where he could see Baraniq. The defector seemed to be
asleep. The temperature had lowered only a few degrees
because the sun was no longer direct and sleep was now
easier to come by.

"Key the receiver, Manny," Mears said to Rodriguez.

The Cuban was now radio operator since Entzion was with Frogpond 2.

"It's on auto, Joe," Rodriguez replied.

"Check it anyway," Mears said, again using his binoculars to sweep the distant horizon. He was now in the awkward position of not having enough light for the binoculars, but a few minutes too early for using the NVOs (night vision optics).

"Yes, sir," Rodriguez said, turning his attention to the radio. A brief click into the transceiver's memory bank showed no new messages had been received. Rodriguez took a last look at the hydropump, insuring that it was clean, clear of even the finest silt, before packing it into its storage place on the DPV.

"You in a hurry to pack up, Manny?" Mears snapped.

"No hurry at all, Joe," Rodriguez responded cooly.

There was not a breath of air. Stars were now out, sparkling through the small pores of the camouflage netting over the Leopard team's head. Sweat was continuing to be pulled out of their bodies by the incredibly dry air. They could sometimes hide from the blistering sun, but there was no way of escaping the water-hungry molecules of air around them.

"Have a drink, Joe," Quack said, offering an open water bottle.

Mears glanced at it, then turned away in irritation. But Quack did not move his hand that held out the water. Mears took it and had a drink. He handed it back to the medic but Quack did not accept it.

"Have another one. I'm buying," he said.

Rather than argue, Mears did as he was directed. This time he took a substantial amount of the stuff into his body before handing it back to Quack.

"Thanks."

"I'm pretty sure they must teach that in Officer's Candidate School, don't they, sir? I mean, don't they instruct you never to put water in your mouth unless it's attached to pubic hair or the frozen part of a drink at the officer's club?"

Mears looked at Quack's straight face for a long minute before looking over his shoulder at Rodriguez. Rodriguez was shaking like an out of balance washing machine on the rinse cycle. He held his hands over his face, rolled over on his side, and continued to vibrate.

Mears slowly shook his head. "Fuck," he said.

He removed one of the NVOs from its protective cover and, snapping on the power source, began scanning the horizon once more. Rodriguez and Quack were also looking into the darkness, now assisted with night vision glasses similar to Mears's.

"We should go," came a baritone voice near them.

"Thus spake the Griffon," Mears mumbled to himself. "We will, Colonel," Mears said to Baraniq.

"It is dark," Baraniq said.

Mears said nothing, but his jaw clenched. He was aware that by now they should have struck the layup and been heading south. McTaggart had used up his time. They were dead. He could not imagine that there could be an alternative, certainly not capture. Mears's course was still over the desert and they would have to cover one-hundred-fifty miles, two-hundred-fifty kilometers, and that was as the crow flies. Their reception committee would wait two nights; then egress from Iraq became problematical. If Mears continued to wait the mission could well be lost. It might even be lost now.

"All right," he said, "let's go." Quack immediately began snapping down water bags and covering holes that had previously been dug to accept waste. Rodriguez bent to the task of pulling camouflage net stakes from the ground. The net slowly collapsed around the DPV.

"What's that?" Baraniq said, looking off into the distance.

"What?" Mears repeated, unable to imagine what the former Iraqi officer was looking at. Mears followed the man's gaze, raising the NVOs to his eyes.

"Dust trail," he said softly. It could be anything or anybody. "Coming this way. Manny, get on the MG. Quack, handle the 60." Mears referred to the rapid fire

Mk-60 grenade launcher that complimented the 30mm low-recoil cannon carried on Frogpond 2's vehicle.

All three of the Leopard team were now wearing night vision equipment as they sighted in their weapons at their five o'clock position. Mears was hoping to see a single vehicle in front of all that dust. If there was more he would not attempt to stand and fight. They would fight, but on the run, trying to gain as much ground as possible before they fell to the enemy. If they ran, he had already determined that they would turn southwest on a course of one-hundred-ninety-six degrees for Saudi Arabia. He had few illusions that the Saudis would welcome the American commandoes with open arms, but it was for sure a higher percentage play than Umm Qsr that was fifty miles farther.

"What do you see, Manny?" Mears asked the Cuban who was fingering the machine gun.

For a long moment there was no response from the gunner who peered into the distance. "Low to the ground. One, I think. Could be—" Rodriguez hesitated. "Well, fuck me!"

"It's them, Joe!" Quack said, standing up in the DPV, holding onto the cage bars for a better view. There was no doubt about it. As the vehicle approached at high speed they could make out the features more clearly with each second that passed.

"Okay, let's be ready. Let's don't spend anymore time here than we have to," Mears said. He began to walk forward, snapping on the safety and slinging his M-4 over his shoulder.

McTaggart was behind the wheel of their DPV, Haggar on the gun mount, and Entzion, instead of riding to McTaggart's right in a bucket seat, was in the center compartment, his head back. Mears could see immediately that none of them looked good, especially the one-time Navy SEAL, Entzion.

"Greetings from the Cradle of Civilization," Mears said to McTaggart. "What's with Tommy?"

McTaggart stepped out of the DPV stiffly. They had driven for thirty hours without stop, without sleep.

"Bad hand, Joe. Real bad," McTaggart said, accepting the offer of water from Mears. "Tastes good," he said after a long drink. "We ran out at noon yesterday."

"Quack," Mears said, turning toward the medic, but Quack was already helping Entzion out of the DPV. Using a thin thermal blanket to cover his light, Quack shined a flashlight onto Entzion's swollen hand. It looked more like a melon with five bumps on it than an extension of a human arm.

"Take it easy, Tommy," Quack said, gently patting Entzion on the shoulder. From his zippered medical bag, Quack removed several items including a stethoscope and placed it on Entzion's chest. He looked into Entzion's eyes carefully, and into his mouth. Then he began to examine the wounded hand again. He worked his way up Entzion's arm and he spoke to the SpecOps man in soft tones, asking questions, not always getting an answer from the nearly delirious soldier. He gently poured water into the man's mouth, careful that Entzion not choke, but continually giving him more of the fluid. Quack set up an IV in Entzion's good arm and started a fast drip of antibiotics and water. The plastic line had an access into which Quack could insert any other drugs while the drip was still going.

Quack removed a book from the medical bag. By now the team had jury-rigged a light shield around the two men and lit a pressurized adjustable camp light. Quack began to read from his book.

"What do you think?" McTaggart asked Mears.

"I think the Dodgers might surprise you with their pitching staff. Problem is they've never been hitters, so that's still questionable this year. And they can't play little ball. It just isn't part of their psyche, if you know what I mean. But they can go a long way with pitching. Look at the D-Backs as a perfect example," Mears said.

He raised his NVOs and scanned the horizon.

"So what do *you* think?" he asked McTaggart in return.

"I think we gotta be out of here in a matter of minutes,

ot hours. I think we're probably up to our assholes in raqi mobile units and just don't see 'em," McTaggart aid.

"Skipper," Rodriguez said to Mears, "we have a message from Limoges. They want an ETA and a position eport."

"Encrypted?" Mears said, his brows knitted.

"Yes, sir. It's our stuff, for sure," Rodriguez conrmed.

Mears didn't like it. Sloppy thinking down the line. ending out position reports even using the encryption nd decryption transceivers they carried was not a smart lea. Technically, it probably didn't matter. With the urst transmitter it wasn't likely that the Iraqis could get triangulation on them and it was even less likely that hey could crack their operational crypto anytime in the ext three-thousand years.

Still.

"Request I.D. of originating American officer. Tell hem to include his AGO number. And Manny, use a Milstar frequency and copy the message to SOCCENT."

"Roger, Joe," Rodriguez said, turning immediately to he task of tapping out the message Mears wanted sent.

The Milstar satellite system turned out not quite as vonderful as the DOD wanted it to be, but it was a nifty actical communication system because it was about as lose to real time as mission personnel, like the Leopard eam, could get when they were out in the jungle. The atellites dedicated to Milstar were elliptical, semi-ynchronous orbits right over where the action was likely o be and they operated on EHF (exceptional high fre-uency). Its architecture was for the war fighter, but the ystem, while new, was becoming obsolete. Meantime, oe loved it because it was slick and quick.

Quack jerked his head at Mears, indicating that he vanted to talk away from Entzion. McTaggart stepped ff to the side with Quack and Mears to listen.

"Joe, Tommy isn't good. You know that," Quack said, hoosing his words before going on.

Mears didn't want to wait. "What've you got for him?"

The medic shook his head. "Nothing that will stop th[a] thing. I've put a lot of antibiotics into him. A lot, but don't have experience enough in whatever the hell h[e] has. I know he has gas gangrene, but there are differe[nt] forms of it, different treatment protocols. Look her[e] Joe." Quack turned his medical reference book aroun[d] so that Joe could make it out while he, Quack, held [a] flashlight. McTaggart pushed closer so that he could rea[d] over Mears's shoulder.

"What do you mean you don't know? You spent tw[o] fucking years doing this stuff. Tell me what you *think* [it] is," Mears said.

"Take a look," Quack said, pushing the book at hi[m]

"I don't have time. What's it say?" Mears wanted to kno[w]

"It looks to me like a deep, localized clostridial myos[i]tis. Spreads rapidly and it's produced by a toxin. Th[e] scorpion bite," Quack said.

"You took care of that," Mears said, his voice risin[g] in frustration.

"I gave him all the antitoxin we had, Lieutenant Colo[]nel Joseph Mears," Quack bit off the words like he wa[s] crunching ice with his teeth. "And I told him at the tim[e] and I told you at the same time that the stuff onl[y] worked in about half of the cases. And here, sir, it de[]scribes the wound site becoming red or bronze, finall[y] turning blackish green. That's Tommy's hand. It's th[e] source of the septicemia. A mortality of seventy to on[e] hundred percent can be expected in the presence of acut[e] renal failure and septicemia." Quack read from the boo[k]

Mears rubbed his eyes. "Christ. So, what are you goin[g] to do?"

Quack shook his head. "I could be wrong about th[e] kind of gangrene he's got. Most of the time it's treatabl[e] The antibiotics will kill the disease in most healthy pe[o]ple. And if Entzion is anything, he's healthy. I wish h[e] had a bullet in him. I know something about that. He[,] I'm a trauma guy. That's what they train us for."

Mears nodded his head, sadly. He patted Quack o[n]

the shoulder affectionately. "You're the best medic in the whole command, Quack."

"I was afraid you'd say that."

"It's your call. What's going to happen?" McTaggart asked, his voice remaining low.

"I think his arm has to come off," Quack said, his voice now firm.

McTaggart felt a shudder go through him. He knew that Special Operations medics were trained extensively in wounds and trauma of all kinds. They were excellent battlefield surgeons having worked for at least a year in big city emergency rooms where knife wounds and shooting victims came through in endless numbers. He also knew that Quack had the equipment with him to do the work. But would Entzion survive? McTaggart asked the question.

"I don't know," Quack said. "I wouldn't rate his chances high."

There was the component no successful surgery could give them. Time. They were totally aware that the delay the operation would take would seal their doom.

"I'll stay here with Quack," McTaggart said, quite calmly. "When he's finished—"

"Two hours," Quack said, his throat dry.

"In two hours, we'll crank up the DPV and be right behind you," McTaggart said.

"Nope. No more splitting up the unit. You get to work, Quack. We'll be right here when you're all through. Lee, help us set up some room for Quack to work. Get more light," Mears said to Haggar.

Within a few minutes the camo net and the big tarp had been raised around Entzion and Quack to contain the necessary light. The team medic had broken the seals on his sterile instruments, and placed a pre-op chemical into Entzion's IV. He began cleaning the arm he was going to amputate.

Entzion's eyes came open wide and he was suddenly coherent, unlike the fever induced semiconscious state he had fallen into a day earlier.

"Hey, Quacker," he said, his voice dreamy.

"Hey, Tommy," Quack smiled back confidently.

Entzion turned his head to look at his suppuratir hand.

"You gonna take it off, Quack?" he said.

Quack swallowed hard. "Yeah. I warned you abou picking your nose or I was going to—" he said, but h attempt at humor turning sour in his mouth.

"It's okay, Quacker."

Quack then inserted the propathol into the IV. Th anesthetic was very fast acting, and would leave no sid effects. The perfect battlefield knockout.

"Joe," Rodriguez said, returning from the team's mai radio. "Limoges transmission identifies Lieutenant Con mander Stockton R. Briggle, Unites States Navy, SPEC OPS Liaison, Task Force 28-B. There's an AGO numbe attached, but I don't know whether its good or bad. Wa me to have SOCCENT authenticate it?"

Everything sounded good. Right man, right task forc SOCCENT would not have Briggle's AGO number i front of them and it would take a while to get it. He wa getting jumpy in his old age.

"Naw. Sounds okay, Manny. But we're not giving ou any position reports. Tell 'em we'll send an ETA in si hours. And tell 'em to stay the fuck off the air unle they hear someone knocking on their door."

"Those exact words, Colonel Mears?" Rodrigue asked.

"Sure. Why not?"

More than once within the time Quack was workin on Entzion they heard engines straining through heav sand or whining at high speed down a highway five kilc meters off. Using ocular amplified light, the team saw a Iraqi unit consisting of specialized recon patrols in BTR the same kind the team had run across in northern Irac

They were probably not seen because they lacked th quality and quantity of special night vision equipment tha Leopard-1 had, Mears thought. Their line units, even th

Republican Guard, did not issue the equipment to every man. Also, it was just a fact that unless the Leopard team ran smack into a SpecWar team just like themselves at night, the Americans would have a clear advantage.

"Lee, how we doing on ammo?" Mears said.

"Ballpark? We got maybe fifty pounds of small arms per man, three-hundred rounds between the launcher and the cannon. Maybe four thousand for the M-240."

"Okay," Mears nodded. They had been lucky. No prolonged firefights. The storm slowed them up, but it got them out of the Baghdad complex, too.

"We're done, Skipper," he heard Quack say.

Mears saw the light shields taken down around Quack's OR.

"Okay," Mears said in a whisper loud enough to be heard among the Leopard team. "We're out of here in five minutes. McTaggart," he called to the young lieutenant.

McTaggart squatted with Mears as the two men examined their area maps and consulted their GPSs.

"Here's the location we meet the navy for a free ride the rest of the way," Mears said, and articulated the precise coordinates to McTaggart who, in turn, punched them into his GPS receiver. He would pass those coordinates on to the others in Frogpond 2. If they were separated for any reason they could proceed independently. "But I don't expect that to happen, Ross. We don't split up our firepower the rest of the way unless it's a tactical situation. Right?"

"Yes, sir."

"We're still looking to avoid a fight. I don't care how far out of our way we have to go to lose these suckers, I don't want to slug it out with them. So we're going to continue to run and hide. We bury us and we bury the vehicles until the danger is past, then we run again. Difference is, by the time the sun comes up we're going to be in different vehicles."

McTaggart blinked. "What's that, Joe? Our people going to drop us something new?"

"Not hardly. Fact is, by the time we get real close to the south we're getting deeper into a bottleneck. Look here," Mears said, pointing to the map of Iraq. "Gets narrow here and that means enemy military presence gets downright concentrated. You agree?"

"No question," McTaggart said, his brows knitting.

"So tonight we run at high speed. Sometime between 0200 hours and dawn we're going to find us an Iraqi vehicle out there and we're going to take it over. We bury the DPVs along with the dead Iraqis. We travel the rest of the way on paved roads as fast as we can push it. Stop for nothing. Nothing," Mears emphasized.

"What if we don't find a suitable vehicle to, ah, commandeer?" McTaggart asked.

"Plan B. The Saudi border. Fact is, we just ain't gonna make it to the navy's folks in these cars." Mears patted a cage bar on the DPV for emphasis.

"Gotcha, Joe. I agree," McTaggart said.

"Okay, now let's talk about strategy."

Mears motioned the other team members to gather around him. He short-handed what he had just explained to McTaggart, then launched into an outline of the tactics he intended to employ against a one-car, two-car, or a three-car takeover, depending upon the targets of opportunity. The team was not new to the game. They had practiced similar actions hundreds of times in a variety of venues. They were like a well-trained basketball team that knew how to put the ball through the hoop in any gym in the world defended by any opponent. Some opponents were tougher than others, but in the end the chances that they would prevail were good. Mears didn't allow himself to dwell on the old sports adage that said "you can't win 'em all."

He remembered a chapter on sports psychology in the book Julia was writing. It talked about winning attitude, how it was absolutely necessary to believe in the team's ability to come out on top and one's proficiency to support that team effort. The confidence came largely from practice and more practice. But part of that chapter in her book included the importance of not letting a single defeat destroy your ability to bounce back and win the next contest. Leopard-1 had practice and more practice behind them, and they had the confidence that came with experience and steel willpower. But they had never practiced returning from defeat. Losing for them was death.

The team that was gathered around Mears was listening to his game plan for getting them out of Iraq. There were no words uttered about coming up short, but it went without saying that if they were not going to live, neither were a whole lot of other people.

"Okay, check your radios as soon as you plug 'em in." Mears was referring to the small intercom each man wore with a headset over his ears and a lip mike touching his mouth. Once inside their vehicles they would wear hats with flaps covering their ears and tied below their chins to keep them in place. The wind that had blown a gentle fourteen knots during the day had subsided now.

"Quack," Mears beckoned to the medic as they began pulling on their headsets. "How's Tommy doing?"

"Not wonderful, Skipper. If he makes it I'll be more surprised than you."

Mears nodded. "We're going flat-out."

"I know. I've got an IV taped solid into his arm. What I'm worried about is whether the fibrin will do the job. A really rough ride could open the wound. Bleeding, you know," Quack stated the obvious. Fibrin sealant was a superglue that was mixed from a powder form with the victim's own blood.

"How long will he be out?"

"Another hour. I didn't give him anything to wake him up. What's the point? He's strapped in as tight as I can get him."

Mears patted Quack on the back before giving the signal to the rest of the team. They mounted their DPVs and took positions behind the guns. They were fully fueled from the almost depleted rubber bladders they carried and ready to roll. No lights. Each man was wearing NVOs to see what they hoped the enemy could not. Rodriguez started the engine of Frogpond 1 while McTaggart took the wheel of Frogpond 2. Haggar was at his place in the rear with the rapid-firing 30mm cannon in front of him. At 23:07 they accelerated out of their layup, the specially muffled DPV engines doing little to betray their reentry into the field.

The night was cool, even cold, but the men of Leopard-1 hardly noticed as they traveled along the once-hot desert sand at speeds of up to fifty miles per hour. Their lights remained out but they still made good time. Their run was due south with no more rivers to ford. McTaggart, now in the lead vehicle, signaled for the trailing car to halt near his. They halted the DPVs in a slight depression of sand and, creeping very slowly up the side of another small elevation, lay prone on the ground to observe a truck and a troop carrier concealed behind a building in a small village. Iraqi units did a minimum of nighttime driving because of the scarcity of night vision equipment. So their technique, Mears and McTaggart noticed, was to occupy key intersections of travel, including roads, railroad tracks, and bridges. The backroads that touched or were near villages were well patrolled.

Mears and McTaggart watched the truck and troop carrier for many minutes in the silence of the night; Rodriguez and Haggar did the same. There were no visible lights in the five crude buildings of the village. It was probably nothing more than a water stop for travelers coming from the direction of Ash Shabicha in the An Najaf province. The team was now fifty-five miles southeast of As Salman in the Muthanna province. Mears wanted to turn more sharply east for a dash past Basrah, but he had no intention of doing so in their DPVs. Tempted though he was by the apparent availability of the Iraqi vehicles, there was a bit too much activity to suit him. Still, he thought, it may not get any better farther on.

"What do you think, Ross?" he asked.

McTaggart made no immediate reply, but continued to watch the village and the vehicles. There was a brief light that showed from within the troop carrier, then went out. Two soldiers stepped out of their troop carrier and walked a few meters to the cab of the truck. One of the men opened the door on the driver's side of the cab and appeared to be speaking with a man behind the wheel. The truck door closed, the sound faintly carrying to Mears's position. Then one man returned to the carrier while the other entered the rear door of one of the buildings.

"Nobody's asleep up there," McTaggart observed.

"Haggar?" Mears asked. "See any targets?"

Haggar was aware of what Mears wanted to know. Could he hit two or more of the enemy soldiers with his sniper rifle to support a fast moving assault by the rest of the team?

"I'd like to know how many in that truck," Haggar said, whispering like the others despite the fact they were almost a quarter of a mile away.

That was the part that had made Mears feel uneasy. If twenty Iraqis piled out of the back of that covered truck while four of the team were busy assaulting the TC, they could take some hits. Mears was certain they would win the battle, but what he was looking for was an absolute, well-defined outcome with no casualties.

"All right. We pass." Mears slid backwards from the crest of the rise and resumed his position in the second vehicle.

McTaggart led them in a wide circle around the village that was so small it had no name on their navigation maps. They continued for the next hour at good speeds that sometimes topped fifty miles per hour, but probably averaged forty. Twice they spotted Iraqi patrol vehicles and once were spotted by them. But the Iraqis sent challenges by blinking lights, and the Leopard team did not respond. Instead, they stepped on the gas and drove ever faster over uneven surfaces. It seemed that the Iraqi patrol was going to give chase, but unsure that it was not simply another of their own widespread forces, they gave up pursuit within a kilometer.

The going was very hard. Each man was strapped tightly into his seat yet was still tossed around when the vehicle would slide almost sideways down the side of a sand dune or strike a rock or a gnarly piece of desert vegetation. In Frogpond 2 Quack watched Entzion carefully, reaching down from the high gun-mount to feel an artery on his neck or to sense the temperature of his skin. The bandages on his stump were completely soaked with blood that had oozed from his wound. Quack had sealed the muscles and the blood vessels in the stump, and had then lavishly applied tissue glue to the closed skin flap of the stump. But as incredibly effective as the tissue glue was, there was simply too much traumatized flesh to stop all blood oozing from Tom's wound.

"Change IV bag, Ross," Quack said. Quack had no choice but to leave the IV line in Entzion's good arm to keep blood expanders flowing into his body. He needed a short stop to set up another bag.

"Roger," McTaggart said, bringing the DPV to a stop. He could see that Mears had done the same a few meters away.

"How you doin', Tommy?" Quack asked his patient while he quickly ripped the plastic seal from another IV bag.

"Good, Quack." Entzion tried to smile. He could have had all of the pain medication he wanted, but he had asked for and received the minimum. He wanted to be alert if and when they ran into the enemy. One arm or not, he could still fire a weapon.

"Sleepy?" Quack asked as he worked quickly. All of the team could hear the dialogue.

"Nope."

"Want something for pain?"

"Don't need it," Entzion said.

Quack threw a glance at McTaggart who merely shook

his head in admiration for their wounded comrade's courage.

Quack put both hands in the air, the signal that he had completed his work on Entzion. But as he assumed his position on the low-recoil 30mm cannon, Mears's voice was heard by all.

"Check nine," Mears whispered over the com radio.

At the team's nine o'clock position was an Iraqi APC squatting near the side of a sand dune. Incredibly, next to the machine, at the crest of the dune, was an improvised flag pole with two pennants attached at the top. They were the Iraqi national flag and the battle flag of the 41st Mechanized Infantry Division. As Mears and McTaggart studied the APC through their high-powered night vision glasses, they saw no movement whatever. As far as they could see from their vantage point, not even a guard. It was 0214 hours, the ideal time for an attack when the enemy would deep into REM sleep, all of their mental senses at lowest efficiency.

With their engines left idling, they were close enough to the APC so that the sound of an electric starter might alert them. The enemy vehicle, common to the Iraqi army, was the eight-wheeled Model 80 with the small turret on top. Mears and the others knew the specs of the vehicle very well and were aware that the machine had full-sized doors on each of its steel-welded armored sides and three firing ports along each side. There was a firing port in the front for the commander and most of the Model 80s mounted 14.5mm heavy machine guns in the turret. It had a diesel engine that would provide them with all of the rapid transportation they would need to reach Basrah and beyond.

Mears turned to speak to Baraniq in the rear seat. "We'll have action now, Colonel. Be silent and don't worry."

"I can help," Baraniq said. He was not eating well and took water infrequently, but his eyes were steady and there was no fear.

"This is a small thing, Colonel. We'll deal with it."

At his signal, the team gathered around Mears as he crouched on the cold desert sand.

"This looks about as good as it gets. Frogpond 2 approaches from their blind side. Top of the dune. Frogpond 1 from their twelve o'clock, with Haggar on Beast for cover. At three-hundred meters we shut down the engine on Frog 1 and approach on foot—assuming they haven't seen us yet. Ross, when you see us begin our approach, you make sure you get to the top of the dune ASAP in case they wake up. Use your suppressors. I want this as quiet as possible, neat as we can. We need their uniforms." Mears looked at his watch. "On the mark, eight minutes to be in positions, nine to start. Mark!"

Each man hacked his watch to begin the countdown to assault.

McTaggart waited three minutes before he moved Frogpond 2 in order to give Mears and his DPV time to circle round to their twelve o'clock position. He then gave a hand signal to Quack, who was behind the wheel, and they began moving cautiously forward. At five-hundred meters they were committed to the fight. If they were spotted by the Iraqis, they would have to move forward at the fasted possible speed, taking the fight to the enemy while he was still not fully aware.

Peering ahead with his NVOs, McTaggart snapped off the safety of his M-4, the suppressor screwed onto its barrel. As they began their ascent up the side of the dune, the Iraqi APC was out of sight, but the tall flagstaff served as a perfect guide to their position. When the DPV was within one hundred meters of the Iraqi machine, McTaggart signaled Quack to stop and shut off the engine. They would crawl the rest of the way.

Before Quack rolled out of the DPV, he got close to Entzion, making sure he was comfortable. Entzion's eyes were open and, because he wore his radio earphones, knew exactly what the team was about to do. He winked at Quack.

At three-hundred meters from their target Mears signaled Rodriguez to stop the vehicle and cut the engine. Mears's eyes never left the Iraqi APC. While Mears and Rodriguez advanced, keeping low, Haggar stayed in the vehicle, the .50 caliber sniper rifle resting easily on the vehicle's upper frame, a full magazine of rounds in the gun. It would be hard for Haggar to miss at this range and he kept his nightscope trained on the turret of the Iraqi APC. He had chambered the first round, an armor-piercing bullet made of spent uranium, knowing that he could put the turret and probably its gunner out of action with the first pull of the trigger. Subsequent rounds would be meant for personnel, not the vehicle, because they needed the machine in as good condition as possible.

When Mears and Rodriguez were at the fifty-meter mark, they dropped flat on the desert sand at the sound of a vehicle door opening with a squeak and clang. They watched as an Iraqi soldier who stood near the vehicle casually unzipped his fly and began to urinate. The American SpecOps men could clearly see the soldier watching his own stream instead of the surrounding desert. Mears knew that Haggar would have him in the crosshairs of his scope. They waited for a full minute after the Iraqi soldier had returned to his vehicle before resuming their approach toward the enemy car.

Mears and Rodriguez reached a position directly under the boat-shaped front of the Iraqi APC without discovery. A few feet away, leaning with his back to one of the four tires on the side of the car, was an Iraqi sentry, chin on his chest, asleep.

Rodriguez was nearest the sleeping sentry. With an nod from Mears, Rodriguez silently slipped his combat knife out of its sheath and moved closer to the guard's side. When he was within reach, Rodriguez sprang upon him, one hand going firmly over his mouth, pulling his head back, and quickly bringing the razor-sharp blade across the sentry's throat. There was no sound, not even the exhalation of breath as Rodriguez kept his hand over the Iraqi's mouth for extra seconds less there be a reflex action in the vocal cords.

Looking quickly up, Mears saw that McTaggart and Quack were in position atop the dune looking down, their M-4s trained on the APC. Their vantage point covered all of the gun ports on one side of the Iraqi vehicle while Rodriguez and Mears, as well as Haggar with Beast, covered the other side. Mears wished that the team had brought at least one flash-bang grenade on the mission, but it was not envisioned that they would ever need to stun their opponents. There were limits as to how much ammunition and explosives could be carried out the back end of an airplane and flash-bangs just didn't make the priority list. Dropping a fragmentation grenade down through the turret into the inside of the vehicle was possible, but it would turn the Iraqi soldier's uniforms into barbecue ash.

Mears was about to whisper instructions into his lip mike for each man to take a gun port from the outside and, on his signal, fire inside. The gun ports were closed, but he guessed they would not be locked from within. He was just about to give the order when the question of gun ports being locked or unlocked became moot. From just a few feet away came a booming voice, loudly rasping a command in Arabic.

"Get out of there, you sons of camels! Get up, I say, and get out. This is Sergeant Akmed Bzaaki speaking to you! Out! Out at once, you pigs!"

Access doors opened on each side of the vehicle and sleepy soldiers, all but one without their weapons, tumbled and lurched through the narrow doors. They looked around in confusion, some barefooted, some without pants or shirts. They milled around outside, trying to adjust their eyes. There were five in all.

"Who is your officer?" Mears said in Arabic.

None spoke. They didn't have to as all eyes stole glances in the direction of the man at the end of the row. He was, if anything, more passive than the others, all now with their hands in the air, surrounded on all sides by the Americans.

Mears stepped in front of the end man. "What is your rank?" he demanded.

When the man did not speak, merely rolling his eyes languidly upward in bored indifference, Mears raised his M-4 and placed the muzzle directly between the man's eyes. Then he shifted the weapon to the man next to him and pulled the trigger. Blood, large and small pieces of skull, gray matter from inside the head cavity, all were splattered against the steel side of the armored personnel carrier as well as upon the other men standing in line. And onto Mears.

Mears swung his assault rifle back to the Iraqi, who had suddenly turned chalk white. He gaped at Mears, who did not bother to wipe the pieces of flesh from his face and shoulders.

The corners of Mears's mouth twitched slightly upward. He had more questions to ask, such as radio frequencies, call signs, and unit commands. Now he would get the answers.

CHAPTER 15

Newly promoted Lieutenant General Bruce Coggin had spent a worried day in the field, deeply involved at his advanced special forces training center. A special operation never went better than the preparations done for the real thing. His warriors had to master the art of combat in all of its aspects—from ancient tactics to the highly sophisticated equipment and techniques of the 21st century. It took constant intensity, dedication, self-deprivation for the good of the team, and courage beyond the average person's imagination. The teams he commanded in the field simply could not accomplish their missions if any of those components were missing. Bruce Coggin sweated and fretted most days, needing to stick his nose into the faces of the new guys coming through the program so that he could judge whether they were all together.

Coggin's parachute harness was being checked behind him for the umpteenth time as he waited for the green light in the C-130. Every man who jumped needed to have his equipment checked by another. More than once. But Coggin lost count of the number of people who went over him and his equipment as though it was his first jump instead of number four hundred twenty-nine. He got this kind of treatment because of his rank. He had three stars instead of two bars or three stripes. For a moment he was tempted to turn his head and snap at yet another poke and prod at his harness, but stopped himself just in time. He should have felt flattered, and indeed he was, that men under his command cared whether or not he survived a jump. Coggin could think back to his long army career and recall senior officers whom he thought deserved a nice, deep, self-made impression in the ground. It doesn't take much for a ground-pounder to lose respect for an officer, and the little touches to his equipment told Bruce Coggin that he had earned respect from his men.

The warning light winked on. Coggin half-turned toward the men behind him and gave a hand signal to stand by as the ramp of the cargo/troop carrier lowered and locked into place. When the light turned from yellow to green, Coggin was the first man out.

He and twenty other seasoned SpecOps instructors were trying out the new French Mach 3 Alpha high-glide parachute. It was designed and built for tactical insertions that included HALO/HAHO, as well as free-fall operations. With deployment at twenty-five thousand feet at a gross weight up to three hundred sixty pounds, the parachute was purported to have the highest glide to descent rate (L/D) of all the parachutes in the world, with the lightest system weight. Special Warfare people were always looking for the lightest, the strongest, the fastest, and the deadliest of everything. Every ounce they did not have to carry was a mile farther they could move in "Indian country."

Coggin had hardly hit the ground a half-mile from the airstrip from which they had just taken off and was rolling up his chute when he stopped what he was doing and switched on his mobile radio. Pulling on its headset he spoke into the lip mike.

"Sergeant Raggio, Coggin. Do you read?"

"Five square, General. Go ahead," Jim Raggio responded. He had been guarding the general's frequency from the time the C-130 took off from Robbins Field.

He had always accompanied his boss when the general made jumps, but was ordered by the medics to pass on this one because of a severely sprained ankle. Even then, it took a direct order from Coggin to prevent his sergeant from attempting to board the aircraft without being seen.

"I'm on my way, General."

Indeed he was. When the first man had hit the ground, Sergeant Raggio had already begun driving toward the DZ and his boss. Raggio skidded to a stop near the general and Coggin dropped his jump harness and chute into the vehicle before Raggio could get out from behind the wheel to help.

"I need a secure landline," Coggin said.

Raggio dropped the vehicle into gear and accelerated quickly. "Base headquarters should have one, sir," he said.

The base deputy commander was only too pleased to provide General Coggin with the privacy of his office as well as his secure telephone. Coggin punched the keys that would put him in touch with his chief of staff, Lieutenant Colonel Irvin Kranz, SOCCENT, at MacDill Air Force Base in Tampa, Florida.

"Irv, General Coggin," he said into the telephone.

"Yes, sir?" Kranz responded, sensing that the general had something on his mind other than asking how business was going back home.

"Are you zipped up?" Coggin wanted to make sure Kranz could discuss secret material from his end of the line.

"Yes, sir, General. Go ahead."

"Get a copy of yesterday's G-2 briefing," Coggin said. General Coggin was briefed every morning, six days per week, by departments of his staff, including G-2 Intelligence three times weekly and more often when required; G-3 Plans; G-4 Operations; and G-1 Personnel. Each officer representing his staff would give a terse, bare-bones outline of events deserving of the general's attention.

"It's right in front of me, General," Kranz said. Like all efficient staff officers, Irvin Kranz tried to anticipate the needs of his boss. He had a number of classified files stacked atop his desk whether the general was off base, in the next office, or on the other side of the world.

"Look at the signal notations in the back of Major Arkin's briefing. See if you find anything referring to any teams operating in Iraq," Coggin said.

Coggin could hear paper rustling as Kranz looked for the pages of signal logs that had been transmitted by or to the SpecOps teams assigned in locations within the Central Command.

"Yes, sir. Five of those. Anything special?" Kranz responded.

"Leopard-1. Anything about them?" the general asked.

"Three signals, General, one from navy liaison, the extraction unit attached to Task Force 28-B. Then there was a transmission from Frogpond to them. They used the codeword Limoges. Then there was one more from Limoges to Frogpond with I.D. authentication. Want me to read them to you, sir?" Kranz asked.

"Yeah, go."

Kranz read the messages sent to Mears and Mears's response to Commander Briggle.

"Why were we copied on the first message? The navy one," Coggin asked.

"As a matter of fact we weren't, General. When Mears responded he copied us with both of them."

"Hold on, Irv," Coggin said, needing to think for a moment. Then he said, "Okay, so why?"

"I'm not sure I have an answer for that. Do you want me to contact Frogpond and ask him?" Kranz asked.

Coggin thought about it but not for long. "No. He's up to his ass in alligators by now. Do we know where he is?"

"No, sir. Last report we got was in a layup in the An Najaf area. Joe doesn't like giving out position reports."

"Smart."

Colonel Kranz was the first to interrupt the silence between them. "Is there something you want me to do, General? Anything you think I should run down?"

While Colonel Kranz held obediently to a silent tele
phone General Coggin was indulging his irritating habi
of chewing his fingernails. "I guess not. Authenticatior
go okay?"

The general again heard pages being turned. Then Col
onel Kranz said, "I don't see the authentication. But i
wasn't unusual we weren't copied. Limoges sent it direc
to Mears. He must have been satisfied or we would have
heard. Anything else, sir?"

General Coggin inhaled deeply. "No. I've got Raggio
with me packing a radio. Don't hesitate to contact me i
anything comes up. I don't care what it is."

"Roger, General," Kranz assured his boss. It was a
long standing order to "bother" the boss no matter
when, no matter where, and no matter what—even if wa
just somebody on the staff who got bad news from his
astrologer, Coggin wanted to know about it.

After hanging up the telephone Colonel Kranz leaned
back in his chair, fingers interlaced behind his head. He
picked up a second telephone that was on the desk, di
aled for an outside line, then dialed a Tampa number.

"Hello?" a woman's voice answered.

"It's me," he said.

"Oh, hi, honey. What're you doing?"

"I'm getting hungry," he said.

"Want me to fix you something and leave it in the
fridge? You can come over here and eat it when you get
off. I'll come straight home from work," she said.

"Like what?"

"Anything you want, Irv. I've got some fresh Oregor
oysters that I could fry and a green salad with bleu
cheese dressing, and some garlic toast. And beer. Does
that sound good?" she asked.

"*Fresh* from Oregon? Margo, think about it. Anyway
I'll get something at the club."

"Aw, Irv, honey, you don't like that food. Want me
to get off early? We could have some wine and—"

"I have to work late. I don't even know why I started
with the hungry bit. You go ahead and work your full

shift. If I get through by ten, eleven o'clock I'll come over."

"Promise? Are you okay? I can call in," she said.

"No. I'm fine. I just wanted to say hello. Anyway. I'll be there. If I can," he said.

"Okay, Irvin. Bye, sweetheart. I love you," she said.

"Me, too. I love you, too. So long, Margo," he said, replacing the telephone in the receiver. He did love her, he thought. She wasn't just a knockout babe, she had a knockout heart, too. They didn't do a lot of socializing with the other officers because sometimes it became awkward when the conversation got around to what the other wives and girlfriends did.

Colonel Kranz walked out of his office and stopped at the door of the admin office he shared with the general. "I'm going down the hall. Luftwaffe."

"Yes, sir," Master Sergeant Hall said, without looking up.

"If the general calls," Colonel Kranz said. Just tell him what you want him to do."

On the other end of the building was the aviation arm of the Special Operations Support Wing. Kranz walked in without knocking, but stopped short at Colonel Robert Levy's door. When he saw that it was open he nodded to Levy's enlisted clerk and walked inside.

"Hey, Irv," Colonel Levy said. He was the vice-commander of the 325th Special Operations Support Group.

"Bobby," Kranz said, remaining on his feet out of respect for a colleague's valuable time. Although he and Bob Levy were buddies Kranz never took advantage of that friendship.

"It's Friday night, man. Call up Margo and let's go party! Fuck this place," he said.

"Coggin is out of town—" Kranz began.

"Okay, I'll call Margo and the two of us'll get drunk. Give us a call tonight or tomorrow when your boss gets back."

"It's Wednesday noon," Kranz said.

"Doesn't make a damn bit of difference in reality, pard. You know the first thing they taught us at the academy? How to fly when we're drunk. Sit down, I'll get us a Coke to put in the Jack Daniels."

"I'll pass," Kranz said, preferring to stand and look out of the window.

Colonel Levy regarded his friend for a long minute before returning to his swivel chair behind his desk. He turned leisurely toward Kranz, but remained silent as he waited for the army officer to speak.

"We've got a Leopard team coming out of Iraq," Kranz said.

"Not by air," Levy said, his attention suddenly sharpened. If any kind of SpecOps aviation was being planned, executed, or even talked about, it would have to be run by Colonel Levy.

"No," Kranz said emphatically.

Levy leaned slowly back in his chair. He was under six-feet in height, just what Kranz had imagined the perfect fighter pilot should look like. But Levy had struggled with his weight for as long as he could remember. He affected a dark moustache that refused to lie obediently on his upper lip. Instead it grew in almost every direction, causing Levy to either brush it frequently with a small moustache comb or shave it off. This month he had chosen to brush. Again. His less-than-perfect physical appearance notwithstanding, Bob Levy had risen to the rank of full colonel well ahead of his academy classmates because he was smarter than most of them, as brave as the definition of that word can mean, and if you wanted your mother rescued from the FLN in the deep jungles of Colombia, you'd want Levy to fly her out. He was, quite simply, The Man.

"So," he said to Kranz, "your boys got a problem?" As he spoke in a low voice Levy left his chair to walk across the room and close the door for extra privacy. His entire staff was cleared for top secret and above, but it was still a good practice to treat everything, including your golf scores, on a need-to-know basis.

"I don't know. Coggin's throat is tickling him," Kranz said.

"And yours is tickling, too?"

"Not really. Well, just a kind of sympathetic feeling for my boss," Kranz said.

"Who's the team?"

"Leopard-1," Kranz said without hesitation.

"Isn't that Mears's old team?" Levy said, suddenly interested.

"Still is."

"Hell, I thought Joe was a civilian. In California somewhere, banging that dynamite sports babe."

"Julia. Bowes," Kranz said.

"Right, and right."

"Coggin got him recalled?" Levy guessed.

"You should have seen it when Mears reported. General Coggin looked him right in the eyes and said he'd gone right to the Pentagon to talk them out of recalling him. Said he put his stars on the line for him," Kranz said, shaking his head.

"Joe knew he was lying," Levy said, amused.

"No, he didn't."

"Yes, he did, but it's all right. Everybody lies." Levy regarded his friend for a long moment. "So he's bringing a team out, but you say he's got no problem."

"We don't know that. That's the problem. We don't know anything," Kranz said. Succumbing to temptation, Kranz slid open one of the bottom drawers in Levy's desk and helped himself to a couple fingers of single malt Scotch. He poured the same amount into a second tumbler and placed it at Levy's elbow.

"Got any guesses about where he is?" the air force officer asked.

"Southern Iraq. The navy has a task force in the Gulf."

"Are they bringing your guys in? Who're you dealing with, there?" Levy asked, interrupting.

"Stockton Briggle. Know him?"

"Damn good man," Levy said, nodding vigorously.

"Knows what he's doing. Just about twice as smart as you think he is."

"Yeah? Damn, that's good to hear, it really is," Kranz said, instantly brightening. "I'll pass that on to the boss. How do you know Briggle?"

"We lifted several SEAL teams out of Afghanistan and other places. I kept running into Briggle on those hops. He's not the only guy in the Middle East who does that kind of work, but I noticed that when he did it, it always went right. I can tell you horror stories about some of our joint mission planners that can't tell what time it is when the little hand is on the three and the big hand is on twelve. Briggle ain't one of those."

"Hell," Kranz said, knocking back the last of his Scotch, "how cool is that? Thanks, Bobby. Glad I came down to see my guru."

"Nothing it is," Levy said, barely sipping his Scotch. "Anything else?"

Kranz shook his head slowly as he looked down at the glass he held in his hand. The silence between them became longer as Kranz continued to be concerned and Levy patiently waited.

Kranz sat down again. He leaned forward in his chair. "What can you do if we need instant firepower out there?"

"Out where? Iraq? Down in the south, you're talking about?" Levy said.

Kranz nodded.

"We'd need a mission order but we wouldn't throw the spears. That'd be the task force you're already dealing with in the Gulf or maybe some Strike Eagles out of Saudi," Colonel Levy said. "But I think you know what the answer is going to be."

Kranz pursed his lips. Things could not be worse in the Gulf at this time. The entire area was like a pool of gas, no irony intended, waiting for someone to strike a match. America had plans, he knew, but not now. Would "they," the administration, sacrifice a Leopard team in order to save a match? Kranz didn't know.

"Well," he said, getting to his feet. "It doesn't matter. Nothing's wrong. If Mears needed something he'd call home."

"Sure," Colonel Levy agreed. "That's assuming, of course, that someone at home would answer."

CHAPTER 16

It was a short forty kilometer drive north from Umm Qsr to Az Zubayr. Cyrille Cosette had made the drive more than once during his more than three decades of service in this part of the world, but he had never sweated more heavily while riding in the cool of the evening in a totally air-conditioned environment. He had not wanted to drive, but the Iraqi SSS officer had already settled into the passenger seat of the Mercedes. Fahdi kept one eye on the rearview mirror mounted on his side of the car, making occasional micro-adjustments, in order to keep the large transport truck following them in sight. On the side of the truck were the Arabic letters indicating that the truck was the property of Iraq Petroleum, a state vehicle.

Cosette found his attention frequently going to the mirror on his side of the car for the same reason. It had become a nervous habit. Should anything go wrong the Iraqi intelligence officer was in his home country. He had nothing to fear. But with Cosette it was a different story. He did not have the protection of citizenship. He could call upon the French embassy, of course, but he had no illusions about being allowed to do so if, God forbid, the Americans should succeed in eluding the entire Iraqi army. Yet, he reminded himself for an unounted number of times, everything that could have een done *was* done. There was no reason to entertain ven the smallest negative notion. On the contrary. Vhile Mohammed Fahdi may have been a monster, he /as in every way a brilliant planning officer. At the mo- nent it was not an exaggeration to say that he was the 10st important man in the entire Iraqi army. It was he /ho was in touch with the American special operations eam that had in its hands Colonel Baraniq.

Cosette considered again. It was he who was the point 1an, the actual designated representative of the United tates Navy and the United States Army units in ques- ion. That fact was no comfort to the Frenchman. On he contrary. He reached for the air-conditioning control nd found that it was on the coldest setting possible.

"You had better drink water, Cosette," Fahdi said, naking no effort to hide his lack of respect for the older py. "I don't want you to die of dehydration just at the ritical moment when you might be of real value to omeone."

"Thank you for your kindness, Major," Cosette said.

"Here," Fahdi removed the cap from a plastic bottle ontaining filtered water.

Cosette sipped at the bottle, prepared to hand it back o the Iraqi, then changed his mind and took several arge swallows. The water was not cool, yet it was surpris- ngly calming to his state of mind. Perhaps the water was icting upon his electrolytes. Yes, in a few hours his bat- eries would be fully charged, he thought as he drove. Ie was, at this very moment, a wealthy man. He had 1ever been one before, so it took some getting used to. After still another drink of the bottled water he felt re- axed enough to look around at the countryside through vhich they drove, if one could describe endless desert in uch generous terms. These were Iraq's most productive iil fields and they went on for miles; row upon row of lerricks pumping black gold from the depths of what 1ad been a seafloor millennia ago.

It was an hour after midnight, Cosette saw as he

glanced again at his watch. He wondered if the Americans were already at the bridge, waiting. Could they find it easily? Of course, he snapped at himself, it is a landmark. If the Americans could not find such an obvious. . . ."

"Go slow," Fahdi said, his voice controlled. "Well? Did you see them?"

"Who?"

"Our forces, of course," Fahdi said, unable to hide the satisfaction in his voice. "Look around. Do you see them?"

Cosette looked through the safety glass of the Mercedes into the night. The darkness was distorted, however, by multiple fractals of light, their source from the city of Az Zubayr, highway lights beginning to appear along their route, and smaller yet intense luminance on the sides and tops of oil platforms. Cosette knew that Fahdi had hundreds—surely not thousands—of Iraqi army troops hidden somewhere nearby.

Now they were passing a power station on their right as Cosette drove more slowly in the direction of Basrah. Az Zubayr was behind them. On his left he could see two large oil pipelines running parallel to the road they were on. They passed a gas/oil separator plant as they crossed the Olmām Anas wadi. Cosette looked for a road indicator that would tell him that they were crossing the span but he could see none.

"Drive into Basrah," Fahdi directed.

The city's international airport passed by his side of the car as Cosette stepped more firmly on the gas pedal. Everywhere he looked he saw oil industry. Lower income housing was scattered among plants of all description that supported the flow of oil from under the ground to pipes to plants to pipes again and finally to the sea. Cosette wondered what the place would look like if Iraq were up to full production. It must appear to be a giant anthill at those times.

"Well?" the Iraqi officer said, now openly smirking.

"You hid them very well, Mohammed," Cosette admitted.

"We have our own special forces, you see. There are none better. They are concealed along that pipeline over there," Fahdi said, pointing. "They stretch for three kilometers, from Az Zubayr to Basrah. The men and their equipment have dug in behind and beneath it and covered it with camouflage. Not even the American satellites can detect them."

Cosette knew that the Iraqi was carried away with his appraisal. They both knew that the American satellites could see through netting as though it did not exist. In point of fact their imaging penetration was more than twenty-four inches beneath the surface of the desert sands. And as to his reference of his special forces, well, Cosette had not yet seen them defeat an enemy in battle. Still, he respected the Iraqi soldier. They were not afraid to die. And if they were handpicked and well trained.

"Your problem, Cosette, is that you give the Americans more respect than they deserve. They cannot fight if they do not bring overwhelming numbers to the battle. Individually, what do they have to fight for? Hamburgers? Automobiles?" Fahdi laughed at his own metaphor of American values. "Turn off here. We'll wait."

Cosette parked the car as directed. They now had a view of what would soon become the battleground of choice for the Iraqi high command. Whether Colonel Baraniq was killed or captured made absolutely no difference to the military nor, for that matter, to the government's Leader.

"Hamburgers to make them fat and automobiles to carry their fat carcasses. I know the people with whom we are dealing."

"You have been to America?" Cosette asked.

"No. But I have seen the pictures. All of the pictures I need."

The conversation was interrupted by a signal received on the radio Cosette had taken from the dead American

naval officer. For a long moment both men could only
stare at the red light blinking between them on the seat
of the car.

"Well?" Fahdi urged Cosette.

Cosette picked up the transceiver and tentatively tried
to accept the encoded incoming signal. He was not familiar with the device except those that had been provided
him through DGSE, and then only occasionally. He had
preferred to work through government offices that had
landlines. As he looked at the compact EHF machine in
his hands he knew that he had to key in an authentication code that would unlock the machine's security mechanism. For several moments Cosette could not remember
the code.

"You have forgotten the authentication. It is in your
pocket," the intelligence officer said.

He had forgotten. Cosette and Fahdi had written down
critical information that Commander Briggle had divulged while he was still able to speak. They had both
taken notes while Briggle spoke in hoarse, pained whis-
pers, each keeping his copy. The notes would only be
valid within the immediate thirty-five hours, until the
American Leopard team arrived and the action completed.

Cosette snatched the notes from his breast pocket,
scanning them quickly. Without looking in Fahdi's direction Cosette knew that the Arab was sneering at his fum-
bling. He was glad that this event would be his last. He
would go directly to Kuwait International Airport and
board the first plane to France. For the first time in his
professional life, Cosette felt he was no longer in control
of his destiny.

"Ah. Here," he said, holding the paper on which he
had penned in the authentication code in one hand while
with the other he switched the radio to the transmit position. Then he plugged the radio's outside power source
into the cigarette lighter. The authentication process did
not allow for more than one mistake, including the se-
quence for entering the combination of letters and num-

ers before pushing the "send" key. Cosette took longer
utting in the seventeen character set than the protocol
llowed. The transceiver's red light turned to orange,
linked for fifteen seconds, then shut itself down.

"What did you do?" Fahdi snapped, clearly concerned
ith Cosette's poor performance with the radio. Still, he
id not want to pull the transceiver from the French-
aan's hands. "Never mind, I know what you did. Calm
own, for God's sake!"

Cosette watched the transceiver, now inert, hardly dar-
ng to breathe. After sixty seconds, exactly the time Brig-
le said the encryption program would reactivate, the
aachine's red light began blinking once more. Cosette
new that if he did not key in the authenticator correctly
nd quickly enough, the radio would shut itself down
ompletely. The EHF device would then order its brain
o destroy itself, taking with it into radio eternity a vast
mount of data, code systems, and satellite communica-
on protocols.

Moving deliberately, feeling Fahdi's eyes boring into
ae side of Cosette's temple, Fahdi pressed the radio's
eypad; then the final "send" key. For what seemed an
ternity, but which was only a matter of seconds, the red
ght turned from blinking to steady state. Then, miracu-
ously, to a solid green. The French spy and his reluctant
raqi colleague watched in utter fascination as the small
creen in the EHF filled itself with straight lines and rows
f numbers and other symbols, with many gaps among
aem. Very quickly the symbols and numbers began to
earrange themselves into English language words.

"What does it say?" Fahdi asked, trying to read the
mall screen by leaning over Cosette's lap.

"They are map coordinates," Cosette said, distracted.

"I know, I can see that. What else? The words!"

"They say the meeting place changed. And there is a
ime group included," Cosette added.

"Impossible," Fahdi blurted in disbelief.

Cosette shrugged.

"What else?" the Iraqi said.

"Nothing else," Cosette said, handing the radio t
Fahdi.

"Idiots. American idiots! Do they not understand orde
when they are given? Their high command orders them . .
here," Fahdi said, thrusting the radio back into the Frencl
man's hands. "Send them a response. Tell them they ar
to arrive exactly as ordered in the place and time agree
to. Sign it Commander . . . wait, sign it from a highe
authority yet. The American SOCCENT. That will mak
them comply."

Cosette turned a dour look at his Arab colleague. '
don't think that will fool them, Fahdi."

"How do you know that, eh? There is no way the
can know the place of origin of the—"

"We do not know the transmit authentication fc
SOCCENT, if you will think about that for a momen
What we have is Commander Briggle's."

The Iraqi made a fist with his hand and touched h
forehead. "Yes. Of course. I should have remembere<
Send the message from Briggle, then, and tell the Amer
can Leopard team that all arrangements have been mad
from the original point, impossible to make changes a
this time."

Cosette referred once again to the notes he had take
from the dying American commander to key in the trans
mit authenticator. It took a short time to key in Fahdi
dictated message, then to activate the encrypt code be
fore pressing the send key.

A return message was not immediate. They sat mc
tionless in the automobile, practically holding thei
breaths as time dragged. An hour passed. Cosette wa
uncomfortable and wished that he had alcohol in som
form with him in the car. Two drinks would have don
wonders for his state of mind. The tension in his hea
was as tight as an ill-fitting hat. He glanced at the Irac
intelligence man at his side. Fahdi sat erect, almost rigic
staring straight ahead through the windscreen of the ca
his eyes fixed on an object that might exist on anothe

planet. As bad as life would become for Cosette should this operation go wrong, it would be exponentially worse for the Arab. Cosette shuddered to think of what would be done to the man at the order of his unhinged leader. It would certainly be longer lasting and far more painful that what had befallen Stockton Briggle.

Unspoken between them was the American Leopard team's reason for changing the rendezvous place and time. If there had been a trap set, the ambush forces would have to move to another location. There was no way of silencing so many vehicles or moving so many men and their weapons across open desert without giving them away. If that had been their motivation for changing the plans, it was simple and it was clever. Also, Cosette felt that Fahdi was compounding the problem by not complying with the American team's directions for the new coordinates for the meeting. Were it him, he would have begun moving men and equipment, even in greatly reduced numbers for reasons of stealth. But it was obvious that Fahdi was counting on a soldier's first tenet of conduct, which was to obey orders. It was simply inconceivable that the American leader of a mere half-dozen men would have the arrogance to countermand orders from superior authorities.

When the transceiver's red light began to flash on and off Cosette snatched it up. Fahdi turned his head very slowly, his eyes fixing upon the Frenchman who was again referring to the authenticating string required to decrypt the coded message. Controlling his nervous system better than on his first try, Cosette managed to correctly enter the string, then pressed the enter key. He watched, lips dry, while the encryption software inside the small machine began to form words in the tiny screen.

Cosette swallowed. "Negative."

"Negative," Fahdi repeated, dumbly.

Cosette nodded. While he was waiting for Fahdi's response, Cosette began to entertain very fast-moving word pictures that could have an impact for him within the next few hours and even days. *A race to the airport . . . no, dispose of Fahdi first, then. . . .*

"Who do they think they are?" Fahdi began, almost strangling on his own rage, his clenched fists shaking on his thighs. Fahdi's eyes narrowed as he willed himself to regain control of his intense hatred of the Americans who were frustrating his carefully laid plans. "Well," he said at last, almost calmly, "they will still be dealt with, but I will innovate. I will spring the same trap, but with a slightly different bait."

Fahdi reached into the backseat of the Mercedes and lifted a hand-set from an Iraqi field radio. He switched the transmitter on and, after waiting for a brief moment to confirm that the machine was ready to operate, he dialed in a scrambled frequency used for troop movements by Iraqi High Command. Fahdi spoke into the mouthpiece.

"Scimitar, Scimitar, this is Hammer. Come in, Scimitar."

"This is Scimitar, Hammer, proceed," Fahdi recognized the voice of Fayed al-Barzun coming to him into his hand-set.

"There has been a delay. At minimum three hours, but do not let your units relax. Move ten armored units into the approaches of Umm Qsr, Major. No more than ten. Do you understand?" Fahdi said.

"Affirmative. Ten armor to Umm Qsr," al-Barzun said. There could be only one reason to move troops from the trap they had planned to spring and that was because the fight would take place at Umm Qsr. He would lead the armor there himself.

The Iraqi officer got out of the Mercedes and walked back to the large truck that had been keeping station with them from the start of their drive north. He returned to the car within minutes.

"What are you going to do? What good will it do to move. . . ."

"Be good enough not to tell me how to do my business," Fahdi snapped at the Frenchman. "Now," he said, placing an area map on his knees, "read the references to me."

Cosette read off the coordinates given them by the Leopard team commander. Cosette leaned over to watch as his Iraqi colleague used a ruler and a pencil under the glow of the automobile's dome light to plot the new position where they would meet the Americans. Fahdi drew a heavy pencil on his map along the roads they would need to travel.

"Drive," he said.

Cosette did as he was told. The new position was west, back along the highway they had come, leaving Ar Rumaylah and the massive industrial chemical processing plants to their right. They continued for approximately thirteen kilometers along an expressway before turning off onto one of the service roads to the west side of the Zubayr oil fields. Glancing into the rearview mirror Cosette could see the large truck keeping pace behind them.

Units of Iraqi armies could be seen at various strategic locations, all waiting for the Americans to appear, but considering the odds against them, they were skeptical that they would actually try to pass through the established blockade. There were any number of places that desert-equipped vehicles could travel without the need for roads. By now they, the American commandos, could be en route to anywhere. That very thought crossed Cosette's mind as they came upon Iraqi vehicles with ever increasing frequency. They passed through these guarded areas unchallenged, but closely scrutinized, as was the Iraq Petroleum transport keeping pace behind them.

"Do you think they will be there?" he said to Fahdi.

"Why would they not? They trust Commander Briggle. He is their only way out. Of course they will be there." The Iraqi Intel officer lit a cigarette, exhaling the smoke into the Mercedes.

Cosette wanted to open his window to disperse the acrid smell, but that would have let in the still-warm

desert air. Better to let the air conditioner filter ou
the smoke.

Referring to the map, Cosette turned south again, stil
following the oil field access roads, this one two kilome
ters from the Ar Rumaylah Southwest Airport, and fol
lowed it directly south. The area was all coarse sand and
rock, endless numbers of large and small wadis all going
in the same direction, toward the sea.

The road was now rough, no longer kept under repair
This part of the Zubayr oil fields was first developed ir
1936 and now much of it was abandoned. While they
were traveling quite slowly, bouncing up and down with
their lights flashing wildly, they came upon yet anothe
Iraqi army element. Two of its men were lazily draped
over one side of their vehicle while a third man, a sub
machine gun slung over one shoulder, stood in the mid
dle of the road, his hand held in the air.

"Hell," the Frenchman said, but was not altogethe
displeased to brake the Mercedes to a stop. He pushed
the electrical button that rolled down the driver's side
window. The Iraqi road guard stooped to look inside
flashing a light into Cosette's face and then into Fahdi's
Cosette did not like that kind of treatment from anyone
and he waited for Fahdi to explode at the insolence o
the common soldier who held the light.

Instead, Fahdi said nothing.

"Are you lost?" the soldier said, not taking his light
from Cosette's eyes. "What is your business out here?"

"You will kindly get that light out of my eyes, you
fool, or I will. . . ."

"We are here to have tea. And we have brought our
teacup," Fahdi said, calmly and in English.

The Iraqi soldier said nothing. He merely looked at
them.

"Yes, that is correct," Cosette spoke up. "We are trav
eling by way of Limoges," he included Briggle's
identifier.

The Iraqi soldier squatted down so that he could see
the men in the car more clearly.

"They better be porcelain," the soldier said.

"Yes. They are porcelain teacups," Fahdi said, visibly relieved that the challenge and the countersign had been given.

The soldier snapped off the light, but said nothing. Instead, he studied both men. When Cosette looked again into his rearview mirror, he could see that an Iraqi soldier had climbed onto the cab of their petroleum truck and was pointing a gun at the driver. On the other side of their Mercedes there were two more soldiers, now aiming their submachine guns at the windows of their car.

"Get out," the soldier near Cosette said.

Cosette did as he was ordered, hands raised. Fahdi did the same from his side of the car, now keeping his mouth closed while they were examined even more closely. Slowly the soldier who had used his flashlight casually lifted his submachine gun so that the barrel pointed upward but his face did not become friendly.

"You don't look like a US Navy officer to me," Mears said in English. "Either one of you. Where is he?"

"Briggle?" Cosette said, regaining his wits, now fully realizing with whom they were dealing. The Americans had somehow got their hands on an Iraqi army vehicle. "Why, he is back there," Cosette jerked his thumb over his shoulder. "Near Al Basrah where we were supposed to meet you. He, ah, could not believe you would be here. He thought it was a trick."

"Who're you?" Mears said.

"I am Cyrille Cosette, French DGSE," Cosette said, still holding his hands in the air while Rodriguez completed his body search. McTaggart looked Fahdi squarely in the eyes while Haggar patted down Fahdi. The Iraqi Intel officer was carrying a .40-caliber autoloader which Haggar took away without comment. Any man, in these circumstances, could and probably should carry a weapon.

"Identification," Mears said, holding out a hand. He then motioned toward the driver who had been brought away from his truck to stand near Fahdi. McTaggart immediately took a wallet from the driver and began to examine his papers under the glow of his flashlight. Mears marched the driver to the rear of the truck and ordered him to stand where he was. Haggar then moved the captured Iraqi APC to a position directly behind the petroleum truck. The headlights of the armored vehicle were now shining at the doors. From the gun turret Haggar trained his machine gun squarely at the rear door of the truck.

"Open them," McTaggart told the truck driver. The driver did not understand English, but there was no mistaking what was required of him. With nervous hands, he unfastened the lock on the doors and swung them open.

The truck was empty.

Mears studied the Frenchman's papers closely, comparing the photos, looking from the wallet to Cosette's face, shining the flashlight directly. He cared not at all that the Frenchman was discomfited by the blinding glare. He slowly lowered the light as he handed the wallet back to Cosette.

"You," Mears said to Fahdi.

"I am Mohammed al-Ammal. This gentleman," Fahdi nodded toward Cosette, "and Commander Briggle have done me the honor of hiring my boat for your safe passage."

Mears wiggled his fingers to indicate he wanted to examine the Arab's papers. Fahdi passed them to him at once. "Is that so?"

"Yes, sir," Fahdi said.

"You're Kuwaiti?" Mears said to Fahdi, still holding the documents.

"Yes, sir. All of my life. My father was a master fisherman. He is too old to work and I now own three boats."

Mears considered for several minutes, but as he stood before the two men who were his welcoming committee he seemed to relax slightly.

"Okay. My name is Joe Mears. This is Ross McTaggart. Where's the boat?"

"Umm Qsr, sir. Do you know it?" Fahdi asked.

Mears nodded his head. "Yeah. I know it." Mears knew it by map references only. But you never want to tell a New York cab driver that you've never been there before. "That's still in Iraq," Mears added.

"Technically, but the city is used by Iraq and Kuwait. It is a shared harbor," Fahdi said, shrugging his shoulders as though it was a commonly known fact.

Cosette took advantage of the situation to ask, "And what about Griffon?"

"What about him?" Mears wanted to know.

"Is he all right? He has not been injured, has he?" Cosette asked.

"Sure. He's okay. Manny, take Monsieur Cosette to look in on the colonel," Mears said. Then he turned back to Cosette. "Go ahead. He's in good shape." Mears grabbed Quack by his shirt sleeve. "How's Tommy doing?"

"He's lost a lot of fluid through the wound. I've used up all the blood expander we brought with us. He needs the real thing. Now. And I mean right now."

Mears looked on as the French DGSE man and his Arab fisherman talked to Baraniq. They were not be allowed inside the vehicle, but there was no reason they couldn't talk through the gun ports. Cosette was the one who spoke to Baraniq through the steel hull of the APC while Fahdi remained to one side. They returned soon, which was fine with Mears because they were going to run out of darkness in a couple of hours and he wanted to be shed of Iraq by then.

"Leave your vehicle here, Joe," Cosette said. "We will transport you in this truck. You will have to change into civilian clothing so that you will look like oil workers in case we are stopped."

"I don't think we much look like Iraqi oil workers, Cosette," Mears said. To himself he admitted that they just might. They had not shaved in weeks—months, in his case. Plus there were plenty of Europeans who worked in the Middle East around the oil fields.

"The army will not stop a state petroleum truck, Joe, but if by some stroke of ill-fortune they do, you must not be caught in uniforms or with those weapons. We would all be killed."

Mears considered for a moment and looked at his team as they waited for him to make his decision. They were a bit ragged, but that was because they had been operating in the desert for some time. And they would look as good as most Iraqi soldiers. They all had their guns and they were a very long way from being too tired to use them.

"I guess we'll keep our weapons, Cyrille, and I guess we'll pass on the truck ride, too. But we'll follow you. You lead the way to Umm Qsr and the boat and we'll be right behind you all the way," Mears said. Out of the corner of his eye he could see that the team was relieved by his decision.

"That will not work," Fahdi objected strenuously.

"Why not?" Mears asked, eyebrows raised.

"Because arrangements have been made. This truck will not be stopped," he urged.

"I have to agree with Mohammed, Joe," Cosette said. "We should go with the original plan."

"Let's get Briggle on the radio and see what he thinks," Mears said. "Manny, use the command radio and call Lieutenant Commander Briggle. Use the task force guard frequency and call him in the clear. If you don't get a response in twenty seconds get off the air."

"Yes, sir," Rodriguez said as he put the command set on top of the APC and switched it on. He placed headphones over his ears and dialed in the frequency.

"I don't understand what your plans are, Joe Mears," Cosette said, beginning to show signs of discomfort. "I doubt that Briggle can respond."

"Oh, he'll respond," Mears said, tightly. "He would never be out of com with us or the ships. Unless you're telling me that he can't respond. Is that what you mean, Cosette?"

"We are running out of time. I think we have done everything we could do," Fahdi said to Cosette. "If you choose not to go with us, then you have no one to blame but . . ."

"You stay right where you are, Mohammed. You're just the fisherman in this crowd. Right? You must be some kind of freedom lover to risk your life and your boats to help somebody escape from Iraq. I admire that. Don't you, McTaggart?" Mears asked, never taking his eyes from Fahdi.

"Sure do, Joe. Fact is I feel a lot safer knowing Mohammed is here with us."

"Candycane, Candycane, this is Frogpond, do you read? Over."

Clearly there was no response to the radio call. Rodriguez squeezed the transmit key again and said, "Candycane, Candycane, this is Frogpond, do you read? Over."

Rodriguez looked at Mears and shook his head. Then he tried the call again.

After a full twenty seconds on the air, Rodriguez changed the frequency selectors and shut down the radio.

Mears looked at Cosette, his eyes drifting slowly toward Fahdi.

The Frenchman was clearly nervous and beginning to perspire. Fahdi's eyes were moving rapidly, as though there might be a source of help off in the darkness.

"Well," Mears said, "he's probably busy doing something else."

"Yes. Exactly. He is, ah, probably. . . ."

Mears's icy stare closed Cosette's mouth for him.

"So we'll just go ahead on our own. Haggar, they won't need that car. Take a look and see what they have in it," Mears ordered.

Haggar strode over to the Mercedes, opened the doors, trunk, and hood. He removed the two radios from the rear floor of the car, then pulled the pin on a thermite device and set it on the engine block. He dropped the hood closed. Within seconds the hood turned cherry red, then white as the aluminum block melted into runny globules.

"Cosette, want to stay alive?" Mears asked in a conversational tone of voice.

"Of course. What kind of question is that?" Cosette said, shaking.

"What happened to Commander Briggle? Don't lie to me, Cosette. I have some kind of gift that tells me when people are lying. I'm a human lie detector," Mears said, his submachine gun inching upward at the Frenchman.

Cosette looked quickly at the Iraqi intelligence officer. The spy pointed at the Arab. "He killed him," he said. He closed his eyes as though to block out what they had seen.

Mears nodded, knowingly. "When?" Mears asked Cosette while never taking his eyes from Fahdi.

"Shut your mouth, you idiot!" Fahdi snapped at Cosette.

"Two nights ago. On the boat. He . . . he. . . ." Cosette was unable to go on.

"He what?" Mears asked. When the Frenchman did not respond Mears turned to the Iraqi. Fahdi stood as tall as he could, thrust his chin up, trying his best to bluff his way to the end. But his knees began shaking until they became uncontrollable and would no longer support him. He slowly sank to the ground. Mears knelt in front of him, spoke softly, almost gently.

"Did you enjoy it?" he asked.

"What?"

"What you did to Commander Briggle. Did you enjoy it?"

Fahdi opened his mouth, but no sound came out. His eyes were wide open, almost bulging. He urinated in his pants, the water puddling on the ground below him. Mears ignored it.

"You had to have the information, didn't you? Lives were at stake, weren't they? So you caused him pain.

Lots and lots of pain. That's what happened, didn't it?" Mears asked.

"Yes," Fahdi said, swallowing hard, trying to get a grip on himself. "I had no choice. There was nothing. . . ." He licked his lips; then closed his mouth. It was important to him that he die bravely before the eyes of Allah.

"I have to kill you," Mears whispered to the man so that the others could not hear. "I don't make judgements of who is evil and who isn't. But you killed my comrade. A brother of mine whom I never met. You should have been a real fisherman, then you would be out on your boat tomorrow."

Mears shot him through the brain, just over the ear. When Mears got to his feet the Frenchman was no longer capable of sweating.

"You said I could live!" he said frantically to Mears.

"No. I asked you if you wanted to live. Big difference," Mears said.

Cosette placed both hands over his face and began to sob.

"I'm not going to kill you, Cosette," Mears said. "Others will do that."

Mears rejoined the team. He spread his map over the trunk of the smoldering automobile. "One hour of dark. Here's where we are, about sixty-five kilometers to here, As Sabiyah. That's on Kuwait Bay. We travel overland from here to this road. It's a main highway south through Umm Qsr. Only fifty clicks left to go. When we get to As Sabiyah we get us a boat. Anything that floats and can move, and we head out into the gulf. Questions?"

"Are we going in that?" Haggar said, pointing to the APC.

"Right. They don't know where we are. There must be five hundred of these rigs running around this part of Iraq. I think our chances are good," Mears said.

"I know our chances aren't too slick if we don't move," McTaggart agreed.

"Ross, give me a hand siphoning the fuel out of this

truck," Mears nodded toward the Iraqi Petroleum truck. "We're going to need all we can carry."

"My pleasure," McTaggart said. Siphon hoses were essential equipment for every Special Operations team operating in country.

As the team began walking toward the APC Mears spoke to Rodriguez.

"Manny, use the burst transmitter to notify SOCCENT and the task force on the guard channel. Tell 'em what we're doing and every six give them our moving coordinates from the GPS."

"Yes, sir," Rodriguez said, dropping himself into the APC.

CHAPTER 17

Moammar Rumallye walked with his head down to protect himself from the cold wind blowing across the water into the dock area of Umm Qsr. There were few people about at this hour of the morning, so he encountered no one as he opened the door of a van parked nearby and sat on the passenger side.

"It looks as though we may see action," he said to Nabil Zibri sitting behind the wheel. "Headquarters has ordered a small armored detachment here." Rumallye had just used a landline to talk with his Hizballah associates.

"Is that all?" Zibri said, a bemused look on his face.

Rumallye shrugged his shoulders. "They are supposed to arrive in the back of a petroleum truck. Without guns and without vehicles. I never thought they would give up their weapons. They would not do that."

"But somebody thinks they would. Who?"

"An Iraqi intelligence officer. I don't know his name but he is very good." Rumallye screwed off the top of a thermos bottle and poured himself some tea. He was very sleepy. And he was drinking too much tea and every few minutes, it seemed, he had to pee.

"Is that what I tell my men? To look for a petroleum

truck? There must be hundreds of them going through
here day and night," Zibri said, pointing out the obvious.

"Yes, well, this one has American soldiers in it. When
it stops, have your men shoot them," Rumallye said, closing his eyes.

Zibri had his men positioned along the roads coming
into the town. He also had two men on the southern part
of Umm Qsr in case the Americans should break through
and make a run for Kuwait. Although he had no idea
how much good that would do them. The Hizballah operated where it pleased when it pleased. As far as that
went, the Iraqis would not hesitate to chase anyone
across their borders into Kuwait. He had seen them do
it before. But if the American desert commandos no
longer had their vehicles and were driving a truck, they
would be easy to bring down. Zibri looked at his watch.
Only an hour left until dawn.

He was almost getting to enjoy it. Rodriguez drove at
full throttle as they swung south of Al Mufrash air base
and cut southeast toward the main highway that ran directly to the border of Iraq and Kuwait. While the sky
was lightening to the east, it was still dark and Mears had
the headlights on bright. He had found a unit pennant in
the vehicle and flew it proudly behind the turret. Tanks,
trucks, and support vehicles were more frequently seen
now. Mears raised his submachine gun in one hand high
above his head, waved with his free hand, while yelling
into the wind at the top of his lungs, "Allah is great!
Saddam is a god!" Almost without exception the greeting
he received in return was vigorous, exuberant.

When they rolled onto the expressway near Safwan
Airport, the traffic was no longer sparse. The wheels of
commerce were rolling and Mears could see why the
petroleum truck would have been a good choice of transportation. Too bad the wrong people had thought of it.

"Road block, Joe," Quack said into his lip mike from
the driver's seat below.

"Roger. Slow down but don't stop," Mears ordered.

All of the Leopard team were wearing their com radios, ready with their weapons in the armor-protected interior of the vehicle.

Haggar sat behind the KPV heavy machine gun in the turret. It would be his initial hits that would likely spell success or failure for the team should a firefight take place. He would take out the enemy's heavy weapons while the rest of the team would use the 7.62-mm machine guns situated in the front and sides of the APC. Mears patted Haggar on the back. Hagger nodded, knowing precisely what was expected of him.

There were dozens of vehicles at a complete halt, some military, some civilian, meekly waiting for a roadblock manned by police and military personnel to interview or search them. Per his orders, Quack aimed the APC between the lines of traffic and kept his foot on the gas. As they approached the roadblock the people behind it began waving frantically, realizing that the APC was moving too fast to stop as ordered. Quack decreased their speed only enough so that Mears could make his voice heard to those behind the barrier as they rolled through.

"Get out of our way, you stupid sons of bitches! Camel dung!" He yelled in Arabic, rasping at the top of his lungs, raising his fist and shaking it at them.

"Joe," McTaggart said peering out of the back gun port of the APC, "you scared the poor guys to death. Jesus, give 'em a break."

Mears kept his eyes on the road ahead, not wanting to make a challenge out of his roadblock run. He only wanted to give the impression of a tough line unit on an important mission.

When Rodriguez placed the burst transceiver out of a gun port and pressed the "send" key, he had no way of knowing who, if anybody, would pick up the message. He hoped their automated reception system would notify the right person that the shit was already in the fan.

They rolled through Umm Qsr without letting up on the gas. This was the place Fahdi wanted them to stop,

Mears vividly recalled, for a boat that was waiting for them. There were probably boats there, all right, but not friendly ones.

Dawn had arrived. They were no longer protected by their greatest asset, the dark. Still, Mears thought they had a chance to make it now. The highway had bypassed the middle of the town and they were headed almost directly south, toward the Bay of Kuwait and the small port town of As Sabiyah. The border of Iraq-Kuwait was less than a kilometer away.

"Tanks at twelve," Haggar said. "Ten and two o'clock," he added. But Mears was already looking at them through his glasses.

"Hold it, Quack," he said. He wanted to get a good look at what was clearly an armored ambush set up for them. They had a short time, he thought, before the ambush commander realized that the APC approaching his position was going the wrong way for the wrong reason. He needed time to think.

"Manny," he said to Rodriguez. "Talk to the tanks. Ask them if they've seen the petroleum truck."

Rodriguez turned on the APC radio which was already set to the Iraqi army command frequency. The Leopard team had the identifiers they needed to talk with other units thanks to the information divulged from the APC's commander when they captured it in the desert.

"We're not going to punch it out with those guys, are we, Joe?" McTaggart said, emerging from within the APC.

"You afraid of a T-72?" Mears asked the young lieutenant.

"No, sir, I'm not. But that changes if there is somebody inside to spin the shiny knobs and aim the great big gun," McTaggart said, soberly.

"Joe, the tank platoon commander wants to know where we're heading," Rodriguez said.

Mears thought for a minute. "Tell him that we're at the southernmost end of our assigned patrol area before we turn west into the desert. Tell him that first we're going to have tea."

"Tea?"

"Yeah. We're not moving until we drink our tea. And rest," Mears said.

Captain Daniel Unrue approached Rear Admiral Carl Nydigger while he was on the bridge.

"Admiral," Captain Unrue said by way of greeting, the formality of saluting done away with aboard ship.

"Hello, Dan. What's up?" Nydigger said. Standing nearby was his chief of staff, Commander Wes Claridge.

"We've got that defector coming out of Iraq," Captain Unrue said.

"Right. We're maneuvering now. We're on schedule, aren't we, Wes?"

"Yes, sir. We're almost complete on the last turn," he said, referring to the carrier's fighting position, into the wind and moving in the direction of potential action while coordinating with the other ships of the carrier group.

"I dropped the ball on this one, Admiral, big time. We were using a fishing boat to get 'em all out of Iraq. Seems that the man we picked to coordinate the boat ride, a Frenchman, was working for the other side." Captain Unrue clipped off his words through gritted teeth.

"Jesus," the admiral breathed. "Are they still alive?"

"They are, sir. They're sending us GPS coordinates every five minutes. Last transmission we received included the information that they are in the middle of a road with tanks in front of them. And they're still one kilometer inside Iraq."

The admiral turned to chief of staff. "Wes, find out what we've got in the air. Whatever it is, start a vector for them. Get two tankers up and put a strike package together and launch them ASAP."

The admiral turned back to Captain Unrue. "Keep feeding your GPS fixes to Commander Claridge. Are your Mark V boats in the water yet? Well, crank 'em up and send 'em. Run 'em right up on the sand if you have to."

"Yes, sir. Admiral . . ."

"We don't have a lot of time to go through this thing now, Dan, but we can't blame the fuck-up on the French. You're going to get a lawnmower run over your ass, but it will hurt a lot more if those Special Ops boys don't make it out."

Entzion was mostly unconscious as the heat started early in the day. There were no more bandages to apply. The upside was that Quack was not short on pain killer, so he could keep Entzion at reasonable ease. But he needed the kind of care found in a hospital, not the bottom of a hot car. With the temperature inching over one-hundred degrees inside the APC, they had few choices. They had been stopped dead on the road for forty-five minutes.

"Joe, the tank commander wants you to come down and talk," Rodriguez said, responding to a radio call.

"Does he sound sociable?" Mears asked.

"Negative."

"Tell him soon."

Rodriguez looked up after sending and receiving another signal. "He said now, Joe."

Mears nodded. The game was about to end. "All right," he said into his lip mike. Like everyone else, his Iraqi uniform was soaked with sweat. Their water was almost gone and Colonel Baraniq's eyes showed fear. Hell, they were all scared.

"Let's get out of these rags," he said.

The team quickly and gladly shed the Iraqi army clothing that had almost worked to get them out. If it wasn't to be, they would die in American uniforms.

"We'll drive toward them, try to get as close as we can. If we can get near enough we . . . we let 'em have it with everything we got; then make a run for it. Little zigzagging behind the wheel, Quack?" Mears said in a wasted attempt to lift spirits. But nobody was laughing. One round from a T-72 gun would obliterate the APC.

Mears pulled his upper body out of the turret and waved his hand, a friendly greeting to the Iraqi tank commander. He could see the tanker, also out of his turret, but he was not waving.

"Okay, Quack, start driving. Nice and slow," Mears commanded.

As the APC rolled slowly forward Mears plastered a smile across his dirty, unshaven face, hoping that he looked more Arab than he felt. As the APC continued down the road, closing the distance between it and the tanks, he watched in abject fascination as the gun turrets on all ten of the T-72s began to track him. His mouth went dry. He licked his lips but his tongue was dry, too.

When one volunteers for irregular warfare in a special unit, there is always the strong possibility that one's life will end abruptly, violently, sooner rather than later. Mears had never experienced paralyzing fear. There were countless times, when danger was very near, that Mears had expected death and accepted it. But now, because of his mistakes, too numerous to catalogue, he was taking five good men with him. And another man who might have been a great asset to his country. He despised himself for his inadequacies.

"Joe," Quack said into his earphone.

"I see 'em," he said, still trying to appear relaxed to the Iraqi tankers.

"Shit," Rodriguez said, listening on the Iraqi command frequency. The same one the tanks were on. "They're getting a message in the clear. They found the APC crew we took out."

Mears was not going to wait for one of their gunners to pull his trigger at his damn convenience. No sir, they would take the first shot even if it was to be their last.

"Lee, take out that sorry son of a bitch in front of us," Mears said, meaning the platoon commander in front of them.

"Roger."

Haggar sighted the KPV heavy machine gun and pulled the trigger.

The Iraqi tank disappeared. One instant it sat squat, menacing, blocking the road in front of them, and in the next split second the tank was gone in a massive explosion of fire. It was mind numbing for not only Haggar, who had fired the shot from his machine gun, and not only for Quack and Rodriguez who occupied the forward-looking positions in the APC, but for Mears who had never experienced a moment in combat like it.

The event must have shocked the other Iraqi tankers because for several seconds they turned their attention to their commander, wondering what had caused the catastrophe to his machine. They had to shift mental gears and do something. Shoot the APC? Were the Americans in the APC? And if they were, what kind of firepower did they have on board that could destroy the T-72 like a toy?

In the following seconds all questions were answered when the first F-18 Hornet from the *John C. Stennis* flashed overhead. Almost immediately another tank exploded like the first; then another. The remaining seven tanks, engines roaring, began moving for cover as fast as they could. But there was really no cover for them.

"Frogpond, Frogpond, this is Navy E-2C One Charlie Niner Victor, do you read, over?"

Rodriguez quickly switched the team's intercoms onto the command radio so all could hear.

"Roger, One Charlie Niner Victor, go ahead," Rodriguez said.

"We can put a laser on all those tin cans in your way. You call the shot, we pull the trigger, over."

"Roger Niner Victor, stand by one." Rodriguez looked up into the turret at Mears.

"Roll it, Quack! Go, baby!" Mears said. Then spoke to Rodriguez. "If they don't give chase, we leave 'em alone."

Rodriguez spoke once more into his radio transmitter. "One Charlie Niner Victor, Frogpond."

"Niner Victor, go," the special weapons officer responded.

"We won't shoot if they don't. We're rolling," Rodriguez said.

"Roger, we'll hang around 'til your water taxi arrives. The Hornets have ten minutes of fuel left. We have a second strike package on the way, if needed."

"You the folks who helped us out up north?" Rodriguez could not help but ask.

"Affirmative," Kong advised as the Hawkeye remained on station far above.

Rodriguez clicked his transmit button twice.

"There," Rumallye said, pointing through the van's windscreen at the road ahead. "We can catch them! Hurry!"

Nabil Zibri increased the speed of the van, but something did not look right. They had passed the wreckage of two tanks. There might have been three. A fight? With whom? And the Americans were in Kuwait now. If they could catch the stolen Iraqi APC now, and he knew that they could, could they get effective shots? As a matter of fact he and Rumallye had every intention of using their superior marksmanship gained in seven months of sniper training to first disable the vehicle, and then to pick off those inside.

The APC was now on the Az Zawr road, less than three kilometers from As Sabiyah. The blue waters of the Persian Gulf were beckoning to them. Mears checked their six o'clock. The van was still following them, but now turning toward the east. If they were armed, and he thought they were, they were angling for a zero deflection shot.

"Frogpond, One Niner Charlie Victor . . ."

"Go, Charlie Victor," Rodriguez quickly acknowledged

"Assume you eyeballed pursuing vehicle," the Hawkeye E-2C technician advised.

"Roger, Charlie Victor, he's not one of ours," Rodriguez said.

"We'll just button up," Mears said to his Leopard team, "they can't hurt us with anything they have inside that van."

One Niner Charlie Victor did not hear that.

Nabil Zibri eased on the brakes, slowing the van, and finally stopping.

"What are you doing?" Moammar Rumallye demanded to know.

"Too late," Zibri said. "We've lost."

"We have not lost! Go. Go now!"

But Zibri had no intention of bouncing the van off-road in a hopeless effort to head off the APC. Besides, it was a beautiful day. Blue sky met blue water, a piece of Allah's art for the eyes. He was not as rabid as Rumallye and his fellow Hizballah. Maybe his father was right. Maybe there was another way. He would visit his father again and talk at greater length. After all, he could always go back to killing.

Like the first tank, the van disappeared in a flash of gray dust and pieces of metal too small to be seen from the APC that was now at water's edge.

"What the hell . . . ?"

"The van," Mears said with no particular emotion.

"How'd you like that, Frogpond? One Niner Charlie Victor put the red dot on that T. Standing by."

EPILOGUE

Leopard-1 was taken aboard the Mark V boats and returned to the task force upon new SOCCENT orders. Joe Mears was detached from the team and reassigned as a military advisor to the Home Defense office in Washington.

Colonel Harun Baraniq is in his third month of debriefing by various U.S. intelligence agencies. His information has, to date, been invaluable in defending against terrorist attacks and in identifying and locating terrorists cells on a global scale.

Fahim Zibri, father of deceased Nabil Zibri, now funnels large amounts of money to various Muslim terrorist groups.

Mustafa Al Jahani, who used thallium poison to assassinate, was never apprehended by U.S. authorities and is believed to be living in this country.

Tom Entzion was treated aboard the USS *John C. Stennis* where skilled navy doctors pulled him back from the brink of death. He was separated from the army and awarded a full disability pension. Entzion returned to college and is in his final year of undergraduate school.

Julia Bowes and Joe Mears are separated geographically by their work. However they continue to seek each other's company when possible. Ms. Bowes awaits the publication of her first book.

In one of the unfathomable realignments of the Byzantine French Intelligence Service, always secret, Cyrille Cosette was posted to Washington, D.C., as a special military adviser to that embassy. Cosette reigned in his appetite for alcohol but not his lust for younger women. To the surprise of almost everyone who knew him, he married Anìce Denay, a widow near her middle-years.

TOM WILSON

A missing daughter.
A deadly assassin.
A desperate pilot.
The hunt is on...

BLACK CANYON

A millionaire's daughter has vanished in the Colorado
mountains. At first, Link's job looks like a simple case of
search and rescue. But when he realizes that an
international criminal is also looking for the girl, he's
caught in the middle of a terrible game of cat and mouse.

"Wilson joins the top rank of military novelists."
—W.E.B. Griffin

0-451-19553-1

WARD CARROLL

"CLANCY MEETS JOSEPH HELLER...[a] riveting,
irreverent portrait of the fighter pilots of today's Navy."
—Stephen Coonts

PUNK'S WAR

This is the real Navy, as seen through the eyes of a veteran
pilot. Set on a carrier in the Persian Gulf, this "remarkably
honest"* book introduces us to Navy Lieutenant Rick
"Punk" Reichert, who loves flying more than anything—
even if his life is turning into one big dogfight.

"For readers of military fiction who want some brains
with their boom." —*Baltimore Sun*

0-451-20578-2

Available wherever books are sold, or
to order call: 1-800-788-6262

Penguin Group (USA) Inc.
Online

Your Internet gateway to a virtual environment with
hundreds of entertaining and enlightening books
from Penguin Group (USA) Inc.

While you're there, get the latest buzz on
the best authors and books around—

Tom Clancy, Patricia Cornwell, W.E.B. Griffin,
Nora Roberts, William Gibson, Robin Cook,
Brian Jacques, Catherine Coulter, Stephen King,
Ken Follett, Terry McMillan, and many more!

Penguin Group (USA) Inc. Online is located at
http://www.penguin.com

PENGUIN GROUP (USA)INC. NEWS

Every month you'll get an inside look at our upcoming books and new features on our site. This is an
ongoing effort to provide you with the most
up-to-date information about
our books and authors.

Subscribe to Penguin Group (USA) Inc. News at
http://www.penguin.com/newsletters